TITAN
THE FIGHTING
FANTASY WORLD

Steve Jackson and Ian Livingstone

Edited by Marc Gascoigne

PUFFIN BOOKS

For Tony, who deserves it, and Chetna, who doesn't

PUFFIN BOOKS

Published by the Penguin Group
27 Wrights Lane, London W8 5TZ, England
Viking Penguin Inc., 40 West 23rd Street, New York, New York 10010, USA
Penguin Books Australia Ltd, Ringwood, Victoria, Australia
Penguin Books Canada Ltd, 2801 John Street, Markham, Ontario, Canada L3R 1B4
Penguin Books (NZ) Ltd, 182–190 Wairau Road, Auckland 10, New Zealand

Penguin Books Ltd, Registered Offices: Harmondsworth, Middlesex, England

First published 1986
This new format edition published 1989
10 9 8 7 6 5 4 3 2

Printed and bound in Great Britain by
Cox & Wyman Ltd, Reading
Filmset in Linotron Palatino by
Rowland Phototypesetting Ltd
Bury St Edmunds, Suffolk

PUFFIN BOOKS

TITAN
The Fighting Fantasy World

Steve Jackson and Ian Livingstone

Edited by Marc Gascoigne

Since its first appearance on the Earthly Plane in 1982, with the publication of Steve Jackson's and Ian Livingstone's famous *The Warlock of Firetop Mountain*, the world of Titan has gradually become explored and better known. While there remain uncharted regions, waiting to be opened up by brave adventurers, book after book of Puffin's Fighting Fantasy series has revealed ever more of this fantasy world.

Here in a single volume is all you ever wanted to know about Titan. Not only are the three continents described and mapped, but the underwater kingdoms too are discussed. The chief races and personalities of Titan – your allies as well as your enemies – have whole sections devoted to them. Here you can learn of their history and their gods, their likes and dislikes, their cities and villages.

Did you know that Logaan the Trickster god first created Man? How familiar are you with the legend of the Dwarf hero Hangahar Goldseeker? What should you do if offered a flagon of Orc ale? All this information and much, much more is to be found within the pages of *Titan – The Fighting Fantasy World*.

Steve Jackson and Ian Livingstone are the co-founders of the hugely successful Games Workshop chain and also creators of the whole Fighting Fantasy series. Marc Gascoigne is co-author of the best-selling *Judge Dredd, the Roleplaying Game*. He also edited *Out of the Pit*, the book of Fighting Fantasy Monsters, and is co-author of *Dungeoneer: Advanced Fighting Fantasy*.

CONTENTS

ACKNOWLEDGEMENTS

A number of entries in this book are based on places and characters invented by the following authors. So many thanks to Andrew Chapman for the lands of the Inland Sea, from *Seas of Blood*; Peter Darvill-Evans for Zagoula and Lake Mlubz, from *Beneath Nightmare Castle*; the other Steve Jackson for Scorpion Swamp and the King's Highway, from *Scorpion Swamp*, and for Atlantis, from *Demons of the Deep*; Paul Mason and Steve Williams for the Riddling Reaver, from *The Riddling Reaver*; Mark Smith and Jamie Thomson for the land of Hachiman, from *Sword of the Samurai*; Robin Waterfield for Pikestaff Plain and the city of Arion, from *Masks of Mayhem*. To all these good people we offer our relieved and heartfelt thanks – Titan would have been a much smaller place without you!

FOREWORD

The world of Titan, according to its history books, was created by the gods from a lump of magical clay discovered by the goddess Throff. In fact, Titan came into being in the latter part of 1981, when we were wearing our quills to the feathers, working furiously on *The Magic Quest*.

The Magic Quest was the current working title for a project we had begun in August of that year – and it was a title that neither of us could bear! But after endless debates we still could not agree on another title for the book. Finally, a compromise was reached. Ian, who had written the first part of the book, had mentioned in the opening paragraph that the whole adventure would take place in Firetop Mountain. Steve, who wrote the final part, had made the ultimate battle one with a powerful sorcerer, Zagor the Warlock. On the day that the book was handed in, the final title was agreed: *The Warlock of Firetop Mountain*.

Thus Firetop Mountain was the first location in what was to become Allansia. It was followed by the Forest of Yore, the Vale of Willow and Craggen Rock from *Citadel of Chaos*, and Darkwood Forest, Stonebridge and Yaztromo's Tower in *Forest of Doom*. The existence of Allansia itself was formally announced in April 1984 when the first edition of *Warlock* magazine was published. Now a collector's item, *Warlock* 1 featured the first map of Allansia ever released.

Since then, the map has been expanded. Now there are not one but *three* continents in the Fighting Fantasy world of Titan. Ian and, to a lesser extent, Steve have continued to develop Allansia. All of Ian's books except one have taken place in the north-western corner of this continent. The Old World comprises Kakhabad (the land of Steve's *Sorcery!*), its surrounding kingdoms and Gallantaria, from *The Tasks of Tantalon*. The third continent, Khul, is largely unexplored, with much work left to be done to chart its unknown reaches.

But since that day in 1981, the world of Titan has been alive for both of us – a retreat from everyday life into another world, a world in which we have effectively been GamesMasters in a huge global fantasy role-playing game. We have enjoyed developing the legends, lore, rumours and plots of the adventures. And we have chuckled at the tricks and traps we have set for our readers. There is Good and there is Evil; there is Law and there is Chaos. But like the Trickster Gods, we have striven to ensure a balance in the world . . .

The task of collating the information contained in all the books based in Titan has fallen on a learned scholar whose excellent work on *Out of the Pit* makes him an ideal candidate for the job – Marc Gascoigne. Not only has Marc had to extract information from nooks and crannies throughout all the books – and some of this was hiding in the most obscure places – but he has effectively had to assemble it into a sort of Encyclopedia of Fighting Fantasy. The result is *Titan – The Fighting Fantasy World* and we would like to congratulate him on his laborious work. It is an invaluable aid to adventurers the world over.

WELCOME, BRAVE ADVENTURER!

Welcome to our humble treatise on the wide and dangerous world of Titan. Within its covers you will find much that will prove helpful to you as you cleave your way across wild lands in search of fame and glory . . . and treasure! With the help of all the information crammed into this essential work of reference, you will finally be equipped to fulfil your destiny as a hero, fighting for the Forces of Good!

You will find geography – masterful charts and drawings of all the settled and not-so-settled lands of Titan. You will find maps of the Old World, home of civilization and of learning; of Allansia, savage land of sorcerers and barbarians; and of Khul, which we call the Dark Continent, the wasted birthplace of Chaos. We will show you plans of Elven villages and Dwarf citadels, of rank human cities and rat-infested Orcish caverns; there is even a portrayal of a citadel of the terrible Snake People of the southern deserts. We have stopped at naught to bring this awesome information to you!

We will present you with a history of this cruel world of ours, starting with the very creation of the many races and the releasing of Time into our world, to bring death to us all. We shall take a stroll through the Celestial Court, and introduce you to the many gods and goddesses who toy with us in all our daily activities. Then we will walk the face of our planet to reveal to you the forefathers of our lands, the legendary heroes and the dastardly villains who shaped our world. Shudder as the foul spawn of Chaos itself rears from the perverted ground, intent on swallowing the whole world in its toothless maw! Cheer as the Forces of Good drive the revolting armies back into the ground to fester and decay!

But what of the world today? We shall introduce you to all the main races, from the dour Dwarfs to the ancient Elves, and from the inscrutably evil Snake People to the crude and inhuman Orcs and Goblins. We will reveal secrets of the world's most evil men and their allies – and of those few brave souls who would oppose them. We will show you traders and merchants, craftsmen and innkeepers, and many other not-ables, whom you may even have the luck to meet on your own adventures.

From where has all this information come, you ask? Well, warrior, it has been compiled over many, many years by a great number of sages and scholars from all corners of the world. We have wandered far and wide, poking our collective noses in everywhere we could, in search of new and revealing information about this complex world of ours. And now, after twelve years compiling all our notes into one volume in the Halls of Learning in Salamonis, we present our masterpiece to you.

For any stay-at-home types, it will perhaps offer a glimpse of something different, and show this world of ours in all its glory and mystery. You will learn many things from the pages which follow, both useful and trivial. Who knows, it may even persuade you that there are more things to life than ploughing fields or selling your wares in the market-place.

For you adventurers, however, we can guarantee that it will prove an invaluable guide throughout your travels, no matter how far they may take you. There are a great many dangers in this world, but with the help of this volume you should be as prepared as any man or woman could be. We begin, just over the page, with what we believe is the first map of the whole of Titan to have been seen outside of the learned enclaves of Salamonis, Kaynlesh-Ma or Royal Lendle. It shows Allansia, Kakhabad and its surrounding lands, the mysterious conti-nent of Khul, and many isolated islands which have been discovered and named only recently. Do not be alarmed by the size and extent of the lands of Titan, however: you will never need to journey far to find adventure!

So, brave adventurer, turn the page . . . and may the gods in their wisdom ensure that you find all that you seek!

12

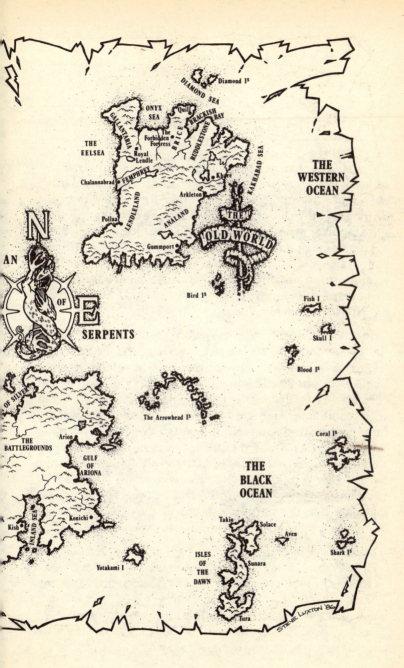

Diamond Iˢ

DIAMOND SEA

ONYX
SEA

Quill

BRACKISH BAY

CALLANTARIA

The
Forbidden
Fortress

BRICE

THE
EELSEA

Royal
Lendle

RUDDLESTONE BAY

KAKABAD SEA

THE
WESTERN
OCEAN

Chalannabrad

FEMPHREY

Khare

Arkleton

LENDLELAND

ANALAND

THE
OLD WORLD

Pollua

Gummport

Bird Iˢ

Fish I

Skull I

Blood Iˢ

N

OF

SERPENTS

OF SILVER

The Arrowhead Iˢ

Coral Iˢ

Arion

THE
BATTLEGROUNDS

GULF
OF
ARIONA

THE
BLACK
OCEAN

Konichi

Takio

Solace

Aven

Kish

INLAND SEA

ISLES
OF
THE
DAWN

Sunara

Shark Iˢ

Yotakami I

Tura

STEVE LUXTON '86

13

THE WORLD OF TITAN

Allansia, Land of Danger

Let us start our journey across Titan with the most notorious of all lands, Allansia. It may offer the greatest prizes for a daring, ambitious adventurer, but it also offers the greatest dangers. Throughout the land, the Forces of Evil are drawing together, growing ever stronger: in the north, corrupt humans bring forth wild magic into the world, knowing little of what they are really doing; and creatures are stirring in the southern swamps, things that will ultimately affect all of Allansia. For these reasons, if for no others, you should study Allansia in far more detail than other lands.

Originally, 'Allansia' was simply the name of one small part of the great continent, the extreme western area between the Icefinger Mountains and the northern reaches of the Desert of Skulls. It means 'the Teeming Plains' in a very ancient, much-corrupted Elven tongue, for the land has always been covered with a multitude of races, each fighting for dominance over the tiny corner of the continent. In recent centuries, however, the name has come to mean the entire landmass, from the Dragon Reaches to the Strait of Knives, from Kaynlesh-Ma and Arantis to the Iceberg Straits. Nevertheless, when most people speak of Allansia, they still mean the small pocket of life cowering alongside the northern shores of the Western Ocean, dominated by the unholy vermin-pit that is Port Blacksand.

Blacksand is a relatively new city, built on the ruined docks of an earlier and much larger city completely destroyed and abandoned in the years following the cataclysmic War of the Wizards. Because of the ruins, however, and because it is situated at the mouth of the Catfish River, another settlement quickly grew up among the ruins of the old. Unlike the earlier city, the new one was not designed as spacious and geometric, but is a ramshackle heap of wood and stone buildings piled high on top of one another, a haven for thieves and brigands, pirates and cut-throats who prey on one another and on more innocent citizens. The city is ruled over by the mysterious Lord Azzur, a tyrant known both for his great ruthlessness and for his quirky acts of 'charity'. We shall return to Blacksand and Azzur in more detail later. Suffice it to say at this point – beware Blacksand!

This corner of the continent is wild – mostly rough moorland interspersed with hills and tangled forests. Its climate varies considerably from sticky, sweaty summers to frigid, snow-bound winters, with many days of torrential rain or sunshine in between; despite the best attempts of sages and weather-mages, the weather in Allansia remains annoyingly unpredict-able. The land is bounded to the north by the frozen peaks of the Icefinger Mountains, which manage to shelter the lands from the colder gusts which billow down from the Frozen Plateau nearly a hundred leagues further north across the ice plains. The Icefinger Mountains are a desolate place, inhabited by wild creatures like Yeti and the subhuman Toa-Suo. The only humans who venture this far north come in search of skins and furs, if they dare come at all.

THE SETTLED LANDS
The southernmost boundary of the foothills of the Icefinger Mountains is marked by the wide River Kok, which brings trading barges and galleys downstream from the strange city of Zengis twenty days upstream, to the thriving town of Fang, capital of the province of Chiang Mai. Fang is a prosperous place, ruled over by the devious Baron Sukumvit. Every year the locals make a monetary killing from the many visitors who arrive for the Trial of Champions, a vicious death-test run by the Baron with a prize of 10,000 Gold Pieces for the warrior who can survive it, but for the rest of the year they earn their money by extracting extortionate river taxes from the traders who pass upstream and downstream.

Beyond the River Kok, the Pagan Plains stretch for many, many days, dotted with the small settlements of simple peasant folk. The north-eastern corner is watched over by Firetop Mountain, whose summit, coloured red by strange plants, once made people believe it was a volcano. Beneath the mountain, there is rumoured to be a subterranean dungeon complex, ruled over by an evil warlock, though some locals swear that he is now dead, killed by a fearless adventurer. (If so, you may have to look elsewhere to make your fortune!) Heading further south, we arrive at Stonebridge, a Dwarf town famous both for its mines and for its rumbustious leader Gillibran, whose legendary magical hammer returns to the hand of the wielder when thrown! The Dwarfs of Stonebridge are friendly towards adventurers, preferring to vent their anger upon the local tribe of Hill Trolls, with whom they have been warring for many decades.

Heading south, we cross the Red River (so called because of its colour, which comes from carrying red soil from its source high in the lonely Moonstone Hills), and immediately find ourselves in Darkwood Forest, a wild and dangerous tangle of trees and brambles which stretches away southwards. It is bisected by the Catfish River, which flows on down to the sea at Port Blacksand. The forest is home to a great many evil creatures, and a prominent local legend has long told of a large city of Dark Elves in caverns deep beneath it. It is certainly true that hunting parties of Darkside Elves roam the forest after dark, burning isolated farmsteads and abducting humans, presumably to be their slaves.

The lower reaches of the Pagan Plains are windswept and less hospitable, for they open out at their eastern end to the Windward Plains, and thence to the Flatlands, an enormous area of grassland and steppes which stretch all the way to the Sea of Pearls, far, far away on the other side of Allansia. There are fewer settlers on these lands, and a traveller would be hard pressed to find a friendly face until he reached the safety of the ancient Forest of Yore and the walled city of Salamonis, which is almost as old as the forest and is situated on the banks of the fast-flowing Whitewater River, where it runs through the Vale of Willow. The forest is many thousands of years old, and the half-Elven tribes who live within its eaves speak guardedly of

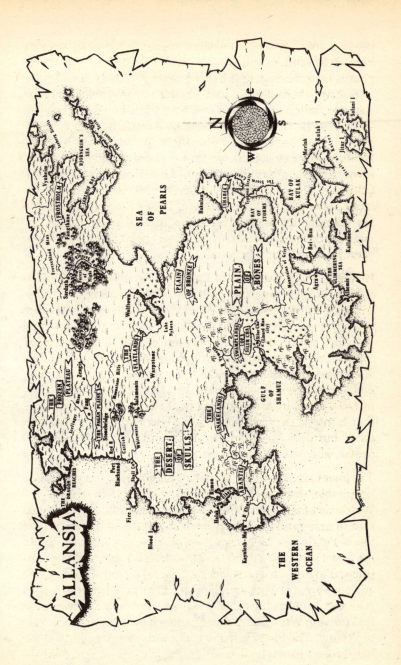

its many ancient secrets. Salamonis itself was built before the War of the Wizards. By the scale of such matters in those days, it was little more than a small walled citadel, but to the present population it is a solid, ancient city. It derives its name from the Salamon line, who have always ruled over the city. The present king, Salamon LXII, is renowned for his ancient library, which is said to contain many important documents relating to earlier ages of Allansia, but also for his laxness in allowing the Craggen Heights and Trolltooth Pass to become overrun with Orcs, Goblins and worse creatures.

Trolltooth Pass is the true gateway into Allansia, for beyond it lie the Windward Plains and the Flatlands. It is a dangerous place, only three leagues wide at its narrowest point, and bounded by the Moonstone Hills and the northern reaches of the Craggen Heights, two ranges of inhospitable highlands which give shelter to all manner of human-hating races. Along its length are the ruins of watchtowers and fortresses, built by

various local rulers through the centuries in an attempt to fortify the pass against intruders. At one point, there are the remains of a massive wall, which stretches for perhaps eight leagues, fortified every two leagues with massive (and now crumbling) gatehouses, before petering away into the scrubland. The ruins are haunted by the ghosts of the thousands of warriors who at one time or another gave their lives to defend this narrow strip of land.

THE FLATLANDS

When an Allansian wishes to express the size of something so big that it cannot be imagined, he simply says 'as wide as the Flatlands'. The gently rolling plains stretch for many weeks' ride, spanning an area far larger than that of old Allansia, until they slowly dip down to the shores of the Sea of Pearls on the other side of the continent. In comparison to the Pagan Plains, they are sparsely populated, but humans and other beings do live there. Many small tribes of nomadic horsemen roam the wastelands, setting up their villages in one spot for no more than a few days, before moving on. They are short, sallow-skinned people, with slanting eyes and coal-black hair. Horses run wild on the Flatlands, and worse creatures too; both are hunted by the tribesmen, who are experts at wielding bow and lasso from the backs of galloping horses. The tribes could offer a great threat to settled Allansia if they were ever brought together as a single fighting unit, for they are hardy warriors; but they are proud people, fiercely loyal to their particular tribe, and it would take a great power indeed to unite them against other peoples.

The Flatlands are intermittently crossed by trading caravans from Zengis, which skirt the safer northern fringes of the plains on their long journeys to the city of Sardath, and from there on to ice-bound Frostholm and the cities of Fangthane and Vynheim. Sardath is an alarming city, built on stilts over a lake, which is itself squeezed precariously between two sheer mountain peaks. It is inhabited by the rough men and Dwarfs who built the city a few centuries ago to house them while they exploited the many resources of the inhospitable region. North of Sardath, in the foothills of the Freezeblood Mountains (known to the Dwarfs as the Kalakûr, or 'Wall of the Gods'), gold mines penetrate deep into the earth, trappers hunt bear, snow-fox and rarer creatures for their luxurious pelts, and lumberjacks work timber from the thick forests. It is a rough land, and it takes its toll of even the strongest, but the rewards are great for those who can survive.

FROSTHOLM

Further north still is Frostholm, a land of mountains and fjords inhabited by a race of hardy, broad-shouldered humans who live alongside Dwarfs in their stone and timber settlements. Vynheim is the only major settlement in Frostholm, though every inlet of Bjorngrim's Sea (named after an ancient giant-slaying hero) is dotted with farmsteads and small villages. The city perches on a plateau overlooking Vynfjord, from where boats set off for the open ocean beyond the Giant's Teeth, even as far as Gallantaria across the Ocean of Tempests. The people of Frostholm are strong sailors and doughty warriors, for they have had their share of conflict, especially in the legendary wars against the Frost Giants which once dwelt in the Kalakûr – wars which are celebrated in song whenever the people get the chance!

The Dwarfs, for their part, respect the northmen as great warriors, and there are many links between the two races. However, there are some things which the Dwarfs will always keep to themselves, and for this reason no human has ever entered the great citadel of Fangthane. Ruled over by King Namûrkill, Fangthane is revered by Dwarfs from all lands as the focus for all Dwarf peoples. Carved from the insides of a mountain in the Time of Legends, while the first humans were still learning how to throw rocks, it is truly one of the wonders of the world.

SHABAK AND THE SOUTHLANDS

Far away, south across the Sea of Pearls (a curious name for a wild, stormy gulf where no man has ever dived for oysters!), the small principality of Shabak thrusts out into the Ocean of Tempests, perched on a peninsula which is part of a much-feared stretch of coastline known as the Storm Coast. Gales blow across the ocean from the east, bringing hurricane winds and whirling tornadoes which batter against this side of Allansia like the hammer of an enormous Giant. Shabak itself consists of little more than the single city-state of Bakulan, which hides away on the western side of the Shabak Peninsula. Little is known of this land, save that some of its merchants occasionally trade with the subhuman peoples who dwell in the Plain of Bones further inland.

The Plain of Bones is another desolate, wind-swept land. It is bounded to the north by the baking Plain of Bronze, to the east by the impassable Bay of Storms, to the south by the uncrossable Mountains of Grief, and to the west by the Swamplands of Silur Cha, known throughout the south as the domain of the Lizard Men. The Plain of Bones takes its name partly from the dinosaurs which roam across it, and partly from the primitives who hunt them. Once, maybe, there was civilization here – at any rate, occasional ghost-haunted ruins of small settlements and fortifications dot the plains – but that must have been many, many lifetimes ago, for now there are only the dinosaurs and their hunters.

Further south still, beyond even the Mountains of Grief, a few small communities cling precariously to the coast around the Glimmering Sea. Isolated from the other civilized parts of Allansia by the mountains and the plains, and visited by few merchants from the far north as a result, they have not grown much beyond tiny city-states, ruled over by dynasties who occasionally trade with one another, and occasionally war with one another, but who never influence the rest of Allansia. Little is known about these lands by the scholars and sages of the north.

SILUR CHA AND THE SWAMPLANDS
Thick jungles and swamplands line the wide Gulf of Shamuz, making it a perilous place for any adventurer. Even worse, they mark the full extent of the Lizard Man Empire, an evil domain which is slowly threatening to spread out across the face of the southlands. The eastern part is known to us as Silur Cha, a Lizard Man term which (very approximately) means 'Home to the Supreme Majesties of all Lizards'. At the heart of the swampland there is the unholy city of Silur Cha itself, which is indeed home to the Lizard Man emperors and their human-hating followers. Except in the scrying pools of

sorcerers, no human has ever seen Silur Cha and lived to tell the tale, for Lizard Men hate all intelligent life and will allow nothing to cross their swamplands – as if anyone could! The swamplands themselves cover an area almost equal in size to the Pagan Plains, and are inhabited by giant snakes, crocodiles and, of course, the Lizard Men themselves.

The northern extent of the evil Lizard Man Empire is currently spread along the Vymorn River, at the mouth of which stands the besieged city of Vymorna. For six years now, the city has been cut off by the inhuman troops, who have slowly pounded away at the walls until they have reached the inner fortifications and the keep. Vymorna is an old city, built to withstand a great deal, but its back is broken and its people cannot hold out for much longer. Over the six years, a few brave warriors have attempted to escape the city in search of aid, but none has ever made it all the way across the Snakelands or the Desert of Skulls, so no aid has ever been sent.

When Vymorna falls, as it surely must, the Lizard Men will find that they are opposed by the equally vile Caarth, the Snake People who dwell in stone cities excavated on the fringes of the Desert of Skulls known as the Snakelands. Even if they win against them, the Lizard Men will simply be faced by the endless wastes of the Desert of Skulls itself. Unless, of course, their attention turns to Arantis . . .

ARANTIS AND KAYNLESH-MA

Just south of that stretch of the Western Ocean known as the Pirate Coast, the city of Kaynlesh-Ma guards the head of the River Eltus, as capital of a land called Arantis. The people of Kaynlesh-Ma are strange, being highly religious and learned, but also hard-working and physical. The city and the land are governed by the Overpriest, who is widely believed by his subjects to be the incarnation of a messenger of the gods, and is therefore treated with incredible deference and loyalty by his subjects. The priests of Arantis are known for their learning, even in old Allansia far to the north, but even more famous are the exotic spices, oils and cloth which merchants bring to the northern lands. Galleys regularly ply up and down the coast from as far away as Fang – making them ideal prey for the pirates of the Bay of Elkor and Blacksand itself!

Not for nothing is the stretch of water around the Bay of Elkor known as the Pirate Coast. While the two cities which face each other from twin peaks at its seaward end, Halak and Rimon, are not especially aligned to Evil, they are havens for thieves, pirates and gamblers, though most of these have their hide-outs among the many inlets of the bay itself. Every so often, the piracy gets so bad that the powerful merchants of the three cities force the rulers into action, and for a few weeks the pirates are driven underground – maybe a few are actually caught and hanged. But when the fuss dies down, as it always does, the pirates re-emerge and continue their dastardly trade as if nothing had happened.

North and east of the Bay of Elkor there is only the arid expanse of the Desert of Skulls, which stretches as far as the mind can imagine. Within these endless wastes great treasures are rumoured to be hidden among the ruins of cities like the legendary Vatos, but few adventurers would be so foolish as to try to cross them without an overwhelmingly good reason. Even the rampaging Lizard Men may have some difficulty adapting to the searing heat of this waterless wilderness. Around the northern fringes of the Desert of Skulls, traders and nomads trek on camels, bringing goods to the few settlements of the northern edges of the Plain of Bronze, but they do not go far into the desert, for they know how inhospitable it is.

Pressing on further north, the desert turns into the broken wasteland of the Southern Plain, which gradually leads back into settled Allansia, where we started our journey. Much of Allansia is uncivilized and very hostile, and it must be said that there is as much adventure to be found in this corner of the world as any other – which is perhaps why so few adventurers need ever explore the world beyond Trolltooth Pass and the Southern Plains.

GARIUS OF HALAK
The greatest pirate of all those who ply their deadly trade along the Pirate Coast is Captain Garius of Halak. He learnt his trade in the service of the feared Captain Bartella before setting off in his own ship, *The Death's Head*, to bring fear and terror to all seamen of Allansia, both merchants and pirates alike – for Garius does not care whom he attacks, as long as it brings in gold or precious cargo. He has a secret hideout somewhere along the coast, but is normally to be found in one of the many taverns in the dockland quarter of Halak – when he is not out on the high seas in search of a heavily laden galleon, that is!

The Old World

The people of Allansia often wondered what lay across the Western Ocean, that vast rolling expanse of monster-infested water which stretched as far as the eye could see. Some said that the ocean just went on for ever, and a ship would sail until its crew died of starvation and thirst, without reaching land. Others said that you would travel for weeks and weeks, never sighting land, until you sailed over the waterfall at the end of the world! But some had heard legends which said that Allansia was once joined to two other continents, which were split apart by the gods for some terrible crime many, many centuries ago. They knew that out there somewhere was another land, though what it was like they could not imagine.

Eventually, however, brave mariners did make the crossing. Sailing due west for many weeks, with dolphins dancing around the prow and flying fish skimming by their side, they finally caught sight of land – and what a land! The first sailors from Allansia to visit the Old World, as its inhabitants called the landmass, landed near Arkleton, the capital of Analand, where they were received by the king. Scholars were eager to learn about the second continent, which they had long suspected to exist. The sailors travelled across the whole of the continent, being shown the full extent of the land they had 'discovered'. Moreover, when they came to Pollua in Lendleland, they met mariners from yet another continent, who had made the long and perilous voyage across the Ocean of Serpents from Khul. Eventually the sailors returned to Allansia, where they at once declared what they had discovered to scholars and anyone else who was interested. Now merchants and adventurers make the crossing quite regularly, with perhaps two boats a year taking goods and travellers to the continent, which ironically they called the New World for a while, until its real name was known!

The Old World is a land of contrasting regions, from the lush grassy plains of Lendleland to the unscalable peaks of the

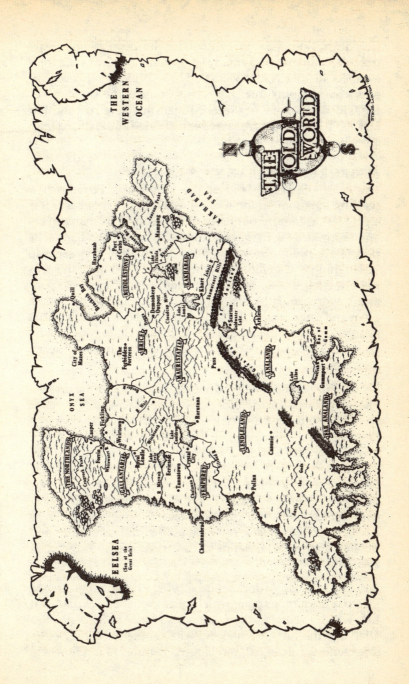

Cloudcap Mountains in Mauristatia. Its people live mostly from the land, but it has many larger settlements as well, for it escaped the cataclysmic wars that have kept the other continents from attaining true civilization. Some of the kingdoms of the Old World have not reached their full development, but just about all of them are more sophisticated and civilized than anywhere in Allansia or Khul.

FEMPHREY, CHALANNA'S LAND

The most important land at the moment is Femphrey, a wealthy kingdom on the western coast of the continent. It is a flat, fertile country of grassy plains crossed by many rivers and sprinkled with small clumps of old woodland. Its people are ruddy, brown-skinned folk who always seem to be laughing and smiling with the joys of life, though this was not always the case. Many years ago, Femphrey was a poor and tawdry land, its soil moderately fertile but its people glum and unenthusiastic. Its decrepit capital Femnis, situated near the coast on the mouth of the Femnis River, was rapidly crumbling around the ears of the king and its poverty-stricken merchants.

But all this changed when King Chalanna found the artefact known as the Crown of Kings. This magical symbol of rulership made him wise and charismatic, and he quickly inspired his people into revitalizing their country. Within the space of just a few years Chalanna had worked wonders. The capital city was torn down before it could fall down, and a brand-new one was built in its place from the proceeds of the nation's new prosperity. Named Chalannabrad after its most famous resident, it is a wide, open city, with pleasant tree-lined avenues running between large, well-built houses and clean parks and public squares, and stands at the mouth of the renamed Chalanna River.

From its impressive docklands, ships sail out into the strange Eelsea, a mysterious place which takes its name from the Great Eels which live there, though it is also home to Serpents, Sea Dragons, the huge horned Bullwhales, the mythical Decapi (frightening, intelligent, ten-legged creatures found nowhere

else on Titan), and worse. As they set out to travel up or down
the coast, or merely to fish, every boat and ship ensures that
there is a fully qualified naval sorcerer on board . . . just in
case!

At the other end of the Chalanna River lies Crystal City, a
wonderful place built entirely from crystals dredged from the
intriguing Crystal Lake. Hot springs beneath the surface of the
waters keep them very warm; sometimes, when the springs
are very active, the water of the lake actually boils. The River of

Fire which feeds the lake springs from the slopes of an active volcano high among the peaks of neighbouring Mauristatia, and brings strange minerals to the lake. These react with the steaming lake and form crystals which are mined by the people of Crystal City, and to a lesser extent by those of Rorutuna.

LENDLELAND
The people of Lendleland are very jealous of those of Femphrey in many ways. Their mining operations in Crystal Lake are nothing like as successful as those of the Femphreyans. The capital city and chief port, Pollua, is small and run down, and the fishing grounds off its coast are not as rich as those of the Eelsea. Its people are poor and superstitious. Much of the land is infertile grassy plain, suitable only for breeding wild horses (which admittedly make the best mounts in the world). In the eastern hills, rebellious barbarians still make raids on the other country, to Lendleland's eternal shame.

Their dissatisfaction came to a head in a very petty dispute with Femphrey over who actually owned the Siltbed River, which flows out of Crystal Lake and marks the boundary of the two nations. After many years of squabbling, Chalanna the Reformer in his gracious wisdom granted Lendleland full rights to the river, and at the same time lent them the awesome Crown of Kings. This tremendous gesture of peace was heartily welcomed by Lendleland: there was even some talk of the two kingdoms merging under the joint rule of Chalanna himself. But in fact the river is a poor prize. It has a thick silty bed and is tidal, so that a great many boats and barges regularly line its banks waiting for the high tide to float them off again. Its waters are also filthy with minerals and waste from the Crystal Lake, and they are not fit to drink. When the Crown was passed on to Gallantaria after four years, the people began to see Chalanna as an opportunistic swindler, and the old squabbles started again.

ANALAND AND THE EASTERN COAST
At the far eastern end of the Anvils of the Gods, the land drops sharply down towards the country of Analand, where it is

immediately blocked by the enormous Great Wall of Analand, built to check the raids of unruly barbarians from eastern Lendleland. It was a foolish gesture to attempt to build a wall around an entire kingdom, however, and the project was abandoned with several large sections missing, before the country bankrupted itself and the king was deposed! Today Analand is a pleasant land with hard-working and honest citizens. In the southern part, known as Far Analand, spices and strange plants are grown, before being carried and shipped all over the continent by merchants and ships from Gummport. Most of Analand's citizens live in the broad plain which runs north from Lake Libra. The lake is revered as a holy site of great importance, for it is said that the goddess of justice, patron goddess of Analand, once appeared to a sick man on the lakeside and cured him of his ills. The lake is now ringed with the monasteries of many religious groups; pilgrims travel to Libra from all over the land. At the far end of the fertile plain, on the banks of the Goldflow River, lies Arkleton, capital of Analand and home to its king. The river has its source in Goldwater Lake, which lies some way to the north. The lake is rich in metal ores, and fine particles of ore can actually be seen floating in suspension in the water! The town of Scarton on its shore recovers the gold and the other metals, and refines them into the ingots which give Analand much of its wealth.

THE VERMIN-PIT

Kakhabad is a wild land, populated by thieves and brigands, monsters and evil inhumans, and many other outcasts from the rest of the world. It is a land tainted by the touch of Chaos, which once festered here, and a place of wild magic and strange natural phenomena. At its centre lies Kharé, known affectionately as the Cityport of Traps.

City it certainly is, though a more disreputable, scummy, violent, ramshackle excuse for a city you could not imagine. Port? Yes – despite being close on a hundred leagues from the stormy Kakhabad Sea, Kharé is linked by the wide Jabaji River, which carries boats, barges and even large ships all the way from the sea to Kharé itself, where they meet with other boats bringing fish downstream from Lake Lumlé to the north. And the traps? Well, unfortunately, these also exist, in great numbers. They were introduced by some of the more Lawful citizens in an attempt at protection from the great many thieves and muggers who infest the city, but the plan backfired somewhat, for the Lawful citizens did not tell one another where their own traps were! Now everyone moves about carefully, sticking to parts of the city they know and avoiding strange streets and alleys.

Beyond Kharé, there are the flat plains of the Baklands, strange barren wastes where Nature's processes are perverted and controlled by the powers of Chaos, which seem to emanate from the land itself! Peculiar plants dwell everywhere; streams bubble as they boil, or creak with slabs of floating ice; bizarre creatures wander its rocky wildernesses. You will need all your wits about you to cross such an unnatural place. Beyond the Baklands, the land rises sharply to High Xamen, where the demonic Archmage has his fortress. The heights are home to deadly aerial races such as Bird Men and Life-Stealers, but if you manage to cross them you will find yourself in Ruddlestone, the first of the northern kingdoms.

THE LANDS OF THE NORTHERN PLAINS
Ruddlestone is a small, rather peculiar place, where people of many different philosophies rub shoulders with one another. The main ruling faction is the religious one, which has a decidedly military bent to it, because of the continual wars with neighbouring Brice. It was these wars which forced the people of Ruddlestone to build the massive Demonkeep Outpost on the edge of the mountains, overlooking the main approach to Brice near the Dagga River which marks the border. It is permanent home to a garrison of a thousand warrior-priests. At the other end of the kingdom – and directly opposed to such warlike organization – there are the ports. Harabnab is peaceful enough, home to all Lawful adventurers and sailors; but just down the coast lies the Port of Crabs, haven to every pirate for fifty nautical miles, who prey constantly on the shipping of the coast. Ruddlestone is a strange land to combine such opposites!

Pirates also raid the coast from the distant City of Mazes in Brice. The kingdom of Brice is very warlike, perpetually disputing with surrounding lands the extents of its shifting borders. It does this, quite simply, because it has few natural resources of its own. Its dictatorial leaders keep the people occupied in always preparing for war, centring their activity around the capital, the Forbidden Fortress.

To Brice's west lies Gallantaria, once the most important land in all the Old World, and a land with a rich history. It has had a turbulent past (mostly because of the warlike ambitions of Brice and the inhabitants of the Northlands), but has gradually settled down a little. Its capital, Royal Lendle, is home to many sages, who spend much of their time sifting through the rich archives of the ruling family's libraries in search of more coherent information about the past of their continent. Gallantaria is generally a peaceful land of peasant farmers and more wealthy townsfolk, though disturbing things still lurk on its borders. The heights of the Witchtooth Line, which divide it from Femphrey, and the Cragrock Peaks, which mark the country's northern border, are home to all kinds of outlaws and strange sects, who may one day become strong enough to threaten Gallantaria itself.

The Old World is a more settled and more civilized continent than either Allansia or Khul. But there are still many threats lurking in the wilder areas, and Kakhabad as a whole is as dangerous a place as you are likely to find anywhere on Titan. Do not think that a little civilization can hide the extreme peril of a land where Chaos once ruled and where it threatens to rule again!

Khul, the Dark Continent

Steer a ship out of Pollua in Lendleland, and head south-west by the light of the Dragon Star. Keep on until it vanishes below the horizon, at about the same time as the land behind you disappears, and you will find yourself sailing in unfamiliar seas under foreign stars. Stick true to your course, though whales and dolphins dance around your prow, and stranger creatures rear out of the water to see how edible you might be, before sinking with hardly a ripple, and in perhaps sixty days or so you will sight land again. A vast, mountainous coastline will grow nearer and nearer until it towers over your frail craft, with no sign of any inlet or bay to ease your journey. You must sail around the coastline for two or three more days before you will find somewhere to beach your craft and at last set foot on Khul.

When the world was still forming, many millennia before the first men set foot upon its surface, Khul and Allansia were joined by a narrow land-bridge, which later separated, as the two continents drifted apart, to create a string of islands. Over the centuries much has happened to the face of the world, and most of these islands have now sunk beneath the waves, allowing the ocean currents to grow stronger and stronger, and creating the all but impassable Ocean of Tempests which now separates Allansia from Khul. Many legends and improbable sailors' stories surround attempts to cross to Khul, including hair-raising tales of Sea Giants emerging from the water to 'play' with boats in scaly hands the size of archery fields, and of manta rays of even larger dimensions which skim along the surface of the water, swooping above it for short distances before gliding back into the water, their mouths wide open as they dredge for fish and other food – including unfortunate ships! Whatever the real truth behind such stories, it is certain that few sailors would ever risk their lives by trying to cross to Khul from Allansia.

The Ocean of Serpents which divides Khul from the Old World

is a safer expanse of water, but since there are few ocean-going sailors in those lands the journey has rarely been attempted. Those who know of Khul's existence hesitate before trying to cross the Serpent Ocean, though – despite its name – it offers few dangers to an experienced seagoer. The crossing to Khul becomes difficult only when you finally arrive at your destination, for the eastern side of the continent is rocky and mountainous, and the only true ports are situated further around the coastline, on the north-western and western coasts.

Those few Allansian scholars who know anything of Khul's history or geography call it the Dark Continent, though even fewer are able to state exactly why it is called by such a name. In fact the name comes partly from the physical make-up of the most settled parts, where the rocks and earth are a very dark black colour, and partly because of the tremendous wars against Chaos which took place in the centre of Khul while Allansia was in the bloodied grip of the War of the Wizards. We will return to the War against Evil and the Battle for Mankind later, when you will learn more of the ancient history of this troubled continent. For now, let it be said that any adventurer to Khul must know of, and beware, the Wastes of Chaos and the Battlegrounds.

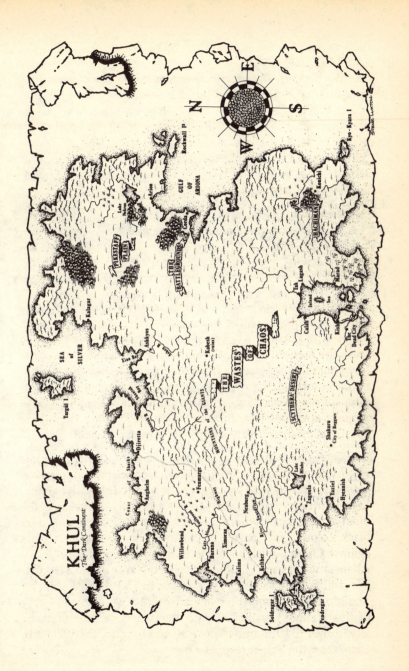

THE WASTES OF CHAOS AND THE BATTLEGROUNDS

The heart of the Dark Continent was once very different to what it is today. In ancient times it was a rugged but fertile region, with pleasant valleys between gentle mountain peaks, watered by fast-flowing rivers which ran in all directions and carried trade to the city-states on the coast. Great Evil and Chaos festered in the mountains, however, and a vast area of land at the heart of the continent was blighted when wild magic was released as Good and Evil clashed.

The Wastes of Chaos are vast areas of ash and choking dust, where life cannot sustain itself. Here and there among the decay are founts of pure Chaos, like disgusting warped oases, where the very fabric of Nature is perverted by the stuff of Chaos as it spews into the Earthly Plane. Palm trees the colour of blood twist and writhe like living beings, while mindless, jelly-like things howl in their shade; living flesh, coloured anything but pink or brown, spouts from the ash as wriggling human limbs, while mouths open in the flesh and scream; everywhere Chaos spawns and dies with frenetic abandon. It is said that the sun never shows itself over the Wastes of Chaos – they are covered by swirling clouds of grey dust which prevent Nature from ever establishing a hold on the area again.

To the north-east of the Wastes, the ash plain peters out into a barren, sandy heath, dotted with ruined towers, walls and other military constructions which culminate in the crumbling ruins of the decimated city of Kabesh. Once the capital of the

whole of northern Khul, the city was besieged by the Forces of Chaos, and finally pulled apart literally stone by stone. Now it is inhabited by the ghosts of warriors and city-folk, and also by small bands of Orcs and Trolls led by evil spell-casters who grub around in the ruins looking for ways to resurrect the dead armies buried under the Battlegrounds, and once again establish a reign of Chaos over the whole of Khul.

XIMORAN AND THE KING'S HIGHWAY

The inhabitants of the small kingdoms and city-states around the edges of Khul are unaware of the storm-clouds which are once again gathering at the heart of the continent. The most developed areas are along the western coast, and clustered around the Inland Sea on the far southern coastline. The city of Ximoran was once home to the Shakista dynasty, a long line of benevolent kings and queens who brought peace and order to the entire western coast, though sometimes more through force of arms than careful diplomacy. They built a wide road, the King's Highway. Although in places it is little more than a dirt-track these days, it can be followed south through fertile farmlands as far as the small port of Kelther at the mouth of the River Swordflow. To the north the road makes a wide sweep east, away from the massive area of wild marshland known to the local people as Scorpion Swamp, before heading north to the ancient city of Djiretta, situated on the unpleasant-sounding Coast of Sharks.

The whole area is still under the protection of the rulers of Ximoran, though since the last king died without leaving an heir over two hundred years ago it has been under the rule of a body known as the Council of Seven, made up of representatives sent from each of the major settlements of the area – Ximoran itself, Djiretta and Anghelm on the north coast, the ports of Buruna, Kalima and Kelther on the west coast, and the small walled city of Neuburg on the far southern edge of the civilized lands. The Council has no real powers, though it does provide a unified focus for the whole area, whose people would probably hide inside the walls of each town and city without it.

THE SOUTHERN LANDS

About a hundred leagues south of Neuburg you may find isolated settlements of short, swarthy humans, who were supposedly the original inhabitants of the lands right up to the Catsblood River, but who have gradually been driven further and further south over the last few centuries. They are crude, violent people, divided into clans and tribes who are fiercely protective of whatever lands they manage to call their own. Border disputes flare up from time to time, and they raid villages and farmsteads, destroying animals and crops and taking hostages and slaves, but swift action by organized troops from Neuburg usually keeps them from doing anything more dangerous.

Further south still, the land becomes more barren, turning from scrubland to wind-lashed steppes, which in turn descend to the edge of the cold Scythera Desert which cuts a desolate swath across the continent as far as the Inland Sea. A few tribes of brutish Goblins live around the edge of the mysterious (and nearly unpronounceable!) Lake Mlubz, though they are slowly dwindling in number under the combined assault of the inhospitable land and their warlike northern neighbours.

South-west of Lake Mlubz lies the abandoned city of Zagoula, once the pride of Khul but now empty and in ruins. Destroyed during the initial stages of the War against Evil, it is a terrifying place, shunned by all but the most adventurous. Some ruined towers and battlements poke above the shifting sands, but most of the city is now underground, and its streets are now tunnels wandered by strange subterranean creatures and a great many undead souls. Legend in the north talks of great riches and forgotten wisdom to be found buried among its ruined temples and palaces, but few have had the courage to explore much of it.

On the southernmost part of the west coast lie two more settlements, Yaziel and Hyennish. Both were once flourishing trading towns under the protection of the rulers of Zagoula, but when that city fell they were quick to follow, overwhelmed by massed legions of Chaotic troops. Some humans survived, however, overlooked when the armies of the enemy turned impatiently to the north to assist at the sack of Zagoula, and there are small fortified villages on both sites, perched precariously among the ruins of the old towns. Life for their inhabitants is hard, for the land has not fully recovered from the ravages of the Chaotic forces – which did not just burn the land, but also emptied it of all life-bearing Goodness – but they struggle on as best they can.

THE INLAND SEA

The cold expanses of the desolate Scythera Desert are home only to nomadic Lizard Men, and to small roving bands of shaggy desert Goblins, who make sporadic raids on the human settlements around the edge of the pirate-infested Inland Sea, which was formed many aeons ago after a massive earthquake dropped the land by several hundred metres and the sea rushed in to fill in the hollow. The area around the sea is quite fertile, and a number of small city-states have established themselves. Competition between them, be it in trade or war, is very fierce, though matters rarely get out of hand. The conniving rulers of Tak, Lagash, Marad and all the others seem to relish their positions, and set up endless alliances with one another against the rest, but then break one partnership and join another, turning violently against their previous allies with great relish. The waters of the Inland Sea are swarming with pirates and privateers, and most trading ships only sail under the protection of a flotilla of warships.

The largest of the Inland Sea's cities is Kish, a dour place which is fortified with immense walls to protect it from the warlike barbarians who dwell in the lands to the west. The people of Kish do not readily welcome strangers to their city, though they sometimes offer the highest prices to any merchant brave enough to approach them. At present Kish is allied with Lagash and Marad in a war against Shurrupak, and the Inland Sea is swarming with war-galleys battering one another into submission for the sake of a few trade treaties.

HACHIMAN, THE ISOLATED KINGDOM

East of the Inland Sea you will find only impenetrable jungles, inhabited by cannibal pygmy Lizard Men and other deadly enemies of mankind. The vegetation gradually rises up the foothills of an all but impenetrable range of mountains which have never been named by the men who dwell on the Inland Sea; in the unwieldy tongue of those who dwell on the other side of them, however, they are called the Shios'ii Mountains. The kingdom of Hachiman which lies in their shadow is completely cut off from the rest of Khul. Being a land of great fertility and natural resources, its inhabitants have never felt any need to attempt to cross the heaven-scraping peaks which isolate their land, and since they are not good sailors, they have never ventured very far along the coast of the Southern Seas.

In their isolation, the people of Hachiman have developed a very peculiar culture, combining deep spiritual belief with a ruling warrior class which has developed the most amazing skills in combat. The ruler of Hachiman is known as the Shogun, who is lord over a number of lesser nobles each of whom controls one of the small baronies dotted around the land. The ordinary citizens of Hachiman are peasants, tied to their feudal lord and master as surely as slaves. They are happy people, however, for the culture of their land teaches them to be content with their lot, and that their place as farmers is as important in the scheme of things as that of their lords. It is perhaps regrettable that other, more violent lands do not benefit from the same beliefs, though Titan would be a sad and sorry place if all lands were much the same as one another – and

SHAKURU, CITY OF BEGGARS

On the south-western edge of the Scythera Desert there sits the foulest city known to man. Called Shakuru, it is home only to the Beggar-King, Holagar the Wretched, and his plague-ridden citizens. Cast out by the rest of the world, they drift to the city in their ones and twos (though no one quite knows how they cross the storm-blown oceans where others cannot), to join their fellow outcasts. The beggars trade with the desert Goblins and the nomadic Lizard Men, to whom all humans look revolting, and raid barbarian settlements west of Kish, taking food and slaves.

Shakuru itself is little more than a massive pile of debris and rat-infested garbage, perpetually collapsing and being rebuilt by its inhabitants. In the rickety temples of the city the beggars offer up praise to Disease and Decay, their patrons and spiritual lords, by breeding rats and flies and releasing them to serve their gods by spreading unholy diseases across the world.

there would be little need for adventurers if that were so! Perhaps we should offer up a prayer that such a thing never comes about?

The Skies of Titan

How many people on Titan never look at the night sky and wonder about those glimmering candles in the heavens? More learned types, the astronomers, believe that the pinpoints of light are nothing less than other suns, possibly even circled by planets much like our own! This is such an outlandish concept that it may seem completely stupid to you, but the learned star-gazers say that mathematics proves their point – though what a few numbers have to do with the homes of the gods only they know.

However that may be, the skies overhead are packed with stars and other celestial phenomena. In the different lands different names have been given and constellations picked out, but in most lands the people firmly believe that the stars represent the forms, deeds or domains of their patron deities. See the two sky-charts opposite for examples of the forms the stars are said to take.

The planet is lit during the day by the bright yellow sun. At night, however, the moon shines like a cold grey lantern as it circles the sleeping world. Like the stars, the moon is called by many names, but every culture surprisingly believes it to be male. The swamp-dwelling peoples of south-east Allansia know it as Kuran, the child of Assamura the sun goddess. Further north the sinister Darkside Elves know the sun only as Brethin's Bane, after a legendary hero of their race who was caught by a Wood Elf's arrow after foolishly venturing above ground during the daylight hours; to them the moon is Tiriel, the Silent Guardian, who they believe watches over and protects them when they hunt under his wan light.

In some parts of the world where the Elemental Planes encroach too greatly upon the Earthly Plane, eddies of great magical power swirl across the face of the land, and all the Laws of Nature are suspended. In the Baklands, the wilderlands at the centre of Chaos-tainted Kakhabad, it is said that day and night never follow each other at equal intervals. At some times there, especially in spring when magical energy is at its peak, the sun appears never to set in the western sky for weeks on end, though in other parts of the world the skies behave as normally as ever. For reasons such as this, it cannot be stressed too highly how dangerous it is to venture into the Baklands and other such areas without very good reason!

HISTORY AND LEGEND

So that is the world of Titan, in all its tarnished glory. But how did it come to be this way? What of its history, its heroes, myths and legends? All we can do is repeat the words of the legendary mystic and scholar Raljak Lying-Jackal, who always started his books with the words, 'Read on, and all will be revealed in time . . .'

In the Beginning

But where shall we start? In the course of our studies for this book, we have drawn on the combined knowledge of the wisest sages of the three continents. As a result, we have collected much information that duplicates, contradicts or ignores other material. If we had given in to our initial urges, simply to tell all that we heard, this book would be ten times the size it is, and we would still be writing it! Therefore, what we have done is chosen the tales, myths and legends which, in our judgement, offer the clearest picture of the past of this world. There is much that we have omitted – though we were loath to do so – and many things have been glossed over. The tale of King Aradax and the Scared Donkey, the legend of Ruritag Half-Orc, the story of the Fall of the Savage Innocents, and many others, must all wait for another book.

But where shall we start? Let us start at the beginning, with the creation of Titan as taught by the priests of Lendleland and Gallantaria. This account is couched in very mythical terms, and it seems likely that much of it was initially invented to explain the unexplainable to the primitive peoples of pre-history.

In the days before Time had been found by the trickster god, Logaan, and unleashed on to the world by Death, the gods sat or lounged around the great palace of the Celestial Court.

There were a great many gods in those days, hundreds of them, and each was different. Moreover, each god was served by a host of lesser beings, demigods or 'lesser gods', who also had their own personalities and their own tasks to perform. And they were bored with their lives. There were no years, months or days, and no one got any older and no one died, but many were being born all the time. And nothing ever happened that was very interesting.

All the higher gods and goddesses had magical powers, so that they could do anything they wished. But even though they were gods few of them had much imagination, and they soon got tired of doing the same things all the time. True, some deities seemed to keep themselves occupied: black Death and his brothers, Disease and Decay had great fun going around disassembling gods and demigods into their component parts, and the other gods had to come along and put their friends back together again. But even this became boring in time, no matter how spectacularly Death and his cohorts presented their peculiar entertainment.

One day, however, the goddess known as Throff was digging with her sister Galana in their luscious gardens. (These gardens, incidentally, were completely different from the 'gardens' of Titan. They were places of great beauty, where glowing crystals and light-beams grew, to the delight of the gods and goddesses of the palace.) She had transformed her hand into the shape of a spade, and was slowly scraping a hole in the soil for a massive blue-green crystal which she wished to plant, when she unearthed a large lump of magic soil, which vibrated and pulsed with life! Throff ran to her sister Galana, and showed her the clay; she knew just what they should do with it.

Throff and Galana took the clay to their father Titan, who divided it in two and then fashioned and worked at one half with his hands until it was perfectly round. And Titan took his creation, and set it among the Planes, so that everyone could see. The gods of the Court were amazed by this new idea, and they wanted to know more about it. But Death and his brothers did not come to look, for they thought it was going to be just another tedious diversion which would soon pale into insignificance.

Now Titan divided the other half of the clay up among the greater Gods. Hydana, husband to Throff, made patterns on the sphere, which were water. Throff herself put down a large mass of clay, which she called land. Galana fashioned trees, flowers and plants from the clay and planted them on the land. And one by one the gods filed up to Titan, and were allowed to take a piece of the magical stuff and make creatures in their own image, which were placed on his creation, which was called Titan after him. Beautiful Glantanka danced around it, the light of her face illuminating it with a golden glow, and she became the sun. She was followed by her brother, who danced in her wake, and became the moon. But while the gods were celebrating their new creation, Death stole some of the clay, secreting it in the black folds of his cloak before gliding away again.

LOGAAN'S CREATION
Soon the creation was buzzing with creatures of all shapes and sizes. And the gods walked on the new world, and played with their creations. Hydana swam in the waters he had made, playing with the fish and the other creatures of the deep which Ichthys and his fellows had created. On the land, Throff, Galana and the other creators danced and played, delighting in the beauty of the things they had made. They gave names to everything they had made, and laughed and were happy. Titan looked down upon it all, and was very pleased. But before him stepped the god Logaan, whom we know now as the Trickster. He had been disassembled by Death and his brothers at the time Titan was giving out clay, but now he wanted to take his turn. Titan had kept back some clay, for he was a wise god, and gave a little of what remained to Logaan.

And Logaan went down to the new world, and looked at what had been made so far. None of it was to his taste, and he decided to make an entirely new shape. It had just two legs, with a pair of arms higher up its body, and it was tall and thin. But to make it special, Logaan took a piece of himself, and placed it inside the head of his creation, and then breathed over it, to set it going. And he called it Man.

THE ORIGINS OF THE GODS

The question of who made the gods of the Celestial Court has vexed religious men and women from the dawn of time. The race of humans who used, before their cities were destroyed in the War of the Wizards, to dwell in the area now marked by the barren eastern coast of the Flatlands, left records among their ruins which show that they believed the gods were made by a trio of primal beings. They called the three Ashra, Elim and Vuh, crudely translated as Light, Dark and Life, and believed that a combination of the powers of all three helped shape the Celestial Court. The strange peoples who dwelt on the Isles of the Dawn before the eruption of the volcano that sank most of them beneath the waters believed that ruling over the Court there was a single god greater than all the others, who fashioned the gods and let them create their own world. They called him Arn, which meant the First, and they believed that when they died they would ascend to the heavens to join him.

THE CREATION OF THE OTHER RACES

When the other gods and goddesses saw Logaan's creation, they laughed heartily at it, for it looked very peculiar as it walked along on its two spindly legs. But they saw it dig in the earth and pull up rocks, and use the rocks to cut through trees, and use the trees to make a shelter from the water which Hydana's brother Sukh was casting on the world. And they saw it take its rocks, and strike them together, and make a light as bright as heavenly Glantanka herself, which gave out heat and kept the chill winds of Pangara away. The gods saw that the creature could think like they could, could reason and create, and they wondered where it had come from.

When Logaan told them he had put a bit of himself into the creature, the gods were horrified! Many of them went back to their creations, shocked that a god had mutilated himself. Only Galana, Throff and Titan stayed to commiserate with poor, foolish Logaan, for secretly they were very interested in learning more about his creation. They asked him to show them how he had made his 'Man', and he did so by making another. But he had already used up that piece of himself which he had placed in the head of Man, and so he placed another part of himself in the heart of his second creation, breathed upon it until it awoke, and called it Woman.

The three deities were impressed, and decided to make their own creatures along similar lines. Titan took a part of his strength and size, and transformed it into a Giant. Throff took a part of her rocky skin and made the first Dwarf. And Galana took her grace and her knowledge, and made the first Elf. They set their creatures on the face of the world, and retired to the palace of the Celestial Court to watch them multiply and spread across the world alongside Man.

This period is known as the Godtime, and it was one of great peace and happiness for the races of men, Dwarfs, Elves and Giants. They lived together at first, but gradually divided as their numbers became greater, each taking one part of the world for their own. Man took the plains, Elves the forests, Dwarfs the hills and Giants the mountains. They dwelt in fine cities and prospered, and grew strong and healthy. They made strange tools and weapons, with which to catch other creatures for their food, and learnt how to use the natural magic inherent in the earth, all under the watchful eyes of their patron gods. During the day, golden Glantanka danced across the heavens, and at night the moon would cast its silvery light upon the world.

VARIATIONS ON THE CREATION MYTH

Various cultures have their own variations on this story. To the people of ancient Arantis, then ruled over by a dynasty of powerful warrior-queens, Logaan gave his brain to Woman, who was created first, and then his heart to Man. Other races have believed that both creatures were made together, and that first Man and first Woman shared head and heart with Logaan. There are also some religions which believed that it was not Logaan (usually a very foolish god in human mythology), but a much more admirable deity such as Sukh the storm god (who is also known as Kukulak).

A rather imaginative warlock once tried to argue that everything was in fact created by Death and his brothers, but his theories were rejected because they explained too much of what was wrong in the world!

DEATH WALKS ON TITAN

But one night, Death and his brothers caught hold of the moon, which did not rise over Titan that night. In the darkness, the evil gods went among the races of men, Dwarfs, Elves and Giants, and did much damage. They set dark creatures on the world, made from the stolen clay and tainted by their evil minds; they made them creatures of Chaos. Xiarga, the horned snake, slithered into the world, accompanied by Arhallogen the spider king, Basilisk the lizard, Gargoyle and the Behemoth, a gigantic sea monster. That same night, the creature known as Hashak the Creator planted his own creatures, the Orcs, in the shadows and corners of the world, where they bred and thrived in the darkness.

When morning came, Glantanka began her dance across the face of the world again, but looking down she could see only thick black clouds, which hid Death's foul creatures from the sight of the gods. By the middle of the day, the gods were despairing of the fate of their creatures, and pondering whether they should risk journeying down to the surface of Titan to investigate, when Death and all his supporters filed into the Celestial Court. With Death were his brothers, Disease and Decay, but also a number of minor gods such as Slangg and Tanit, and a great force of demigods, who were ugly and bestial to look upon. Between them they carried a large sack, in which a number of objects writhed and wriggled. Death spoke to the stunned gods gathered there, a chilling leer in his voice and a bottomless pit in his night-black eyes.

'My dear friends,' Death began. 'My dear friends, I have watched your laughable attempts at creation with great amusement and enjoyment. The time has come, however, to show you how it should be done. Follow me . . .' Saying this, Death transported the gods to the surface of Titan, amid gasps of shock and indignant protests. Looking around them, the gods could see only darkness and smoke, but when Death raised his hands it lifted, to reveal a landscape of carnage and utter devastation. The lifeless bodies of men and animals lay everywhere, and feasting on their corpses were the foul creations of death.

Shaking the wriggling simpleton Logaan out of the sack, Death continued his speech: 'This . . . ah . . . creature is a complete fool, but he can be very useful now and again. While nosing about in one of the furthest Planes, he came across something strange, a new god, who possesses a power which has not been heard of before. Gods and goddesses, I give you Time!'

At that the sack was upended a second time, and a repulsive figure fell out. As it cowered in front of the assembled gods, it seemed to change form. First it was young and smooth, like a new-born child, then it was middle-aged and rough, before changing again into a wrinkled old man. As it changed from one to the next, the god Decay began to laugh deeply, while Death outlined his terms:

'I want this miserable little creature of yours, all of it, and you are going to give it to me. Otherwise I shall release Time into the universe, and everything shall become mortal, and eventually die. Time has this power, for he represents the replacement of everything that was by everything that is to come. If Time is released there will be no more immortality, and even the gods will be susceptible to my power – they will be able to die!' As one, the gods said, 'No! This shall not be!' – at which Death and his forces turned and stormed from the room. The First Battle was about to begin.

THE FIRST BATTLE
Death and his forces of evil retired to one of the Outer Planes, where they readied themselves for battle. The evil gods had not been idle while waiting for the others to react to their assault on the world, and they had created many more creatures of Chaos, which they formed into a gibbering, writhing army, and marched on the Celestial Court. When they arrived, however, they found it completely empty, for the other gods had gone down to Titan to pull together the Forces of Good for the battle to come.

At last the two sides faced each other across a wide, grassy plain. On one side were the Forces of Death, led by the unholy god and his twin brothers, wrapped in their black robes. Alongside and behind them were snakes, wolves, basilisks, spiders and a great many formless creatures, revolting slimy beings which continually sprouted parts of other beings in

cruel mockery of the creations of the Lawful gods. Flying above the army was a cloud of bats, vultures and other creatures which had been tainted by Death's touch. A large horde of Orcs, Trolls and Goblins stood ready for battle. And at the rear were the demigods, including the repulsive Sith, Ishtra, Myurr, Relem and Vradna. They had dressed themselves in hard steel armour forged especially for the battle, and they formed themselves into a square around Time. The black banners of Death's army bore no motif.

Facing them were the Forces of Good, led by a vanguard of the greater gods, including Titan, Throff, Sukh and many others. Even gentle Galana was with them, veiled so that none should see the fear in her eyes. In a long line to either side were soldiers from all four races, armed and ready for battle. Eagles and other birds of prey, led by the Hawklord himself, swooped above them, crying out warnings to their opponents in anticipation of the coming hunt. There were other creatures too – centaurs, lions, tigers, and many which exist no longer. Bringing up the rear were a host of gleaming golden Dragons, Glantanka's own creations, prepared especially for the battle and led by Kilanirax, once the sun goddess's servant, but now Dragon king.

From the ranks of the evil armies, a skeletal warrior stepped forward, and blew one harsh, discordant note on a horn; and the battle began. The streaming Forces of Evil swept howling down on the thin line of their enemy, while magic burst in the air above them. The line of Dwarfs, men, Elves and Giants held, and they returned with an assault of their own, but heavy casualties were sustained by both sides. More attacks were made; again and again the armies clashed. Bodies were falling everywhere, and the gods of Good were looking at one another in despair. Screaming in anger, Death and his brothers gathered their powers and let a thunderbolt fly at the gods opposite them. It struck Throff, burning her skin terribly, but was answered with another bolt from her sister Galana, the Dragon king Kilanirax and the sun goddess Glantanka. The bolt flew straight through the heart of the evil armies, passing through the creatures of darkness and Chaos as if they were

not there, just as the sun chases away shadows, just as strength and goodness will always cut through the worst excesses of Evil. It struck Time and blew him apart, with a thunderclap that reverberated across the cosmos. The dark gods were surrounded; without Time they were powerless to fight back and their forces fled in disarray. But Time was scattered throughout the world of Titan, and thus all its peoples are mortal, while the gods are not.

Titan, as spokesman for the gods, asked for the captured Dark Lords to be killed, but Throff pleaded for them only to be exiled, for killing them would be an act of Evil. And so the Dark Lords and their minions were banished into the Void, where they could do little harm. And the gods left the surface of Titan, feeling ashamed that they had already brought so much pain and suffering to their beautiful creation. Now they look down on the planet from the sky every night, for ever frozen as the stars in the poses they took up while trying to protect the world from the effects of Time. They will never grow old, for they are gods, but now mortal beings will always age and die, after their allotted span. Some races are protected by the gods, who help them stay alive for more than their time, but in the end all will go to their graves.

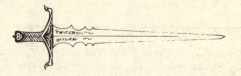

The Time of Heroes

After the gods had departed from the world in the aftermath of the First Battle, the races returned, battered but unbowed, to their respective homelands. At about this time, writing was first invented, and a number of puzzling records have survived, painted on fragments of pottery and stamped on sheets of metal.

For many hundreds of years, scholars have been digging such things out of the ruins of the ancient cities of the world, and they have begun to work out what they actually say in the peculiar languages of the planet's first civilized peoples.

Now that the gods kept their distance from earthly affairs, the first human heroes began to make their names known. The names of kings, warriors and magicians, including vague references to people like King Harar of Granat, Birel Brother-slayer and Zergoul Whitelightning, begin to figure strongly in these ancient writings, though there is still a good deal of religious writing as well.

THE UNITED CONTINENT

At this time, all the lands of the world were still joined together into one massive continent, which these early records call Irritaria. It was not until almost a thousand years after the beginning of Time that they were divided in the drowning of Atlantis, by which time the kingdoms of the world had risen and declined and risen again. But in those early years, there were few such kingdoms. Men regressed from the Golden Age of the utopian cities they had enjoyed under the patronage of the gods, and now they struggled to survive in competition with the teeming Orcs, Trolls, Goblins and (after a few hundred years) the first foul Chaotic Ogres.

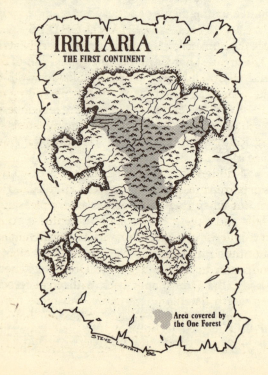

IRRITARIA
THE FIRST CONTINENT

Area covered by the One Forest

The Dwarfs had slipped away to their underground domains, where they were digging ever deeper into the earth in search of riches. In ancient mountains in the far north of Irritaria, the Dwarf lord, Hangahar Goldseeker, was making the first tentative bores which would eventually turn into the enormous undying city of Fangthane, immortal home of the Dwarf people.

The Elves, meanwhile, had returned to their beloved forests, and were investigating their own powers of magic and intellect. The first of the great Elven sorcerers, remembered only as the White Lord, was communing with Galana at the heart of the One Forest, delving deep into the fundamental forces of magic and ritual. The One Forest, which stretched right across the continent at that time, was the home of the greatest number of Elves the world has ever seen: their decline has always been in direct relation to the destruction of their forest homes.

THE TALE OF THE HALFHAND CHIEFS

But it was the humans on whom those early archivists concentrated. The greatest heroes of the time were a pair of brothers, Rerek and Myzar Halfhand, who cut a bloody swath through the western lands as leaders of a tribe of horse-riding nomads. Their battles with the Orcs of that region are remembered by us in the form of two folk-songs, though the minstrels of today who sing 'Riding with Halfhand' or 'Tie Down the Warrior' do not realize it!

They had ridden with their tribe across over two thousand leagues of barren grassland, in search of a fertile land in which to settle. But when they came across a very pleasant area of gentle hills and valleys overlooking the endless ocean, they found it teeming with Orcs, who were taking advantage of the fertility of the area. The tribe was despondent after its long trek, and immediately engaged the Orcs in pitched battle! Surprisingly, the Orcs fought back with great ferocity. The area was worth defending, certainly, but more importantly there was the principle involved – humans should not be allowed to ride around stealing other people's lands, like spoilt children who cry every time they see something they want.

The running battles against the Orcs continued for around twenty-five years, with both sides slowly chipping away at each other. Many heroic confrontations took place, and the names of the Halfhand brothers became known to humans across many parts of the continent. Their dramatic ambushes, the rescue of their kidnapped children from the Orcs' cooking-pots and the burning of the Orcs' major town were sung about from one side of the world to the other, and the numbers of the humans were swelled as warriors flocked to join them. Eventually, the sheer persistence of the human invaders drove the Orcs into a complex of caves in the hills, where every one of them starved to death in three months! It is a lesson to us all to reflect that it was very definitely the humans who were in the wrong in this case, but it is also the humans who are celebrated as the heroes!

THE SPLITTING OF THE LANDS

Gradually, the wandering tribes began to settle down throughout the continent, for agriculture took over from hunting as the main source of food and the distant lands were explored and found to be fertile. Slowly but surely, mankind gathered itself together into small villages, which grew into towns, and then into small cities, and finally into nations. Trade began, and nation communicated with nation. But at the same time, nation fought with nation – as is the way of humans who compete for the best things, be they land, precious metals or whatever. It is believed that it was at this time that the tyrant Faramos XXIII – really the Demon Prince Myurr – rose in Atlantis, which was promptly sunk beneath the waves by the combined actions of the outraged gods. Unfortunately, very little information has ever been discovered about this time, for most contemporary records seem deliberately to have blotted the whole epoch from their memories. It is as if the whole world wished to forget whatever atrocities the people of Atlantis had inflicted. For what few details we have managed to glean of this time, you should read the later section on the underwater kingdoms of Titan, which gives more background to this cataclysmic event.

As penance for the crazed actions of the Atlanteans, the gods apparently split the lands and formed the three continents. Such drastic action cost the lives of many beings and creatures, as gigantic waves flooded the coastal regions while the landmasses were driven to their new resting-places. The One Forest of the Elves was split into many parts, and the long, slow decline of the Elven peoples began. Sections of the One Forest still survive in some lands, such as the enormous Forests of Night near present-day Sardath in north-east Allansia, and around Lake Nekros in Khul, but they are a pale shadow of the magnificent, continent-spanning wall of greenery that the One Forest must have been.

The Rise of Civilization

After the long, slow haul to civilization, the cataclysm surrounding the splitting of the continents set mankind back at least five hundred years. When the blackened skies had finally cleared and the waters had receded, man found himself scattered across the globe. The only cities which had not been turned to ruins by the wrath of the gods were those built into mountains by Dwarfs. But slowly, by degrees, mankind began to organize again.

The first major settlements in the new lands began to grow about 350–400 years after the sinking of Atlantis, on the coasts of all three continents; again, small villages turned into towns, and towns eventually became cities and then states. The central eastern coastline of Khul was home to a thriving collection of small trading towns, which eventually began gathering themselves into a unified state known as Klarash around the year 1510 OT (or Old Time). On the shores of the Onyx Sea, in what is now Gallantaria in the Old World, Orjan the Builder started gathering his tribe around him and building a town. And along the edges of Allansia, a few states began to establish their power; the city of Vynheim, which still exists, was founded as a small fishing settlement in 1530 by the father of the legendary northern hero, Bjorngrim Giant-slayer.

BJORNGRIM OF VYNHEIM

Bjorngrim Bjorngrimsson was a typical northman – large, broad-shouldered and red-haired, and with a lust for strong ale and honourable battle. On the death of his father in 1583 OT, he became chief of a thriving port, which traded with other settlements further down the treacherous coast and, across what was then called the Witch Sea, with the people who dwelt on the string of islands known as the Giant's Teeth. The Witch Sea was a very dangerous place, fog-bound in the summer and full of deadly icebergs in the winter: the people of Vynheim believed it was haunted by the ghosts of those mariners who had been wrecked there, and who still wailed forlornly. After four boats were lost in a month, the people of Vynheim became afraid, and would not set sail.

So it was up to their leader, Bjorngrim, to prove both his bravery and the safety of the waters. He set out single-handed in a small ketch, *The Lusty Dwarf*, either to prove that there was nothing to be afraid of, or to face up to whatever was haunting the Witch Sea. He sailed for eight days, being blown north towards the Iceberg Straits by fierce gales. The temperature dropped and icicles formed on the boat, while icebergs bobbed around him, but the northman kept his tiller straight, knowing that his gods would see him through. On the ninth day a fog closed in, and from its depths he heard a wailing, moaning sound. Suddenly a heart-stoppingly tall Sea Giant rose out of the waters with a crash of grinding ice, and reached out for the boat with one massive green hand. Bjorngrim gritted his teeth, muttered a hasty curse, and made ready with his axe. But as the hand scooped down, he saw a better plan.

His heart in his mouth, he leapt on to the hand, and kept on running. Although the Giant was covered with ice, its skin was also pitted and gave the northman the grip he needed to reach the titanic shoulders. There he paused for a split second, gazing up into the eyes which regarded him with an intelligence so slow he felt sure he could hear it creaking, before swinging a colossal blow at the Sea Giant's neck. The axe bit deep, and a gush of freezing blood knocked Bjorngrim backwards, down into the water. When he surfaced again, he was only a few arm-lengths from his boat, which he pulled himself into just as the Giant's brain received the message from its body that it was dead, and that it should fall over. Ten days later, Bjorngrim Giant-slayer sailed into Vynheim Sound, towing the body of the Sea Giant behind him. The people of Vynheim bestowed his nickname upon him immediately, and also renamed the Witch's Sea, so that even now it is known as Bjorngrim's Sea.

THE AGE OF WIZARDS
Around the year 1650, the continent now known as Allansia was divided up into a large number of peaceful kingdoms and principalities. The largest of these was Allansia itself, which stretched from the Whitewater River as far north as the River Kok. Its capital, Carsepolis, was a wide, well-constructed cityport, which managed to be both a seat of culture and a place of protection against the tribes of Orcs and other inhuman races which still rampaged around the northern plains. Ruling over Carsepolis at this time was the Dynasty of Swords, founded in 1601 by King Coros Sword-bearer, and now represented by his grandson Coros III (also known, it appears, as the Oath-breaker, though no records that we have seen indicate why or how the young king acquired such a damning name).

From the River Kok north and east the country of Goldoran ran as far as the northern edge of the Flatlands (which even in those days were desolate and primitive, home only to the superstitious builders of stone monuments and to nomads). South of the Whitewater River, the Southern Plains were crisscrossed with the trails of merchants and adventurers, who travelled between the small interior town of Salamonis and the two walled city-states of Cutsilver and Balkash, which lay in the middle of the plains and on the coast respectively. The Desert of Skulls, to the south of the plains, was much smaller then, and apparently less dangerous too. There were several small cities clustered along the southern extent of the Craggen Mountains, where you will now find only a few villages on the rarely used road between Warpstone and Wolftown. Merchants travelled far and wide across the continent in search of new markets, and returned to the northern lands with fragrant oils and spices, and tales of the exotic eastern lands which at that time circled the Sea of Pearls and the Shabak Peninsula.

Further south, the city of Kaynlesh-Ma, founded around 1585 OT as a small port at the mouth of the River Eltus and now nominal capital of the country of Arantis, was growing in prominence, and trade was just being started with the tiny cityport of Halak (its partner Rimon started as an overspill for Halak two hundred years later) and the country of Allansia and its neighbours. Kaynlesh-Ma, however, was a very different place from the northern city-states, for it was home to an increasing number of sorcerers.

High magic at that time was very much the province of the Elves, who had a long tradition of its use and practice. By now, however, the Elves had withdrawn into their forests, and their high sorcerers were never seen by any but the very luckiest humans and the unluckiest Orcs. What most people thought of when magic was mentioned were the tricks of hedge-wizards and old women for keeping fleas off or for making village maidens fall in love with you. The shamans of the Orcs and Goblins still practised their magic, but it was so warped and perverted from the pure beauty of the original that it could not be considered in the same context. The magic of Orc shamans tended, and still tends, to be a very repetitive cycle of conjuring up the spirits of ancestors to ask for guidance for the future, and the casting of luck spells before battle, all tied up with a great deal of very tedious mumbo-jumbo.

In the depths of Arantis, a number of scholars had discovered an ancient temple, purporting to be from the earliest ages of

history. It was haunted by the spirits of a trio of ancient sorcerers, who had re-appeared on the Earthly Plane because they had decided it was time that the world knew of sorcery again. The scholars, who – the histories tell us – numbered five, but who obviously did not have very memorable names, immediately leapt at the chance of learning secrets which had been lost to mankind for many millennia. They refurbished the temple at Aranath, as the place was known, and began the slow task of learning the deepest secrets of high magic. As the sorcerers grew more and more engrossed in their studies, they were commanded to travel the earth, acquiring knowledge for the temple and teaching their skills as they went.

This began in the 1690s, and by 1712 the noted sorcerer Erridansis had arrived in Salamonis and founded the school of magic based at the centre of the nearby Forest of Yore (which in those days stretched from the Vale of Willow to the very fringes of Darkwood). Wizardry became a much-respected profession, as every nobleman in the land tried to better King

Salamon by sponsoring a greater sorcerer. Several schools of wizardry were founded, in Carsepolis and in Gar-Goldoran, the capital city of Goldoran, and the air over the northern lands was always full of staff-riding sorcerers and the flash of magic!

There were wars in those days, of course, for there are wars wherever man hoards gold and other possessions and keeps them away from other men. But with the advent of court sorcerers, a good deal of bloodshed was avoided by sending them away to desolate moors and making them fight a duel, with appropriate penalties being incurred by the country of the loser. Moreover, the threats of Orcs and Goblins receded for a time as they met with frightening resistance in the form of fire-wielding sorcerers who blasted away with wild magic and cut great holes through their ranks! For a while, at least, Orcs were reduced to sneaking through settled countries at night, for fear of attracting the attentions of the sorcerers who led the armies of Allansia.

THE CITY-STATES OF THE OLD WORLD
While sorcerous powers were growing in prominence in Allansia, far across the Western Ocean other things were happening. The Old World has always been a far more civilized continent than either Allansia or Khul, which can in part be put down to the fact that there have, in recent years, been few wars cataclysmic enough to set the rise of civilization back at all.

As the darkened skies created in the destruction of Atlantis slowly began to clear, the varied peoples of the Old World were already beginning to settle down and take the first tentative steps on the road towards civilization. Before the continents had been split by the gods as penance for the evil of Atlantis, the peoples of the one continent, which we call

67

Irritaria, wandered far and wide, bringing some uniformity to every land. After the split, the same people could still be found on each continent, so that there were horse-nomads on the Flatlands of Allansia and in the corresponding area on the other side of the Ocean of Serpents, the plains of Lendleland.

But gradually the many peoples began changing, and different lands produced their own cultures. Isolated from the other two continents, the Old World developed a strange, rather quirky series of cultures, very different from those of Khul and Allansia, which, in turn, are different from each other.

At the centre of the Old World there are the nearly uncrossable heights of Mauristatia, which have meant that man has tended to settle on the coastal plains around them. The first major settlements we have records of were on the coast of the Onyx Sea. In 1430 OT, the character every Gallantarian schoolchild knows as Orjan the Builder brought his tribe down across the plains from the southern highlands they had roamed for many hundreds of years, and began building a small village where two rivers joined. He called it Lendle, an old mountain-man's word for flat plains, which described the countryside around the village very well. Orjan's people found other small villages on the plains, inhabited by men and women much like themselves. Trading began, and slowly the villages grew into small walled towns. After his father's death in 1464, Orjan's son, Regulus the Unifier, took over the leadership of Lendle. As the prosperity of the region grew in leaps and bounds, more and more settlements began to grow in the shadow of Lendle, until, in 1498, a treaty between eight of the largest towns created the nation of Gallantaria. Its ruler was Regulus, and its capital was Lendle or, more properly now, Royal Lendle.

Gallantaria grew quickly under the inspired leadership of Regulus. His warriors brought the benefits of his rule to neighbouring lands, and slowly but surely the borders moved back as other towns and villages realized the benefits of belonging to Gallantaria. Gallantaria spread northwards, bringing peace and prosperity to the people who were beginning to settle along the Whitewater River. Further north,

however, the Gallantarians found themselves faced with the insurmountable mass of the Cragrock Peaks.

They also found themselves faced with the Netherworld Sorcerers. These mystical spell-casters lived in a small colony high up in the Crag-rocks, from where they looked down on the southern lands. They had been living there for as long as any of the local hillmen could remember, and they were a perilous people. In Gallantaria, and indeed in the whole of the northern lands, spell-casters were few and far between. As the tribes had slowly settled down and founded villages, their shamans became sorcer-ers, but the tradition of high magic in Gallantaria was only a hundred years old; the Netherworld Sorcerers had been practising it for centuries before the continents were broken up! They resisted every attempt by the forces from Gallantaria to bring 'civilization' to the Cragrocks, turning Regulus's first son into a standing stone, and his second and third into a pair of stunted oak trees.

The Gallantarians, therefore, looked in other directions for the expansion of their realm. Heading east across the wide, fertile lands as far as what is now called the Border River, they found small hamlets and villages who stated that they owed no allegiance to King Regulus, for they were already pledged to the lords of Brice. Another nation had risen and spread quickly across the rolling land as far as the Brackish Bay beyond the Onyx Sea. And beyond Brice, the tiny kingdom of Ruddlestone was slowly rising in power under the leadership of their priest-king. Emissaries arrived in Royal Lendle from a place beyond the southern peaks, which called itself Femphrey, and they revealed that the southern lands were slowly being settled too.

In the space of perhaps a hundred years, the continent became covered with many small nations. Regular trade-routes linked the major towns, which slowly turned into cities. Caravans crossed the continent, from Royal Lendle in the north as far as Arkleton, the new capital of the nation which now called itself Analand. True, the way was still fraught with danger, especially when passing the Demon-haunted heights of the Witchtooth Line and hastily crossing the eastern parts of Lendleland, where horse-nomads and primitives still hunted each other, but as trade became ever more important the routes attracted other settlers, who began to civilize many more areas. But with trade there always comes war, it seems, for soon Gallantaria found itself drawn into conflict with Brice, which wished to expand its borders to take advantage of the better farming-land further west. Many battles were fought during the reign of Regulus's great-great-grandson, King Werkel, until a truce was finally agreed, which made the newly renamed Border River the new boundary of the lands.

Having had its taste of battle, however, Brice wanted more, and looked eastwards towards Ruddlestone. The people of the small nation were very religious, ruled by a priest-king who they fully believed to be the divine representative of their gods on the Earthly Plane. Spurred into action by forays into their land by soldiers from Brice, the good people of Ruddlestone built their massive Demonkeep Fortress, and filled it with a garrison of fanatical warriors, who have kept an unsleeping eye on Brice ever since. In response, Brice turned into an increasingly warlike state too, with things coming to a head in the First and Second Ruddlestone Wars of 1735 and 1805.

ANALAND AND ITS WALL

While the lands of the north were fighting among themselves, the southern province of Analand was slowly becoming more and more civilized under the influence of several hundred years of benevolent rule by the Arkle Dynasty. The kings of Analand became known for their careful, considerate rule, which turned Analand from just another collection of small trading towns into a civilized centre for trade and learning. But outsiders looked at Analand with envy and greed. Surely, ran the thoughts of every two-bit sorcerer and brigand in the southlands, if the land is so peaceful and contented, it must be wealthy beyond compare.

So, from all sides, Analand was suddenly assailed by raiders, who burnt villages, desecrated temples, and put whole areas to the sword. The whole tone of Analand changed, as warriors became more commonplace than farmers or traders on the roads leading north and west. Relations with Lendleland, whose citizens many of the raiders ostensibly were, became strained almost to the point of war, which was averted only after careful diplomacy on both sides. After forty years of incessant raids, King Arkle XIX could take it no longer. With his team of advisers, he drew up a plan which would help protect Analand from all opportunistic brigands and mercenaries. His plan was simple – build a wall around the land and the raiders would not be able to get in!

In 1845 OT, the building of the Great Wall of Analand was begun. It was an immense project, planned to take a hundred and twenty years, but it suffered immediate setbacks when the first section was torn down stone by stone by a massive force of raiders. The Analanders drove them back, but they returned again and again, hindering the work with carefully planned attacks. The deadline for the wall came and went, with only half of its length completed and the land near to bankruptcy and revolution as all resources were poured into keeping the wall going. Finally, in the year 1970 OT, work on the Great Wall of Analand was stopped for good. It was incomplete in three places, and in many other places it was already crumbling as a result of the repeated poundings of raiders from Lendleland, but to be fair it did protect Analand in many places, and it is often awesomely impressive.

Now that the Great Wall was officially 'finished', Analand could concentrate on rebuilding its trade and economy, and continue its path towards civilization. Across the whole of the Old World, the nations were settling down. Disputes were still too frequent, but by now they had fallen into a routine of threat, counter-threat, border skirmish, diplomatic protest, major battle, and then peace. Brice still squabbled with anyone it could; raiders still used Lendleland as a base for attacks on isolated parts of Far Analand; pirates began to prey on merchants rounding the northern capes, but they had little effect on the volume of trade; dark things still lurked in the highlands and the vermin-pit of Kakhabad, and made occasional forays into the lowlands, only to be driven back again. Everything carried on much as normal.

The Spawning of Chaos

While Allansia and the Old World were slowly pulling themselves towards civilization, in the far land of Khul stranger
things were beginning, things which would eventually affect
all of Titan. At first, however, the growth of this continent was
very similar to that of the other two.

Khul was originally a very fertile land, with a semi-circular arc
of gently rolling steppes enclosing a wide central area of flat
moorland and grassy plain, cut by wide, slow-moving rivers.
The early people of this land were mostly uncivilized hunters
and foragers, experts at tracking and killing game, but not so
good at writing or counting. In the western lands, however,
game became scarce and people took to living off the land.
Eventually a few villages began forming along the coast, and
then further inland. Around 1510 OT, a number of small towns
along the west coast were unified under the rule of King
Klarash Silverhair, and the nation of Klarash was formed.
Under his rule, the nation slowly grew, until by the year 1565 it
stretched from the southern edge of Scorpion Swamp (then, as
now, a perilous place of danger and adventure) to the River
Swordflow. Incidentally, the latter received its name in 1542,
when the first exploratory party of warriors from Klarash came
under attack from a horde of diminutive Goblins while
attempting to ford it. Up to their chests in water, the warriors
attempted to draw their weapons, but were swept off balance
and rushed away by the current to their deaths.

As Klarash grew in size and stature, it began sending its
merchants further and further afield. They travelled across the
central plains to small settlements like Remara, Varese and
Kabesh, and south to the small fishing villages on the edge of
the Inland Sea, and eventually even further afield, rounding
the Mountains of the Giants and heading north to Ashkyos.
Soon merchants were travelling back and forth so frequently
that small settlements grew up at intervals along the route,
eventually turning into towns themselves.

Klarash grew rich and powerful, and in the reign of Silverhair's grandson, Klarash III, work was started on a new capital, Shakista, in the centre of the kingdom, on the banks of the Kasbled River (now known as the Catsblood). The kingdom was expanded further north, as far as the small port of Djiretta on the Coast of Sharks, but to the south the way was blocked by tribes of primitives and Goblins, who fought tooth and claw to remain on their lands. Eventually, however, the armies of Klarash pushed them back. To keep them from returning, the city of Zagoula was founded in 1611 OT. Designed by the best stonemasons and architects the king could find, it was a very beautiful place, a haven for scholars, artists and sorcerers, who felt they could fully get to grips with their subjects in such a stunning city.

Kabesh grew too, expanding into and around the rocky outcrop against which it had been built. Under the rule of Khan Gyorgir, a descendant of the legendary horse-nomad chief who once swept across the central plains driving all before him, it expanded until Kabesh was the capital city of an empire which stretched from Kalagar in the north to Tak in the south. His was a benevolent rule, though perhaps a little too tolerant, for he did not mind who dwelt within his lands, as long as they declared allegiance to him. On the fringes of the Mountains of the Giants there dwelt a great many Orcs and Goblins, but the Khan allowed them to reside there in peace once they had sworn loyalty to his throne. As soon as the Khan's representatives had left their lands, of course, the Orcs went back to raiding the local villages, slaughtering and murdering their inhabitants as if nothing had changed.

In the far eastern corner of the continent, the city-port of Arion grew up, supposedly on the ruins of a much older settlement from before the dividing of the continents. It thrived on trade with Ashkyos and Kabesh, and rapidly grew in stature until it was almost a match of the Khan's capital itself. And around the coast of the Inland Sea, a great number of trading settlements grew until they were small walled city-states themselves. Competition for trade between the cities of the Inland Sea was fierce, resulting in sporadic wars – usually settled by naval battles – as several city-states allied against the others to try to enforce their own sets of tariffs and trading terms.

In Klarash, the Shakista Dynasty built the King's Highway from Djiretta – via the capital – to Kelther to unify the kingdom, and the volume of trade crossing the kingdom increased even further. Merchants and adventurers travelled all the way from the Shantak River in the north to far Zagoula, the city of knowledge. It was a peaceful land, its tranquillity maintained by swift and decisive action from the soldiers of the king at the first sign of any trouble!

THE DEAD CITY'S PRISONER

Such a long-lasting peace was far too good to last, of course, though this time the danger which threatened was all-encompassing. The sorcerers and sages of the city of Zagoula were curious, as all scholars are, and they began travelling about the world, seeking out new knowledge wherever they could find it. From their magnificent city they wandered north, studying the Goblin tribes who dwelt alongside the stagnant Lake Mlubz. They journeyed south, taking in the small southern garrisons of Yaziel and Hyennish, which by now marked the southernmost extent of Klarash. Travelling further afield, they discovered on the fringes of the Scythera Desert the old leper colony, which was now Shakuru, the revolting

City of Beggars. They even braved the seemingly endless expanses of the desert itself, running foul of Lizard Men and shaggy Goblins.

And eventually, as if it had been pulling them towards it all along, they found the river and the Dead City. A party of five adventuring sorcerers and warriors chanced upon the river, which seemed not to be flowing anywhere at all; it was just *there*, its surface black with foul weed and giant insects. They named it the River of Decay, and followed it eastwards. After three days they came to the city, lying abandoned in the sand. How long it had been there none could guess, but it must have been very, very old, for its buildings were strangely shaped – pyramids and diamonds seemed to dictate their forms, rather than curves and squares – and much of it seemed to be very inaccessible to beings shorter than about three metres tall. Everything was decorated with images of fish and octopi – bizarre and disturbing images to find in a desert city. Nothing lived in the city – no monkeys, birds or plants of any kind – and a strange atmosphere hung over the whole place, so that the adventurers almost felt that they were desecrating a holy shrine.

Exploring further, the adventurers came to the largest building of all, an immense cathedral-like structure. When they entered, they were plunged into darkness, for it had no windows. Someone found a tinder-box, and as the flickering flames danced from their candles, they gazed around and caught their breath in wonder and shock! Everywhere was decorated with statues and murals of writhing, tentacled creatures, which were devouring humans and other creatures, but all drew the viewers' attention towards the large dark shape at the far end of the building. Their fluttering hearts heaving inside their chests, the adventurers stepped forward.

When they approached, they could see it was a tomb, and a large one at that. The atmosphere in the building was hot and oppressive; voices seemed to dance in their heads, saying over and over again, 'Open the tomb, open the tomb!' Almost as if they were being forced

against their wills, their hands stretched out, and pushed at the stone slab covering the sarcophagus.

Slowly, so slowly, it slid back, until it fell off the back with a deafening crash that echoed around the building, and seemed to bring the adventurers to their senses. They gazed around in bewilderment, until the scaly hand inching its way over the edge of the crypt caught their eyes. They stared transfixed, rooted to the spot as the nightmarish creature sat up in its coffin, its tentacles writhing as if sniffing the air. Somehow, one of the adventurers tore his eyes away and screamed! His fellows started, and fled the mausoleum and the city.

Many months later, one of the adventurers was found by a merchant travelling from Zagoula to Yaziel. Half-dead from exhaustion and dehydration, he babbled out his story. He had survived the crossing of the Scythera Desert by killing and eating his weaker colleagues, but now his strength failed him and he died. The story of the Dead City and of its solitary inhabitant spread like wildfire. Closely following it across Klarash, however, were reports that Goblins and Orcs in the Mountains of the Giants had abandoned any pretence of peace, and were preparing for war!

The War of the Wizards

The releasing of the nameless Chaos-spawn from the tomb in the Dead City in Khul was the spark that lit the flame, which eventually grew and grew until it became the conflagration which was the War of the Wizards in Allansia, the Great War against Evil in Khul, and the Rise of Kakhabad in the Old World. For centuries, Orcs, Goblins and Trolls had been nibbling at the edges of civilization, testing the strength of the defences. Attracted by the ascendance of sorcery in Allansia, many evil mages had trained in solitude until they had mastered the techniques of bringing the dead back to life as their servants. In the Mountains of the Giants in Khul, the inhuman races had gathered their resources under the ignorant eyes of Khan Gyorgir and his people. In the Desert of Skulls, the Snake People were developing magic which would raise the temperature of the sandy wilderness and cause its sterile wastes to expand. In every dark corner of Kakhabad, shamans and witch-doctors manipulated the natural forces, changing day to night and back again within the space of a few hours. Everywhere you looked, Chaos was slowly seeping into the world through ever-widening cracks.

The first engagement came in southern Khul, in the spring of the year 1998 OT. As the month of Skies in Darkness turned to Land's Awakening, the skies did not lighten in Zagoula. A sandstorm blew across the southern lands, darkening the sky for three weeks and bringing with it a plague of locusts and snakes which infested the city. Messengers were sent north to report what was happening, as everyone in the city knew that the storm was not of natural origin. On the twenty-third day of the storm, with the terrified inhabitants of Zagoula cowering in their homes, the Forces of Chaos came striding into the city, the Chaos-spawn from the Dead City leading Trolls and Orcs, and many formless Chaotic beings. The city was sacked, crushed beneath the weight of the obscene armies which swarmed everywhere.

Once the southern lands had been destroyed, the Forces of Chaos split. One army swept north-east, gathering more and more momentum as it decimated the fertile lands at the heart of the continent, and turned them into barren expanses of ash. The host arrived at Kabesh, and met up with a smaller force of Orcs and Goblins which had swept down across the northern plains. The city was besieged, while a breakaway force writhed and slithered north-east, heading for the city of Arion. The other army pushed towards Shakista, the capital of Klarash, but was halted in the Anvil Pass through the Mountains of the Giants by a large force which had responded to the messages of disaster coming from Zagoula. After holding back the tide of Orcs and Goblins for five days, the armies gave way, retreating back through the pass to take up a new position closer to the capital, where they were joined by reinforcements from the coastal lands. Plans were made to abandon the capital if it became necessary . . .

THE REAVING OF ALLANSIA

The first engagement of the War of the Wizards in Allansia was an assault on Gar-Goldoran, the capital of Goldoran, which stood close to where the modern city of Zengis stands today. As the first warm days of summer were beginning, patchy bits of news began spreading about the rampaging Forces of Chaos on Khul. Sorcerers and mystics complained of tremendous elemental forces disrupting the natural magical fields of Titan, and of the presence of Chaos on the Spirit Planes. Reports reached the lord of Gar-Goldoran of a massive host of Chaotic creatures assembling in the eastern parts of the Icefinger Mountains, but before he could even dispatch messengers to warn the surrounding lands, the hordes of Chaos were howling at the gates of the city. But he had forgotten the versatility of his court sorcerers, who managed to break through the disruption of the magical fields caused by the strong presence of Chaos, and alert their fellow spell-casters in Carsepolis of the situation, before joining the battle for the city.

Gar-Goldoran fell quickly, far too quickly, for it had been unprepared, but some of the Forces of Chaos next marched east for Fangthane, the sacred capital of the Dwarf race, which was anything but unprepared: the Dwarfs had been expecting this event, sooner or later, for five hundred years. Now that the day had arrived, the Dwarfs did not worry that sacred Fangthane was finally under attack. Abandoning the city in front of Fangthane, they retreated inside the mountain and waited for the Forces of Chaos to break against it like so many boats against a rocky coastline.

When the attackers arrived, the Dwarfs were mildly disappointed, for they were mostly cowardly Orcs and Trolls, with few creatures of Chaos to offer them any sort of challenge at all. After allowing the repulsive army to burn the city and then batter itself against the impregnable defences of the citadel for two weeks, the Dwarfs became impatient and went out to meet the Forces of Chaos with cold steel. Three days of solid fighting, and the invaders were no more, but with typical grimness the Dwarfs realized that the main strength must have been diverted elsewhere, and that they should march to reinforce the humans of the western lands. Leaving behind merely token defences, the Dwarfs marched for Allansia.

The main force had, in fact, turned for the Flatlands, and swept across them like a forest fire through dry brushwood, heading for Trolltooth Pass and Allansia. The citadel of Durang on the edges of the Flatlands proved only a minor irritation to the Forces of Chaos, and was pulled to pieces by a mass of formless monstrosities. At Trolltooth Pass, however, a force from Salamonis awaited them, reinforced by the Grand Wizard of Yore and five other spell-casters. As the unstoppable black tide of writhing, howling Evil slid towards them through the narrowest part of the pass, the forces of Salamonis broke rank and fled back through it. But at the far end they turned and stood their ground, as the sorcerers raised a massive wall of flame across the pass, dividing the evil army in two. Now that the enemy had been cut down to a more manageable size, the soldiers of Salamonis laid into them for all they were worth, and drove them back into the wall of flames, while on the other side the unstoppable army of Chaos pushed more and more bodies into the fire.

Eventually the commanders of the Forces of Chaos managed to call back their troops, and they retreated into the Moonstone Hills. Here they met up with reinforcements in the form of several thousand Orcs, and a dozen Dark Elf warrior-sorcerers, who guided the foul army through the hills and on to the Pagan Plains, where they raced towards Carsepolis, hard on the heels of the heroes of Trolltooth Pass, who reached the capital just in front of them. As the Forces of Chaos swirled around the hastily prepared defences, many of the ancient city's citizens fully believed that the end of the world had come.

THE BATTLEGROUNDS OF CHAOS

As the breakaway section of the Forces of Chaos slithered across Khul towards Arion, it was met and ambushed by soldiers from that city led by the legendary hero Brendan Bloodaxe, who had hidden among the trees of the Old Forest near Corda, before sweeping round in a pincer movement which caught the evil armies by surprise. Many men were lost that day, as the armies battled back and forth across the plain, but in the final rays of the setting sun that evening Bloodaxe looked down over the field of carnage to see only humans standing. They worked throughout the night, burning the foul corpses of the vanquished foe lest they corrupt the land, before marching for Kabesh in the light of dawn.

They arrived far too late, and found only smoking ruins and a great many corpses. The evil army had pulverized the city, and then raced away to the west, to reinforce the other army at Shakista, which was finally being pinned down. Pushing his troops to the limits of human endurance, Bloodaxe raced across the ash wastes left by the Chaotic horde, and fell on them from behind just as they reached the edges of the battle for Shakista. The human defenders had held the disgusting invaders back for eleven days, and were finally winning against them. The arrival of the armies of Arion cut off any hope of retreat for the Forces of Chaos, who were squashed like an apple in a vice, and with much the same result. The fighting lasted for nine more days, but at the end of it the armies of Chaos were no more, though much of Shakista had suffered too, and it eventually had to be demolished. The incursion of Chaos into Khul had cost all the parties concerned very dear. The Orcs and Goblins were all but finished as a major force for several hundred years, the humans had lost many fine cities and thousands of warriors and civilians, and worst of all, the centre of the land had been blighted by the taint of Chaos, and would never recover.

THE LAST BATTLE

The final battle was the Siege of Carsepolis. At the start of the battle, the defenders of the ancient capital of Allansia numbered around eighteen thousand, including women and children, who readied themselves for battle alongside the men. The Forces of Chaos were uncountable, but lined much of the horizon beneath thick clouds of giant bats and choking black smoke. As the battle commenced, hordes of Goblins brought up siege-engines – catapults, battering-rams and siege-towers. As a hail of black arrows rained down from the sky to keep defenders from the battlements, the Goblins manoeuvred the engines into position, and began smashing their way into the city. Whenever they breached a section of the wall, they met with very strong resistance, but no matter how many human warriors held out against them, their numbers were ultimately limited, while the Orcs and Goblins just kept on coming. After three days – during which time great piles of Orc and Goblin bodies were heaped up, but at a heavy cost to the defenders – the walls were abandoned, and the defenders took to the streets, ensuring that the evil armies paid for every step of the way in hundreds of black-clad corpses.

THE SIEGE OF CARSEPOLIS

The fighting continued in this manner for two weeks, after which almost three quarters of the city had been demolished and two thirds of the defenders were dead. The rest were gathered around the palace of the king, awaiting the final assault. But as the familiar shapes began creeping across the rubble towards them, an uproar arose from the rear of the evil army. A combined force of Dwarfs from Fangthane and Elves

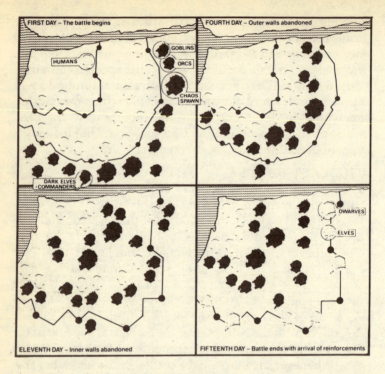

FIRST DAY – The battle begins

GOBLINS

ORCS

HUMANS

CHAOS SPAWN

DARK ELVES COMMANDERS

FOURTH DAY – Outer walls abandoned

ELEVENTH DAY – Inner walls abandoned

DWARVES

ELVES

FIFTEENTH DAY – Battle ends with arrival of reinforcements

from Darkwood and from the Forests of Night had arrived, catching the Chaotic Forces by surprise. The sound of Dwarf voices raised in a battle-hymn accompanied the flash of Elf magic as it lit the sky in a hundred places. The defenders took heart, and went out to meet the enemy for the last time.

But this time the gods were with them. One moment the humans were crushed by a wall of Goblins and Orcs, and the next their enemies were dead, and there were only Dwarfs and Elves there, each and every one covered from head to toe in the foul blood of their vanquished foe. The war was won!

The New Age

In the aftermath of the War of the Wizards and the Great War against Evil there was much to be done, but there was also much that could not be undone. In Allansia, many cities and towns had been destroyed by the armies of Chaos, but in Khul they had poisoned the earth itself, turning vast areas into ash wastes, fit for nothing at all. In view of the apocalyptic nature of the events of 1998 OT, a new dating system was introduced. It took the year which would have been 1999 OT as Year One of the New Age. From then until the present day, we have referred to dates as AC, or After Chaos; as you no doubt know, we are now in 284 AC.

ALLANSIA AFTER CHAOS

In the two and a half centuries since the incursions of Chaos across Allansia, little has happened to the continent. So many settlements were destroyed, and so many people killed, that the old kingdoms like Goldoran ceased to exist. In a few places new kingdoms immediately sprang up to replace the old ones, and life continued much as before, but in most areas life had been blighted by the war. In the early years of the New Age famine and plague were common, finishing off the gruesome job that the powers of Evil had started.

The ruins of Carsepolis were tainted by Chaos, and many ghosts were seen wandering the battlefield late at night. The city was abandoned by its survivors, most of whom were given refuge in Salamonis and the Vale of Willow, and in newer, expanding towns like Chalice and Shazaar. In time, most of the ruins of Carsepolis gradually crumbled, but those of the dock area – which had hardly been touched by the war – remained. They attracted brigands and thieves, who used them as a ready-made hideout, perpetuating the stories of their ghostly inhabitants to keep inquisitive people away. Soon a whole colony of evil-doers was living in the ruins, which were slowly turning back into a town. Over the course of perhaps fifty years, the city which is Port Blacksand rose from the ruins. Its first ruler was Prince Olaf Twohorse, who will be remembered in history as the man who started a prison colony on isolated Fire Island. He was succeeded by Baron Valentis, another corrupt nobleman, who in turn was replaced by the infamous Lord Azzur.

In other parts of Allansia the reminders of the past faded or crumbled away. The Flatlands are still littered with the ruins of villages and fortifications from the war, now home only to rats and ghosts. The Dwarfs and Elves from the north-east were fêted for many months for their part in the defeat of Evil, but eventually had to return home. The Elves went back to their forests, and slipped out of sight of man again. The Dwarfs returned to sacred Fangthane, and slowly set about rebuilding the city at the foot of the mountain. Some ruins still remain, reminding the Dwarfs of the war, but most were cleared away and replaced by completely new buildings and streets.

Civilization has been notoriously slow in returning to Allansia, which is as uncivilized a place now as it was a thousand years ago. The land is wild, with monsters and inhuman races lurking in the hills, and even daring to raid the lowlands now and again. Dark sorcerers still dabble in powerful magic, though they do not understand much of what they are playing with any more. And heroes still stalk the wilderlands, looking for adventure – and finding it!

KHUL AFTER CHAOS

Unlike Allansia, Khul clung on to some civilization, though it had been sorely shaken by the war. The ruins of Shakista and the surrounding countryside were abandoned, and a new capital was built at Ximoran. The ruling family was reinstated, but after only sixty years the last king died without leaving an heir. The land is now ruled by the Council of Seven, made up of representatives from each of the major towns of the land.

In other parts of the world, the recovery was not so quick. Zagoula faded into ruins, abandoned by humanity because of the terrible ghosts which clung on to some semblance of existence there. The southern towns of Yaziel and Hyennish escaped almost intact, and they survive to this day, but with the decline of Zagoula they have become isolated from the lands further north. Kabesh has gone the same way as Zagoula, though its ruins are very difficult to find now. They have been buried beneath the Wastes of Chaos, the name given by all inhabitants of Khul to the desolate ash wastes which choke the heart of the continent.

North-east of the ruins of Kabesh are the Battlegrounds, the remains of the plains where Brendan Bloodaxe's army defeated one of the armies of Chaos. It is a pleasant area of grassland, but here and there are great bare patches where nothing grows, and which animals will not cross. People who know the area say that these are the places where the bodies of the dead warriors of Chaos are buried, and that at certain times their spirits wander the plains, howling out for resurrection.

The city of Arion fared better than most, being left unscathed by the war – though many of its warriors did not return home. Over the last two centuries it has grown slightly, and become the largest city in the north-east, ruled over by the descendants of Brendan Bloodaxe himself.

THE OLD WORLD IN WAR AND PEACE

Surprisingly, it is the lands of the Old World which have changed the most in the years since the wars, though they touched them only briefly. Despite the minor interruption which the Rise of Kakhabad constituted, the politics and power-struggles of the Old World have continued much as before.

Brice continued making threatening displays of its military might which fooled no one, until it suddenly attempted a mass invasion of Gallantaria in the year 175 AC. Warriors poured over the Border River and began advancing across the plains towards Royal Lendle itself! At the same time, rebellious subjects from the Northlands began encroaching into Gallantaria via the Cragrock Peaks. The War of the Four Kingdoms had begun.

King Constain of Gallantaria immediately rode to repel the Northlanders, while dispatching another force to intercept the invaders from Brice. The king and his retinue, including

the queen, were being escorted back towards the garrison town of Forrin after spending several days inspecting the troops in their positions in the Northlands. The royal party's guide was Baron Tag of Casper. Unknown to the king, Tag had made a pact with the regent of Brice: if he could dispose of the royal family, the regent would allow him to take the throne as king of Gallantaria. On that fateful day, the unsuspecting King Constain accepted Tag's offer to guide the royal party back through the treacherous Narrow Pass in the Cragrocks. When they arrived there, however, they were attacked by a band of Northlanders in the pay of Tag, and the entire party were slain, Constain being finished off by Tag himself.

In the absence of any heir, the court sorcerer Tantalon took control of Gallantaria for the last two years of the war. Eventually, after devising a set of tasks to eliminate all but the most suitable candidate, a new regent was found, and Gallantaria settled down to an uneasy peace again.

In recent years, Femphrey has taken over from Gallantaria as the centre of attention, under the leadership of King Chalanna, known as the Reformer. The wise ruler has obtained a magical artefact called the Crown of Kings (thought to be a gift from the devious Netherworld Sorcerers of the Cragrock Peaks), which bestows awesome powers of leadership and justice on anyone who wears it. King Chalanna brought peace and prosperity to Femphrey through the power of the Crown of Kings, but more importantly, once Femphrey had benefited from the Crown, Chalanna decided to pass it around the other nations as well. Every four years, the Crown of Kings passes to another ruler, who may use it to establish order and peace within his kingdom and then join the Femphrey Alliance. The kingdoms of Ruddlestone, Lendleland, Gallantaria and even warlike Brice have taken their turns under the rule of the Crown.

Recently the Crown of Kings was passed to the King of Analand, who was using it to great effect in improving the morale of Analand – until it was stolen by Bird Men in the employ of the Archmage of Mampang, in northern Kakhabad. It seems that the evil despot wishes to make Kakhabad his own kingdom, using the Crown of Kings to organize the various

Chaotic factions under him. Should he succeed in this, Kakhabad will become a tremendous threat to the whole of the Old World. Without the power of the artefact, Analand is crumbling again. Analand is now desperately seeking a brave adventurer to retrieve the Crown of Kings and bring peace and prosperity back to Analand.

THE FORCES OF GOOD

When you set off on your travels around the world, you will come across members of other races. To some of you this will not seem unusual, for in your parts of the world you may rub shoulders with Dwarfs, Elves and others as a matter of course. But for many of you, talk of such creatures, and of worse things such as Orcs, Goblins, Lizard Men or even Dark Elves, will be unusual and may even be terrifying. The following sections, therefore, aim to provide you with more information about your fellow creatures. They will warn you whom to be wary of, and whom you can trust on your travels – for there will be races everywhere who will appear to offer friendship, shelter and safety, but who will just as quickly stick a dagger in your back. You will quickly learn who is who on your travels, but it is perhaps wise to have some idea of the ways of the world before you leave your front door.

The Forces of Good, with whom we start, are more of a 'tendency' than an established power bloc. There are no organized armies of Good in the same way as there are armies of Evil and Chaos, for example. But there are races who follow the gods of Goodness, such as Dwarfs and Elves, who may be thought of as races allied to the cause. And there are in-dividuals in this world who stand up for Good against an overwhelming tide of ignorance and malice, and who will be able to offer aid or advice to one such as yourself when you are hard pressed by the Forces of Evil.

The lands of Titan are still wild and uncivilized, with few centres of learning remaining after the War of the Wizards, and most lands are ruled by a combination of strength, ignorance and fear, if they are ruled at all. Only a few exceptions cling hard to the path of Good – such as Analand, which has to cower behind a massive wall to protect it from other nations, and the old kingdom of Ximoran, now slowly crumbling as its people isolate themselves in their walled cities. In their quest for peace, most nations allow the worshipping of all the gods, whatever their philosophies: only a very brave ruler would have the courage to tell the worshippers of Slangg, for example, that they are no longer permitted to kill other citizens! But in small corners of the world, the worship of the more peaceful gods goes on – quietly maybe, but at least they are remembered.

The Gods of Good

You have already read of the events of the Godtime, when, according to many modern priests and scholars of mythology, the gods created Titan and then battled with Death and his foul minions for its control, until Time was released and then killed in an ironic reversal of his own powers over mortality. After the Banishing, all the gods returned to the Celestial Court with the exception of Logaan the Trickster and a few of his cohorts, who stayed on Titan and watched over the rise of his creation, Man. Many of the gods of Good still gather in the Celestial Court to watch over their world, but some have now left the palace for their own domains. Pangara, god of winds, and Sukh, god of storms, for example, now dwell on the Elemental Planes with other creatures of air. Hydana, god of the waters, has dwelt at the bottom of the ocean since before time began.

THE CELESTIAL COURT DIVIDED
There are two main parts to the Celestial Court. One is made up of the original gods who helped create parts of the world of Titan, and who still govern its physical aspects. But there are also newer gods, who came into being around the time of the Banishing. Before the First Battle they were minor deities (their evil counterparts, Slangg and Tanit, served Death on the side of Evil at the First Battle), but since the rise of mankind and the other civilized races they have grown in stature and influence. These new gods govern emotions rather than physical things, and they sit in judgement over the actions of all intelligent beings in a part of the Celestial Court known as the Hall of Mind.

They are eight in number, and they are led by Sindla, the goddess of luck and fate, who is also a member of the other part of the Celestial Court and who is sister to Titan, the Father of the World. She is known by many names in different lands. In wild Kakhabad they call her Cheelah; in nearby Ruddle-stone and unruly Brice she is Gredd. In northern Allansia she is Avana; in Frostholm she is Lady Luck or Mistress Fate (and sometimes represented as two separate entities); in Arantis she is Zaragillia, and she is worshipped, along with Galana, goddess of plants and fertility, by all those who depend for their livelihood on the regular floods of the River Eltus. In other parts of the world she is Castis, Bismen or Juvenar. Wherever she is known, she is worshipped, and is a favourite god for appeals and blessings. 'May Cheelah protect you' or 'Walk with Sindla as your guide' are common sayings, and every nation has similar ones.

Her daughter is Libra, goddess of justice and truth. Also known as Sicalla, Bersten and Macalla, among many other names, she is the patron goddess of Analand and of a number of smaller lands. Under her watchful eye, an adventurer will be shown all aspects of the world, for Libra is said to understand all aspects of both Good and Evil, Law and Chaos, and to be able to see the reality behind any conflict. She is a powerful goddess, and is worshipped by many common people, who need her protection. She is usually portrayed as a beautiful woman holding aloft a set of balances in one hand, with her other hand raised in admonishment or blessing (it is a source of discussion among her priests as to which she is portraying).

Asrel, known also as Culacara, Jerez and Ooraseel, and by many other names, is the goddess of beauty and love. She is sister to Libra and Usrel, goddess of peace, and is also related to Galana, but is rarely worshipped these days. The local village witch may make offerings to Asrel for you if you want a love-potion made, but few other humans worship her, though all know her name.

Usrel is the goddess of peace, sister to Asrel and Libra and mother of Courga, god of grace, and Fourga, god of pride. She is worshipped most fervently in war-torn lands, where besieged citizens entreat her to end the fighting. She is also known by the names Liriel, Enkala, Ageral and Westrëa, and is most often portrayed as a motherly figure, her arms spread wide as if to enfold the world in peace.

Her children are, as we said, Courga and Fourga, the twin gods of grace and pride. They are said to be opposing gods, who fight each other to produce different degrees of pride and humility in the characters of people. Various myths tell the story of their conflict, but none make much sense. The name of Fourga, especially, is also subject to a good deal of abuse, as pride is rarely considered a virtue any more. In places such as Kharé, the vile city of thieves and cut-throats in wild Kakhabad, Fourga is portrayed as a vengeful god, who wreaks great retribution on those who are over-proud. His priests preach at great and tedious length that pride comes from within, and should not be confused with arrogance or pretensions – but few of their people seem to take much notice. Fourga's son is Telak, god of courage, who is sometimes also associated with Rogaar, the lord of lions, and who is often portrayed as a lion or a Dragon, or as a hefty warrior armed and ready for battle. He is the patron of all warriors and professional mercenaries – many, you will find, bear the golden sword which is his symbol tattooed on the backs of the hand which grips their own weapon. His name is common to many parts of the world, though he is also known as the Shieldbearer, the Swordbearer and the Warrior.

The final member of the Hall of Mind is Hamaskis, god of learning. He is another who is also a member of the Celestial Court itself, and is the patron of all scholars and sorcerers (including the authors of this book). He is usually depicted either as an elderly man or as a fresh-faced youth, preaching wisdom from a book which he holds open before him. He is also known as Serion or Tyralar in other lands, but his worship is restricted to those lands where knowledge is a virtue: in uncivilized lands Hamaskis is not known, and the Hall of Mind has only seven occupants.

THE RUNE OF GOOD
Magical power is often derived from the application of powerful runes which represent the symbolic qualities of the force one is trying to manipulate. They also serve as badges of allegiance. The Rune of Good is an arrow, signifying one purpose, one will, the path of Goodness.

THE OTHER GODS

In the main chamber of the Celestial Council, the other gods and goddesses watch over the physical aspects of the world of Titan. There are a great many gods, and each is served by lesser gods and demigods, drawn from their own children, legendary heroes who have ascended to the heavens to sit with the gods and so on. The 'elder statesman' of all the gods is Titan, Father of the World, always represented as a very old man, with a benevolent smile playing on his lips but a stern look in his deep eyes. Few worship him, but all know of him and offer pleas for his blessing almost as commonly as they entreat his sister, Sindla, for good luck.

Titan has many children. His daughter Galana is goddess of plants and fertility, and is the patron of farmers and Elves, whom she is said to have created. She is also known as Erillia, Kachasta, Zaran or the Gardener in other parts of the world. At planting and harvest times, most farmers partake of a special ceremony in worship of Galana, where seed and scythes are blessed and everyone present prays that she will look kindly upon them and grant them a good harvest. She is also associated with Varantar, the patron of shepherds, and a character known as the Ploughman, both of whom seem to be either her children, or minor gods under her protection.

Throff, the earth goddess (also called Alishanka, Kerellîm and by many other names), is her sister, and is the major deity of the Dwarfs, who revere her and construct shrines in her honour in their bejewelled subterranean cities. Her husband is Filash, god of fire, the brother of Glantanka, the sun goddess. Their children include Verlang, patron of smelters and metal-workers, and Lorodil, god of volcanoes, who is sometimes associated with Chaos but is in fact a very Lawful deity who simply has scant regard for any unfortunate creatures who get in the path of his sacred lava.

Glantanka herself is revered in many lands, though some primitives worship her as the unique deity, rather than as one of many. Some peoples believe the sun to be male, giving female characteristics to the moon; as with the worship of Lunara in Analand. Glantanka is also known by many different names in various parts of the world, including Assamura, Herel, Numara, Sevena and Ariella. Her priests often dress in very bright robes, and spend much of their time at the top of their temples or pyramids chanting prayers for her protection. Some cultures regard Glantanka as the wife of Titan, call her the Mother of the World, and attribute yet more characteristics to her.

The other 'elemental' gods include the storm god Sukh, known for his violent temper (and for being worshipped by several quite evil races, including the nightmarish Life-Stealers); his brother Pangara, god of winds; Hydana, god of the waters; Aqualis, god of rivers; and Farigiss, god of ice and cold. All have many different names in different parts of the world, and are worshipped by humans and non-humans alike. They are associated with other gods, including Solinthar, the patron of mariners, and his brother Fulkra, the patron of travellers. You will find many small shrines to both gods wherever you travel, and you may care to make offerings at them and pray for their protection on your wanderings.

THE CONSTRAINTS OF GOODNESS

As you encounter servants of some of the gods of Good on your travels, you may begin to wonder why so many 'evil' races worship them! Surely, you would say, foul creatures like Orcs would not wish to worship a goddess like Galana (who they know as the Lady of Corn and pray to for good harvests in the few areas where they still bother to grow crops), and in return Galana would not bestow her favours upon servants of Evil and Chaos, even if they were also farmers? This is part of the very nature of Goodness, it seems: the powers of Good are such that they can *forgive* the creatures of Evil enough to grant them their blessing when they need it.

Creatures such as the Life-Stealers, who worship Sukh, are considered servants of Evil because they live by violence and killing, which they seem to do in the name of their god. In such matters, religion breaks down a little, it must be said, and priests have argued with one another for centuries over such points. In the case of Sukh, it is generally agreed that Life-Stealers kill their victims only because that is the way they are. Certainly, no one seems to argue much when humans slaughter Orcs or Goblins, though most servants of Good would agree that killing is – at least in principle – always an act of Evil.

Whatever the convoluted tangles priests and philosophers get themselves caught up in, you may rest assured that if you act in the service of Goodness you can count on the patronage of the gods of Good to help you as you venture through this evil world of ours.

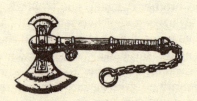

Dwarfs – The Delvers of the Deep

There are only a few inhuman races who follow the path of Good; the most important are the Elves, whom we shall come to in a while, and the Dwarfs.

You already know of the creation of the Dwarf race by Throff, the earth goddess, after she had seen Logaan create Man.

Dwarfs are dour people and you would not, perhaps, associate them with deep religious feeling, but they worship the earth goddess with an intensity which is surprising. In every Dwarf settlement you will find a small shrine to the goddess – whom they know as Kerillîm, the Earth Mother – decorated with precious gems and more gold than you are likely to see in many years. In the Dwarf capital of Fangthane, they have built a cathedral to her way up near the peak of the mountain inside which most of the city resides. It is a place of unearthly beauty, which shows off the exquisite skills of the Dwarfs when working with stone and precious metals.

Kerillîm is always depicted by the Dwarfs as a tall, benignly smiling and very beautiful figure, dressed in flowing light-brown robes and with an undying flame burning from the palm of her outstretched hand. This flame symbolizes, it is said, the spirit of the Dwarfs, which was breathed into them by the goddess, and which will never diminish in their hearts. When they die, the Dwarfs believe the fire from their souls rises to the heavens, where their spirits dwell with their goddess in a land of gold and gems.

Alongside Kerrilîm, the Dwarfs worship a great pantheon of lesser gods and goddesses, and many demigods and legendary heroes who are believed to inhabit the heavens while always keeping a benevolent eye cast earthwards over their relations. The gods include Verlang, patron of metal-workers, who they know as Dûrevendil, and Filash, god of fire, who they call Akkalladûn and know as the husband of Kerillîm. There are hundreds of minor gods too: each clan of Dwarfs has its own patron, as does each guild of miners, metal-workers and warriors within a tribe. Among their heroes, the Dwarfs count a great many warriors and miners, but above all shines the name of Hangahar Goldseeker.

HANGAHAR GOLDSEEKER, FOUNDER OF FANGTHANE

Way back at the beginning of civilization on Titan, Hangahar Goldseeker was chief of a small tribe of Dwarfs who dwelt on the fringes of the northernmost range of mountains called the Kalakûr (now the Freezeblood Mountains of north-east Allansia, which was still joined to the other lands in those days). He acquired his surname because of an unerring nose for finding the richest seams of gold. He would be walking through the hills, not doing anything in particular, when

he would suddenly stop, sniff a little, and then point to the ground saying, 'There's gold down there, lots of it!' He was also a great explorer, and helped map most of the mountains as far north as the icy plateau beyond them.

It was while he was taking part in his final mapping expedition that he found the place which would change the lives of all Dwarfs. He had been travelling for three months in the roughest territory, dogged all the way by skirmishes with bands of local Orcs, which had slowly depleted his band, who now numbered only seven. They were determined to reach the coast, where they thought they could defend themselves from the Orcs, and which they knew had to be near, and they kept pushing ever forward, even though they were dropping from exhaustion. As they passed through a deep gully, they caught a glimpse of an inlet of the sea, which is now known as Jarlhof Bay to us humans, but which the Dwarfs have always called Grinderthûl, the Welcome Waters.

Just as the Dwarfs were cheering at the sight, however, a screaming pack of Orcs burst from the rocks at the top of the gully and tore down towards them, firing arrows and wielding axes and knives above their scrawny heads. The Dwarfs turned to stand their ground, but Hangahar shouted for them to run. The warriors hesitated, for Dwarfs do not flee from Orcs, even when they are outnumbered fifty to one as they were here; but their chief called again, and they obeyed him. The party of Dwarfs scuttled down the gully and out of the far end into a clearing which led down to the shore – and stopped in amazement! There, in the distance, was the most beautiful sight a Dwarf could ever behold. At the far end of the craggy bay, a mountain loomed from the foothills, its summit glowing dully in the wan light. It was what Dwarf legends had always insisted existed – a mountain capped with pure gold – and the Dwarfs had found it!

They turned with a start as several dozen of the leading Orcs emerged from the end of the gully, and made ready with their battle-axes. But the Orcs looked beyond the Dwarfs, with alarm on their faces, then fell to their feet and wailed – as if the mountain were some kind of god! The Dwarfs seized the opportunity and quickly made good their escape. Hangahar and his companions returned to their distant village, but almost immediately set out again, this time making straight for the coast and sailing around it and into the bay, taking the entire village with them! Hangahar and his people settled around the mountain and, despite the rabid attentions of the local Orcs, who were angered beyond endurance by the 'desecration' of their mountain-god, began to construct their city inside it – the city that would one day become Fangthane, spiritual home of all Dwarf peoples.

·Fangthane·

THE DWARVEN CAPITAL.

INSIDE THE CATHEDRAL
OF KERILLÏM

THE DOORS OF
FANGTHANE

CATHEDRAL OF
KERILLÏM

HIGH
RESID

HIGH CLASS
RESIDENTIAL

TRADERS

KAZARKÛL
RESIDENTIAL
LEVEL

AZÛRKÛL
RESIDENTIAL
LEVEL

T

TRADERS
LEVEL

TRADERS

NIMLOTHAN
RESIDENTIAL
LEVEL

STORES
LEVEL

AKALLAZATH
RESIDENTIAL
LEVEL

ERÉTHANE
RESIDENTIAL
LEVEL

KING NAMÚRKILL

BEYOND BELIEF

NAMÚRKILL'S
PALACE

SS
NTIAL

GARRISON
LEVEL

STORES

GARRISON

STORES

ARADIN
RESIDENTIAL
LEVEL

TH
ENTIAL

GARRISON

TRADERS

MANUFACTURE
OF WEAPONS
AND JEWELLERY

METAL SMELTING

METAL SMELTING

GOLD MINES

IRON MINES

GARRISON
LEVEL

THE DOORS
TEN DWARFS
HIGH

THE CITY —
OVER SIX THOUSAND
INHABITANTS

DWARFS TODAY

As we write, in 284 AC, Dwarfs are quite common visitors to human habitations in many areas, especially northern Allansia. Indeed, in the centre of old Allansia there lies the Dwarf town of Stonebridge, a regular stopping-point for many adventurers and merchants as they cross the Pagan Plains and travel up the Red River. Dwarfs themselves are leaving lives of mining and exploration behind them and becoming adventurers too. The names of Dwarfs such as Bigleg, Stubb Axe-cleaver and Morri Silverheart are known to many of those who wander the northern lands in search of adventure.

Stonebridge welcomes adventurers and others who fight for the cause of Good, for the town is regularly assailed by local tribes of Orcs and Hill Trolls, who seem intent on capturing the town's most prized possession (after the diamond mines which lie behind the town) – the magical war-hammer belonging to its ruler, King Gillibran. Gillibran's famous hammer has

served as the standard for the Dwarfs of the town, who rally around to defend it whenever they are attacked. The hammer is magical, for once it is thrown at an opponent it will strike and then return directly to the hand of the wielder! The Forces of Evil would very much like to obtain the war-hammer, for its loss would demoralize the Dwarfs, who are the only beings which stand between the Orcs and Hill Trolls and the rich pickings of settled Allansia, even as far as Port Blacksand on the coast.

In other lands too, Dwarfs fight against Evil alongside adventurers and heroes. They are also surprisingly good sailors, who take to the oceans in their immense wooden ships as they search for distant islands where they hope to find the gold and gems they desire so much. Their men-of-war regularly patrol the coasts and escort the galleys which carry their gems and precious metals to distant cities for trading, on the look-out for pirates and privateers who would rob them of their rich cargo.

DWARF WEAPONS

The weapons Dwarfs use are large and bulky compared to those of humans, but they are manufactured with a precision which no human weapon-maker could match. They are always cast in the finest steel, and are decorated with Dwarf runes. Their weapons have developed from the tools they use underground, and include hammers, picks and axes. Their mail armour is famous the world over for being light, but very hard and able to protect one from the hardest blows.

War-hammer War-pick Battle-axe Mail Shirt Helmet

DWARF PLEASURES

Dwarfs are simple creatures at heart, though they pursue their pleasures in a very sophisticated manner. Above all things, they love the treasures of the earth – gold, silver, platinum, diamonds, rubies and so on. More correctly, they do not love them – they *lust* after them. Many Dwarfs can almost sniff them out, wherever they are hidden in the earth, so keenly attuned are they to these things. But when they have them, they become afraid, for they fear that other creatures will try to take them away from them again. So they hide their precious jewels away in vaults, behind large stone doors with enormous locks, and they guard them devotedly.

Apart from this paranoid flaw in their characters, however, Dwarfs are quite admirable. They are hardy warriors, and though they do not like to kill, they look on battlegrounds as places where they can prove themselves in the eyes of their fellows. The other good thing about battles, of course, is that they are often an excellent source of tales and songs. Dwarfs love rousing songs and stories, especially if they are accompanied by a flagon or three of strong ale, and a pipeful of tobacco.

Dwarf ale is very, very strong, but will not harm humans who drink it in moderation, unlike the Orc ale, Guursh. They also distil a number of special spirits, including the infamous Skullbuster spirit, but these are very much an acquired taste, and are also very expensive unless you are drinking in a Dwarf tavern. Dwarfs love a good pipe of smoking-weed or tobacco to help their conversation flow. They usually trade for it with humans, who in turn acquire it from the southern lands where it is grown. Famous Dwarf brands include Gurny's Leaf, Pure Axehead and Dragon Smoke.

Even when they are relaxing, however, Dwarfs will always keep their weapons close by, for they know that sooner or later Orcs and Trolls will assail them again. Life for a Dwarf seems to be one long round of fighting, drinking and prospecting down a mine – but you would never hear a Dwarf complain about it!

DWARF RUNES

Dwarf writing consists of runes, simple letters developed because they are easy to chisel into stone. They do not use punctuation, but mark new sentences with a larger capital rune. Here is what they all mean:

ă	bat	j	jewel	r	rule
ā	late	k	kill	rh	cover
b	battle	kh	kick	s	sail
ch	chief	l	live	sh	shield
d	dead	lh	kill	t	town
dh	the	m	man	th	thief
ě	end	n	nail	ŭ	under
ē	even	nd	rend	ū	salute
f	father	ng	hang	v	vile
g	gold	ŏ	lost	w	wind
gh	ghastly	ō	over	z	rubies
h	hall	ö	bought	zh	treasure
ĭ	inn	p	pick	&	
ī	light	q(kw)	queen		

Note: Dwarf runes spell everything as it sounds, rather than as it is normally spelt. 'Cat' is really 'kat'; 'pick' is really 'pikh', 'caught' is 'köt' and so on. ᚠ, the rune for D, is often used as the symbol for the Dwarf race as a whole, and is known as the Dwarf Rune.

Elves – The Children of Galana

The other main race of good creatures could not be more different from Dwarfs. The Elves of Titan are the epitome of beauty and grace and intelligence, and believe strongly in the power of magic and the strength of peace. It is often difficult for humans to understand Elves, for their culture is so far removed from ours, and these differences have caused the

Elves to be misunderstood in the past. The blemish of their Dark Elf relations aside, Wood Elves and Mountain Elves are probably the purest servants of the Forces for Good there are.

THE ELVEN GODS

As you know, the Elves believe they were created by Galana, the plant goddess, at the same time as Throff created the Dwarfs and Titan created the Giants, in imitation of the men which had been made by Logaan the Trickster. Galana, who is known by the name Erillia, or just Elf Mother, is still worshipped by all good Elves, who revere her with an intensity that surpasses even that with which the Dwarfs worship the earth goddess Kerillîm (Throff, known as Elluviel to the Elves). All Elven forests are dotted with shrines to Erillia, where Elves will stop and keep silent for a few moments as they pass. The goddess is never portrayed by Elves, who consider that no statue would be able to capture the true unearthly beauty of their goddess, but they describe her as being fairer than anything on Titan, with silvery skin and long, flowing, white hair; she also has the delicately pointed ears and deep-green eyes of the Elves. She is the Elven ideal of beauty, and any Elf woman who shares similar characteristics is admired by all Elves.

Elves also worship a number of lesser deities, who are known as the Children of Erillia, though this is thought to be a symbolic title rather than fact. They include Argowen, god of trees; Aëgraven, goddess of flowers; and Istarel, god of forest creatures. They also know and give offerings to Hamaskis, god of learning, whom they name Livurien the Sorcerer, and his companion, the demigod and Elf hero from prehistory known only as the White Lord (Téla Oriens in High Elvish). Some animal gods may also receive prayers and offerings. In his or her natural forest habitat, an Elf's day will be full of small rituals and prayers to many gods and deities; such practices keep them at peace and at one with their surroundings in a way similar to the 'meditations' of a mystic or sorcerer before casting a spell.

A LONG, LONG LIFE

One of the things that influences Elven attitudes to other races is their longevity. Barring accidents or death at the hands of others, most Elves live for between two hundred and two hundred and fifty years (and this in an age when most humans do not reach their fiftieth birthday, what with one thing and another), and they rarely show their age. In an Elf's lifetime a city could be founded as a village, rise to statehood and collapse again; generations of humans would come and go – and seemingly changeless, the Elf would witness all of it.

Time, therefore, means very little to an Elf. There is no need to rush anything. They are cautious and forward-looking people, who see everything in terms of the future rather than of the present. In the few times of war when they have joined forces with Dwarfs and men, they have frustrated their allies with their 'wait-and-see' attitude, which is in direct contrast to the urgent need for action usually demanded by Dwarfs and humans.

Because they live for a long time, Elves have found a great many ways of passing their time. They do many things which other races would consider wastes of time: for instance, they sing songs, talk to forest creatures and take great pleasure in simply watching natural things like plants. It seems to shorter-lived beings that they do not know the value of time, but really they know it all too well – they just have a lot of it to use up as best they can.

Their longevity has also given Elves their peculiar love for life and all living things. While this is understandable when one sees the sheer beauty of the Elven groves at the heart of their forests, it is hard to comprehend how anyone could love Orcs and things of Chaos. The Elves, however, seem to look upon such repulsive creatures with a very neutral attitude: they don't much care about them one way or the other – they know that they will die before they themselves have reached full adulthood.

THE ORC WARS

In the past, however, Elves have taken exception – grave exception – to Orcs and other creatures of Evil and Chaos. In the years around 600 OT, twelve years after the beings which would later turn into the Dark Elves broke away from the Elven Council and fled underground (see the section on Dark Elves later for more details of this event), the northern Elvish kingdoms of the Mountain Elves found their forests under heavy attack from large, organized armies of Orcs led by a pair of human sorcerers, the Dark Twins. In the past, Orcs had trespassed in the Elven forests, hunting and killing in indiscriminate searches for food, and had been met with brisk opposition in the form of a few well-aimed arrows which dropped the first Orcs where they stood and persuaded the rest that they were better off not staying in the forests any longer than they had to.

But this time, the Orcs came in much greater numbers, whole legions of the foul things, and they were led by people who knew what they were doing. As the front lines overran parts of the forest, other units would come up behind them and burn the trees, clearing away the beautiful greenery and leaving only sterile ash. Elvish records say that the Elves could hear the trees screaming for many leagues around. The Dark Twins were aiming to acquire some deep secrets of Elvish high magic, but they reckoned without King Glorien Thelemas, Lord of the Elven Council, who had been slow to act when the Elves of Viridel Kerithrion rebelled, but who was now spurred into action.

The Orc Wars began, with Elves harrying Orcs across much of the northern part of the one continent, losing a few battles, but winning most of them by a mixture of careful planning, skill and sheer fury at the atrocities committed by the Orcs. The inhuman armies fled, burning the trees as they went in a vain attempt to stop the vengeful armies which dogged them, but they only goaded their pursuers to greater and greater action.

The armies of the Elven nations chased the foul creatures for a year and a half, as far as the edges of the ice plateaux in the extreme north, where the sorcerers halted the remains of their once-mighty armies for a final stand. But after all his haste, Thelemas wanted to taste his vengeance slowly. The Elven armies stopped, and appeared to be waiting. In the freezing conditions, the Orcs suffered terribly, and they died in their hundreds, but the Elves – many of whom were hardy Mountain Elves – kept warm by using their magic, and by reducing their body temperatures to a state similar to hibernation for all but a few hours every day, leaving perhaps a quarter of their number on guard.

What the Elves were waiting for was the arrival of nine very powerful Elven sorcerers, who had been summoned from their retreats deep within the forests of the south. When they arrived, eventually, spring was coming to the frozen regions. The Elven armies marched north, and finally faced the evil forces. The Dark Twins were challenged to magical combat by the Elven mages, and owing to the code of all magicians they had to agree. The contest lasted only two rounds, before an awesome gout of flame issued from the ground and consumed the Dark Twins; the Elven armies marched home, without fuss, and in silence.

There is only one race which is really hated by Elves – the Dark Elves. The accursed creatures are opposed to everything that Wood Elves stand for – truth, light, peace and justice. Should a Dark Elf meet up with a surface Elf, they will have to fight to the death, because neither side will show any mercy whatsoever. For a good Elf to have any dealings with Dark Elves, he must betray all the principles of his people and his goddess. Even the poor Black Elves, who were originally part of Viridel Kerithrion's rebellion, will have nothing at all to do with the demonic creatures now that they have taken up the worship of the foul Demon Princes. If good Elves regarded Orcs with anything like the same depth of hatred as they do their evil relations, it is likely that there would be few Orcs left to trouble anyone on Titan.

If a Wood Elf is captured by the Dark Elves – and that is not a likely occurrence, since he would fight with a suicidal fury against the foul beings – he is most likely to be sacrificed to one of their inhuman gods after much torture and abuse. During ordeals such as this, Wood Elves have a 'safety mechanism', a form of hypnosis of half-sleep that they can slip into at will by communing intently with their goddess. After a while, their bodies go into the same sort of hibernation that the Elven forces used in the last battle of the Orc Wars. While in this state, an Elf cannot speak or respond in any way, though his eyes may be open and he may remain upright. Dark Elves will not be taken alive by Wood or Mountain Elves, who will run them through even if they surrender.

ELVEN ADVENTURERS AND ELVEN WEAPONS
Since the Orc Wars, the armies of the Elven nations have come together only once, and then only for the closing moments of the War of the Wizards, though individual clans fought long and hard for many years beforehand. But there have always been Elven adventurers, wandering the wild lands alone or in

the company of humans, and even (occasionally) Dwarfs. In their desire to find things to occupy their time, Elves travel the earth, righting wrongs wherever they are able, and generally helping the cause of Good. They have a rather strange attitude to adventuring, for they are not looking for fame and fortune, having no need or desire for either; they do it simply because it is interesting! Their human and Dwarf colleagues can rarely understand such an attitude, though they quickly accept it when they realize that the Elf will not need his share of any treasure they acquire.

Elves are exceptional warriors, especially (thanks to many, many centuries of hunting in their forests) in using the Elven bows, which have become legendary. Elven bows are enchanted weapons, which seem almost 'alive'. When he fires his bow, an Elf attunes his mind to the entire action. He feels the sleekness of the shaft, the control of the flights and the power of the bowstring propelling the arrow forward. His mind merges with the act of shooting the arrow, and together they guide the arrow to its target with unfailing accuracy. Elves hit what they fire at, and if they really need to fire their bows, they will usually fire to kill. All this takes just a few seconds, and is quite astounding to watch, should you ever get the chance.

Other creatures have tried to use Elven bows – indeed, less intelligent creatures like Orcs often attempt to steal them from the Elves, believing the weapons will make them truly invincible warriors. They don't realize that part of the power of Elven archery comes from within the mind of the Elf himself, and that the other part has developed slowly through a history of empathy with the trees from which the wood of their bows is made. Nevertheless, those who have seen an Elf bring down a small black speck in the distance that turned out to be an Orc will have imagined what they could do if they could use a bow like that.

Elves also use swords, usually long and thin in design, almost like fencing rapiers. As with all Elven weapons, their swords are unusually light and strong, almost as if they were not made from iron and steel. Some Elven swords have been known to

be enchanted, with spells ensuring that they remain sharp and do not break traced into the flat of the blades in swirling Elven runes. They may also glow with a faint light in the presence of evil creatures, and tingle in the hand of the wielder to alert him to the presence of such danger.

One such weapon was the legendary Sword of Jeren, originally given as a gift by the Elven peoples to Prince Gethel Aranang, who ruled over a small land known as Bellisaria on the northern edge of the Plains of Bronze in Allansia, around the year 1600 OT. Prince Aranang had earned the gift by helping the local Elves in cleansing a Dark Elf settlement from a network of deep caves in the hills on the edges of his land. It was known as the Sword of Friendship, and it was a wondrous thing to behold – sleek and golden, with many spells of warning and sharpness woven into it.

Before they were defeated, however, the witch-king of the Dark Elves cast a curse on the family of Prince Aranang, which manifested itself around the Sword of Friendship. Many who saw the sword were immediately struck with a great desire to possess it at all costs. Gethel's brother was killed by the prince himself after he had tried to steal it one dark night; courtiers and palace guardsmen met similar fates; even the ruler of a neighbouring country was killed attempting to steal the blade during a visit to Bellisaria's capital. The blade of the sword gradually turned from gleaming metal to matt-black, and the runes on its surface slowly changed from ones warning against evil to ones encouraging it. In great alarm, Prince Gethel returned the blade to the Elves, but they could not bear to approach it and commanded him to remove it from their forests immediately. The prince could think of only one course of action: he rode down to the Sea of Pearls, and threw the blade as far out as he could. But knowing the stormy waters of that stretch of coast, the sword will one day reappear, bringing its ghastly curse with it.

ELVEN NAMES

Elves have not one but three names, each of which serves a different function in their long lives. Firstly, they have a *common name*, by which they will be known most of the time, especially to other races. Such a name will not be very fancy, and may be derived from the name of a plant or tree, such as Ash, Hazel or Willow; or it may be like a nickname, such as Redswift or Hawkeye. The second name is their *Elven name*, by which they will be known to other members of their race. This usually consists of a first name and a family name; Redswift, for example, was known to other Elves as Larel Anorien. The third is their *true name*, the name by which the goddess knows them, and through which they invoke Elven magic. Elves believe that anything can be controlled if you know its true name, which is why they never reveal theirs to any other living being. It is not known what form such names take.

ELVEN SETTLEMENTS

The Elven peoples today are scattered far and wide across the world, and are far less numerous than they used to be. Today there are few Elven towns or cities, and most Elves live in small villages secreted in the heart of old woodland. Such villages are sometimes similar to human villages, consisting of a number of small but exquisitely worked cottages, but many more are still built in the traditional style, on wooden platforms among the tree-tops, connected to one another and the ground by rope ladders and narrow walkways. Such villages are breathtaking when first chanced upon, for it seems amazing that any beings could live their lives perched high above the ground in that manner.

However, you will chance upon an Elven village only if its inhabitants have decided that you are not a threat to it. Elves protect their villages with strong magic which obscures them and makes anyone they do not wish to enter wander around in circles, never able to find them. On the fringes of their villages, Elves post guards who keep their eyes and ears peeled for threatening creatures – though according to Elves, humans and other beings unused to woodland make so much noise that they can hear them from several leagues away, and rarely need to be warned of their approach! If you enter an Elven forest on a warm summer's evening, however, and are very careful as you creep through the undergrowth, you will hear the light voices of Elves, singing in the distance as they celebrate the joy of being alive in the beautiful forest with songs to Erillia, the moon, the stars and everything else they consider beautiful. It is rare to find such beauty alive in our savage world today; even battle-hardened adventurers such as yourself will find enchantment in the singing of the Elves.

Close to their villages, and usually within the protection of their warding spells, Elves construct shrines to their goddess: they plant groves of very young trees and bright forest flowers in her memory, and – a typical Elven practice – wrap small gold and silver ribbons around nearby branches, and sometimes set up a small six-sided plinth cut out of pure white stone and

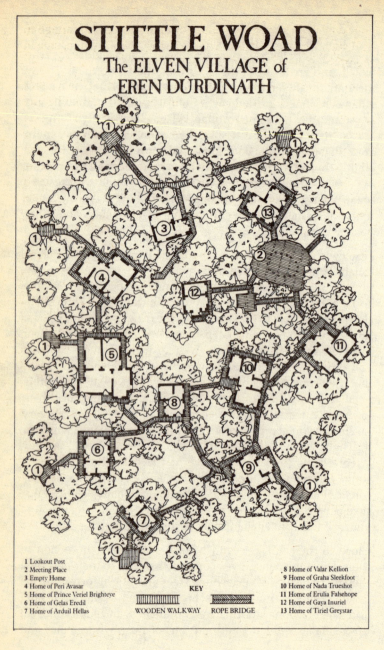

STITTLE WOAD
The ELVEN VILLAGE of EREN DÛRDINATH

KEY

1 Lookout Post
2 Meeting Place
3 Empty Home
4 Home of Peri Avasar
5 Home of Prince Veriel Brighteye
6 Home of Gelas Eredil
7 Home of Arduil Hellas

8 Home of Valar Kellion
9 Home of Graha Sleekfoot
10 Home of Nada Trueshot
11 Home of Erulia Falsehope
12 Home of Gaya Inuriel
13 Home of Tiriel Greystar

WOODEN WALKWAY   ROPE BRIDGE

engraved with prayers to Erillia. Should you ever manage to find such a grove, you will be able to rest there a while, safe in the protection of the plant goddess herself.

Humans sometimes have difficulty understanding the ways of Elves, but that should not stop them appreciating their beauty and strength. They are powerful beings, but use such things in the service of Good rather than Evil, a factor which makes the blasphemy of the Dark Elves even more repulsive. Despite their occasional slowness, they are an important force in holding back the powers of Evil. Should you chance to meet Wood or Mountain Elves in the course of your travels, you will soon learn the meaning of friendship, if you deserve it.

ELVEN LANGUAGES
Elves speak two languages, one of which is a very watered-down version of the other. *High Elvish* is a very complex and courtly language, spoken by Elven nobles and other dignitaries. Prayers are usually said or sung in it. It is also the language of sorcery, and is a necessity for all serious spell-casters who wish to know more than a few explosive party-tricks, as the Elves call most human magic. *Common Elvish*, or *Low Elvish*, is the language that most Elves speak every day. It is also the language of Sprites, Pixies, Woodlings and other forest creatures. It is quite difficult to master, but you may find it useful to pick up a smattering of it; if you spend any length of time in the company of an Elf adventurer, you will learn a few key phrases just by listening to him – especially curses in combat!

The Lesser Races of Good

Apart from Elves and Dwarfs, there are a few more inhuman races who serve the cause of Good, though it must be said that some serve it in very strange ways. They are not only lesser in importance, but they are also all smaller in size, even smaller than Dwarfs. None of them are properly organized into nations, and they do not have armies, but in their own ways they contribute to the continuation of Good on Titan, and may be able to offer you some small assistance as you travel the world.

GNOMES – THE QUIET GARDENERS

Gnomes are strange, grumpy beings related to Dwarfs. Indeed, it is thought by some scholars that at one time they actually were Dwarfs of a clan who did not wish to live in the harsh mountain regions inhabited by most Dwarfs, and who left to live in seclusion in the Elven forests. There, it is supposed, they slowly changed from their original form, becoming shorter and more wizened, and even more withdrawn than normal Dwarfs, until they were recognizable as a separate race, the Gnomes.

Whether or not this is true is difficult to say, for Gnomes are very reclusive and solitary, and have little time for the affairs of larger beings. However, in the records of the Elves of the Forest of Yore, which we consulted over a number of points in our book, a different story is told. Dwarfs, as you know, are very wary of magic. True, they use some spells, but these are very specialized, for casting sharpness into an axe, or for searching out the purest seams of gold ore deep underground – mere cantrips compared to Elven or even human sorcery. But one clan, the Elven records say, became fascinated by Elven high magic after seeing a demonstration of its power from Elven dignitaries visiting the celebrations for the five-hundredth anniversary of the founding of Fangthane. It seems that they wanted to know more about magic, and left the Dwarf capital to wander the world in search of its source. They found a little knowledge, but ended up shunned by the Elves; for they were still rough, unsophisticated Dwarfs. They settled in isolated parts of the forests, where they could be close to the magical powers they lusted for, and gradually evolved into Gnomes.

Whichever of these tales is correct, it is certain that Gnomes do know a little magic, and what they know they are very proficient in. They soon give demonstrations of it to anyone who approaches them, for they use it to ensure that they are not disturbed. They are solitary creatures, who seem to like nothing more than just sleeping in the sun amid the natural splendour of the Elven forests. But Elves have also seen them tending plants, trees and forest animals, using other spells and a good deal of skill. Just as Dwarfs care for their underground world with a deep intensity and reverence which humans find hard to understand, it seems that Gnomes look after the land, albeit in their own small way. As they are nature-loving creatures, they dislike larger beings who they see as destructive vandals, and they get annoyed even by Elves, who they feel patronize and talk down to them, when they deign to talk to them at all!

PIXIES AND WOODLINGS

Both of these forest races, which are related, seem to be descended from a mixture of humans and Elves, though somewhere along the line they shrank! Woodlings stand about as high as Dwarfs, leading to suggestions that they are related to them, though this is extremely unlikely. Woodlings bear little physical resemblance to Dwarfs; apart from the obvious – faces, arms, legs and so on – and their height, they have little or nothing in common. It is thought that they were once humans who simply regressed and grew shorter and shorter, in the isolation of their forest homes.

Pixies are even smaller still, perhaps half the height of Woodlings. Their pointed ears, woodland habitat and happy-go-lucky attitudes to life would seem to point to some relation to Elves, though what it is is not recorded, and there are few theories to explain their resemblance to the noble race. Pixies themselves do not know much about their own history. They live very short lives (no pun intended), their life-span rarely exceeding thirty years, and they have never developed writing, so they have no records of the past history of their race. A few folk-tales seem to talk of a time when Pixies lived alongside some taller, more civilized race of beings, but they give no details, which is very infuriating to us scholars, who would prefer to know these things.

Both races live in thick woodland, building small villages of huts from wood and leaves. They are gentle gardeners, like Gnomes, and tend their parts of the forest with quiet, but great, fervour. Neither race is particularly fond of larger beings, for both learnt long ago that such beings seem to delight in tormenting creatures smaller than themselves. Pixies, in particular, get picked on by cruel men, who take advantage of their dislike of Sprites to hold evil contests in which a Pixie and a Sprite are released into a ring, while spectators bet on which one will survive. Woodlings take their fear of large beings to extremes, however, and disguise their small villages to blend in with the background and wear green and brown clothes as camouflage, to hide themselves away from the attentions of larger beings.

SPRITES, MINIMITES – AND THE PERILS OF MAGIC

Sprites and Minimites were once thought to be two separate races, for while they share similar forms (they are very small winged humanoids), the former are simple and unsophisticated while the latter are very clever and civilized. Sprites dwell in woodland areas, like the other races detailed here, where they live peaceful lives caring for plants and animals. They are a gentle, timid race, who fear men and other large beings. They get on well with Elves, however, with whom they feel a keen affinity, as fellow plant-tenders and magicians. Sprites seem very smug about the fact that they can cast a wide range of magical spells, though in truth these are little more than cantrips, and certainly no more sophisticated than those practised by any aspiring apprentice in his first few weeks of magical training. The Elves share the Sprites' delight in magic, however, and sympathize with their enthusiasms.

Minimites are far more sophisticated than Sprites, and they usually do not acknowledge the fact that they are related. They have a long and detailed history, and their culture was once

very sophisticated. In the centuries before the War of the Wizards decimated much of the world, Minimites dwelt alongside men in some of the great seats of learning in the Old World. There, the race was recognized as one of great intellect, and respected for their tireless efforts in collecting, as best they could, the history of the world. Minimites could discourse for hours on Brician battle tactics, tell long sagas about Bjorngrim Giant-slayer or Jinna Arajar the Hermit, and perform long and very intense magical rituals. They were easily the equals of men in the practice of high sorcery, despite their tiny frames, but they were dedicated to the cause of Good and they never used it to work ill.

When the Forces of Chaos began seeping out of Kakhabad, the Minimites were very afraid. News of the wars raging across

Allansia and Khul was infrequent and terrifying, and everyone began to suspect that unless something were done the third continent would be engulfed too. Their best scholars and magicians began the long but necessary task of searching through their extensive archives and ancient spell-books for clues to the solution to this problem. But after five months nothing had been found, and the Forces of Chaos were now hammering at the gates of Analand and Ruddlestone. In desperation, the Minimites began frantically to hunt through other, more dubious works.

In a treatise written by an insane mystic known only as Aughm Lightchaser, they found what they thought was an answer. Among the crazed jottings they found a long and very dangerous technique which would summon and unleash the very power of Goodness itself in one devastating split-second burst of power! The Minimites had to try. Pooling their resources with those of the greatest human sorcerers, they gathered on a peak in Mauristatia to perform their ritual. Slowly, as they danced and wailed and chanted, they could hear the Forces of Chaos gathering around the base of the mountain, called from all over Kakhabad. The tension rose and rose, the pitch of the chanting reached insane levels, the creatures of Chaos howled beneath them. And suddenly, in a cataclysmic flash, bolts of golden light flashed from the heavens and struck the Forces of Chaos. Where they struck home, they counteracted the power of Chaos, and the two vaporized each other. In less time than it takes to blink an eye, most of the Forces of Chaos had been blasted into their component particles, and the rest were fleeing back into Kakhabad.

But the victory was not without its cost. The Minimites who had wielded this wild magic became enamoured of such power and taught others to lust after it. A dream arose that Minimites would become the benevolent rulers of the world, guiding their subjects by their wisdom and sorcery. Other Minimites, however, saw that this dream was a dream of tyranny. There was only one solution: since a single Minimite on his own has no great magical power, they had to be prevented from working together. The race became nomadic, condemned to wander the world, and prevented by intricate spells woven into the very fabric of their being from ever joining forces with others of their kind.

Allies

As you travel across the world of Titan in search of adventure, you will quickly come to realize that the Forces of Evil and Chaos far outweigh those of Good. Everywhere you go, humans steal from humans, Orcs raid Elves, Trolls assail Dwarfs, evil sorcerers promise death to everyone. Members of non-human races like Dwarfs and Elves may be able to aid you, but they are few and far between, and they have their own troubles too, for Evil is vying for dominance everywhere.

But here and there, if Sindla is keeping her eye on you, you may be lucky and find a friend on the road, or someone who can offer you shelter for the night. In the more settled lands, there will always be places for you to stay in relative safety. But once you are out in the wild lands, you may be very much on your own, unless you can find a few allies. Such allies may crop up in the strangest places, and at the strangest times, for the servants of Good always have to stay one jump ahead of the enemy in such places. But allies are there, carefully working away at Evil's influence, and trying to reinstate the cause of Good in lands which had abandoned it.

COLLETUS THE HOLY MAN

In the wildest parts of Kakhabad, for example, the last person you would expect to come across would be a blind holy man, but in Xamen several adventurers have had need of the services of Colletus. He serves Throff, the earth goddess, who is also the goddess of healing – for Colletus has the power of healing disease, granted to him by his goddess for his efforts on her behalf in some of the wildest lands on Titan.

Colletus wanders the perilous lands of Kakhabad, tapping every step of the way with his staff. How he avoids being waylaid and killed by the servants of Evil is astounding; it is almost as if he is so good that they cannot harm him. This was plainly not always the case, however, for Colletus was not born blind. In his youth, he was an adventurer who saw Evil beginning to fester within the fortress of Mampang as the Archmage began to take his first tentative steps towards his ultimate goal of imposing tyranny over the whole of Kakhabad. The foul sorcerer had made pacts with Orcs, Goblins and the accursed Red-Eyes, who were then starting to raid the few settled parts of Kakhabad, intent on giving good demonstrations of the potential power of the Archmage as a warning to the leaders of other nearby nations.

Colletus, then innocent and unworldly, but full of the courage of the young, journeyed long and hard, until he came to the very gates of the Fortress of Mampang. Proclaiming that he wished to pledge his sword to the Archmage and fight with his armies, he gained entrance, and quickly began finding his way about. Eventually, after two months' exploration of every aspect of the travesty of life which goes on in that place of Evil, he put his plans into operation. He got himself picked as a special herald to the Archmage, with the job of bringing him news from the commanders of his armies as they reported from the furthest corners of the land. His chance came soon, when many of the soldiers of the fortress were repelling an attack from the Samaritans of Schinn, the Bird Man resistance who had been making quick in-and-out raids against the fortress for several months. Bursting into the Archmage's rooms, he surprised the sorcerer kneeling in communication with his foul demonic gods, and without the staff which held most of his power. The brave warrior rushed forward, his sword swinging around his head, ready to deliver the blow that would bring peace to Kakhabad again.

Colletus had reckoned without the Archmage's demonic patrons, however. Through the dimensional gate linking the sorcerer with the Internal Abyss, they sent a ball of black fire, which burst into the room with a flash which blew the Archmage across the room and blinded Colletus. The warrior stumbled from the room, pushing aside the remains of the charred door, and in panic ran without knowing where he was

going. Eventually he found himself on the desolate rocky slopes which lead down from Mampang. Wandering blind, Colletus drifted through the wilderness, until he eventually found sanctuary with the Elven sorceress Fenestra. Under her care he recovered his health, though not his eyesight. He became an initiate of Throff a little while later, and was granted the power of healing through his hands by the goddess in lieu of his lost sight. Now he wanders Xamen, thwarting the Archmage by healing and preaching the word of Throff, rather than by sabotage and violence.

The sorceress Fenestra, incidentally, is a most unusual character, because she is a renegade Black Elf who has turned her back on their evil ways and joined her powers to those of the Forces of Good. She dwells in her lonely house in the heart of the Forest of Snatta in the Baklands, where she studies the deeper mysteries of high magic and watches over the surrounding area. Surprisingly (for an Elf), she used to live with her father, also a sorcerer of some repute. He was killed by the Serpent of Water, one of the demonic Seven Serpents

summoned by the Archmage to bring yet more terror to Kakha-bad, and she now collects any scrap of information that she can about the infernal creatures, while plotting her revenge. She is a great source of information about all the northern Baklands, but she is wary of strangers and rarely receives visitors. Should you ever encounter her you will need to convince her of your good intentions before you can safely ask her advice.

It seems that your best hope of finding allies against Evil lies in magicians, for there are still some who continue to use their powers to fight for Good. You have just heard of Fenestra and Colletus who may aid you in Kakhabad; in Khul, sorcerers such as Selator the Green and the flamboyant Agravert Peltophas may be called upon for aid, though they may require some persuading. And in Allansia, there are three you may need to consult, three who at one time were all that stood between Allansia and total Chaos, but out of whom only one still practises high magic.

SOUTHERN MASK MAGIC

The Healer's peculiar skills use specially enchanted masks to draw sickness from the body of the sufferer. They work on the principle that every sickness of the body is also a sickness of the soul. Each of the masks is enchanted to react to a particular ailment, soothing the soul of the person who wears it, while the Healer casts a spell over them as a cure.

For a common injury, such as a broken leg, for example, the sufferer wears a mask in the form of a Giant, which holds back the pain while the Healer resets the bones and wraps the leg in strips of cloth soaked in healing salve. For a more serious ailment, however, there are rituals which both the Healer and the sufferer must perform, slowly working a magical cure together. The curing of a heavy curse or the healing of insanity take especially strong magic, which can sometimes damage the patient instead of helping him. Mask magic is erratic, but when it works it works well, and it is the only cure for some ailments.

THE STAR PUPILS

In the heart of the Forest of Yore in the southern part of settled Allansia, near that seat of learning known as Salamonis (where your humble authors reside at this very moment), there is the school of the Grand Wizard of Yore. Founded over a hundred and fifty years ago by Vermithrax Moonchaser, then just an ordinary wizard, it has trained many great sorcerers, though it is unlikely to be training many more, for Moonchaser is finally nearing the end of his magically extended life. About fifty-five years ago, his classes were blessed by the presence of three star pupils: Gereth Yaztromo, the son of a priest from Salamonis; Arakor Nicodemus, whose father was a rich merchant in Fang; and Pen Ty Kora, a peculiar fellow from distant Arantis, whose father was something like 'Chief Overseer of Scriveners to the Overpriest'. Between them they amazed Moonchaser with their innate magical abilities and willingness to learn even more. Most young men who acquire a few magical spells seem to spend all their time bragging to village girls about their amazing powers, and running around the countryside scaring cattle and wasting their energies with silly pranks. But not these three! From the start they were keen and attentive, humble and respectful in the face of the Grand Wizard's far superior powers, and fully aware of the limitations of their own.

Eventually there comes a time when a master can teach his apprentices no more, and they must make their own way out into the world to put all the theories into practice. And so the three left the safety of the Forest of Yore, and set out to learn about the world, and to prove themselves master sorcerers. Pen Ty Kora – a short, dark-skinned man who spoke with an unusual accent and who used to perform the most peculiar combinations of spells, to great effect – travelled south again, and returned home for a while, where he became an initiate of the temple of the earth goddess in Kaynlesh-Ma. There he learnt the peculiar southern healing magic, which he took to with great fervour. In time healing magic became his speciality, and as he travelled the world, heading slowly but surely back to the northlands, he became known simply as the Healer to those who came to him for cures.

NICODEMUS AND THE DEATH SPELL

Meanwhile, Nicodemus had set off into the Flatlands, which were as harsh in those days as they are now. After several years of extreme hardship, living on roots and anything he could catch, he had slowly worked his way as far as the eastern edge of the Moonstone Hills. Intending to strike north for Kaypong and the exotic city of Zengis, he began crossing the Moonstone Hills, but there he chanced upon a great evil which would eventually threaten his life. Travelling in the rolling hills, he arrived one evening in a small farming village leagues away from anywhere. The citizens were gloomy and depressed, and did not welcome him with the normal good humour of country folk.

Upon asking the reason, he discovered that a curse had come to their lands, inflicted by an evil shaman who, they said, dwelt in a cave further in the hills. Once a fortnight the shaman would come and stand on the rocky crag which overhung the village, and give them the same speech, in which he demanded that they move away from the area immediately. The citizens of the village had decided from the start that they were not going to let some petty spell-caster tell them what to do, and had refused to move. But the shaman returned with a large force of Orcs and Goblins, and showed the full extent of his power. He blighted their fields, killed their animals, and made the sky so overcast that nothing would thrive.

Nicodemus was spurred into action. Taking on the form of a Man-Orc through the use of an illusion spell, he worked his way inside the caverns of the shaman, until he discovered the reason why the evil sorcerer wanted the villagers to move away. Centuries ago, long before the War of the Wizards, a titanic battle had taken place at this point between the two Elven sorcerers and three evil human necromancers, known as the Dark Ones. The Elves had won, eventually, and the ashes of the humans were buried in the valley where the village now resided. But now the call had come down to the shaman from the evil deities which he served, to make plans for the resurrection of these important servants of theirs.

The warding spells the Elves had placed on the ground where

the foul sorcerers were buried were such that the spilling of blood (the usual technique for resurrection) would ruin the ashes, making resurrection impossible. For this reason shaman was not risking an armed confrontation with the villagers, which would certainly lead to bloodshed. But now the villagers had had enough of being threatened, and of starvation and misery, and were preparing to leave the village to the shaman – though they were still very puzzled as to why he wanted it so badly, but apparently not badly enough to kill them all for it in the usual manner of the servants of Evil.

As soon as the last villagers had fled the little hamlet, the shaman's forces (including the disguised Nicodemus) moved in, and began making preparations for the resurrection of the Dark Ones. The time came, and under a moonless night sky

the shaman started the long ritual which would culminate in the ashes re-forming into bodies which would then rise from the ground. There was an almost tangible feeling of Evil in the air, and Nicodemus, waiting near the front of the crowd of Orcs and Goblins, was sure that the unearthly spirits of some very evil beings were somehow present.

The shaman began his dance, wailing in a tongue Nicodemus had never heard before (the 'Demon's Voice', a language used for all dark magic). The chanting of the shaman was joined by three other voices, groaning and keening from beneath the soil! Nicodemus broke from the ranks of Orcs, waving a large jagged-bladed sword as he ran towards the shaman, who was too involved in the approaching climax of the ritual to notice. The sorcerer split him from end to end with one almighty slash of the sword, and the shaman's blood soaked the ground. Screams came howling from the ground, but slowly faded away, as Nicodemus cast a spell of purification over the blood-stained soil. The Orcs and Goblins, stunned for a moment but now galvanized into action by the demonic spirit voices screaming in their heads, streamed towards him, but carefully aimed fireballs kept them at bay long enough for him to flee the village . . .

A year to the day later, Nicodemus found himself exploring an ancient ruined temple in the middle of the Pagan Plains. In a crypt beneath the nave of the temple, he found a large black chest, which gave off powerful magical emanations. Perhaps it was greed for new magic, perhaps just a natural curiosity that caused him to be less cautious this time. Whatever it was, as he opened the lid of the chest, the crypt shook with demonic laughter and three smoky black shapes swirled and solidified, until in front of him stood three cowled figures, and a great aura of evil filled the crypt. The central figure spoke: 'At last, Arakor Nicodemus, we are revenged on you! You will not escape a Death spell!'

Nicodemus gazed in horror at the runes engraved on the inside of the chest's lid. The cowled figures of the Demonic Servants faded into thin air, and already the wizard could feel

a sickening trembling start in his bones. Fleeing from the temple, he headed east, making for the Dwarf town of Stonebridge, where he had last heard tell of his fellow sorcerer, the Healer. If there was anyone on this world who could help him now, it must be him. The Healer was not at Stonebridge, but the Dwarfs told him that he was heading for Fang. Nicodemus borrowed a horse and galloped north across the plains, his every jolt echoed by the panicked thumping of his failing heart. After three days' hard ride, pausing only to swap his exhausted horse for a fresh one at a small farm he passed,

134

the dying sorcerer caught up with his old colleague, as he was laying on hands in the market-square of the village of Anvil.

Pen Ty Kora took one look at his friend, now so near to death, and swore under his breath. He led the shaking Nicodemus out of the village and on to the plain. Holding his friend upright, he pointed to the glowing peak of Firetop Mountain away to the east. 'There, my friend, we will wait for the dawn,' the Healer said obscurely. After three hours of desperate struggle, the pair arrived at the foot of the mountain, and began the long, painful job of ascending to the top. When they at last reached the summit, the Healer pulled a large mask shaped like the sun from his pack, and placed it upon the head of his friend, who by now had gone a ghostly white, as Death's clammy hand began to squeeze ever stronger on his spirit. The Healer began his ritual . . .

At dawn, the sun rose painfully slowly, but as its rays touched his body, Nicodemus sat up and yawned, saying he had dreamt of a phoenix which carried his soul back to the land of the living. He was alive! Nicodemus had cheated the vengeance of the Dark Ones and their demonic masters.

But this time the Healer was not spared their wrath. He was struck down, within a week, with an extraordinary disabling ailment which disfigured his body and made his every movement agonizing. The Healer fled the world of men and became a recluse, hiding himself in a lonely cave on the fringes of the Icefinger Mountains. He is still there today, helping the sick and the injured, but refusing to see anyone who does not require his services. Both Nicodemus and Yaztromo have visited him, but both times he refused to see them. If you find yourself in the northern lands, and in desperate need of a healer, you can be given directions to his cave by anyone – but do not expect his aid if you do not require healing.

Nicodemus himself went on to have many more adventures, being called upon several times to thwart the plans of the servants of the Forces of Evil. Eventually, however, he tired of constantly being asked to sort out the problems of the world, and went into retirement in the decadent vermin-pit known as

Port Blacksand, the City of Thieves. Why he did this we will probably never know – it is certainly unusual for such a servant of Good willingly to settle in such a den of Evil, unless there is some very good ulterior motive. Perhaps he is just keeping an eye on Azzur for Yaztromo? But what of Yaztromo during all this?

YAZTROMO, DARKWOOD'S KEEPER

When he left the school of the Grand Wizard of Yore, Yaztromo initially returned home to Salamonis which, although close to his school, he had not seen in fourteen years. There he set himself up as a commercial sorcerer, selling charms and potions from his home half the time and spending the other half researching in the extensive libraries of Salamonis, which date back to long before the cataclysmic War of the Wizards. He learnt much about the magics of other lands and other races, but eventually wanderlust took him, and he set off on his travels. Over the next few years, his wanderings took him across the whole of settled Allansia, from the border between Chiang Mai and Kaypong to the southernmost fringes of the Southern Plains, from Oyster Bay and the ruins of Balkash to Trolltooth Pass and the edge of the Flatlands.

Everywhere he travelled, he saw the cruel hand of Evil pulling the strings in the background, and he was sorely troubled, for he could see no way of ever being able to fight more than a small portion of it. For a long while he considered simply hiring a boat and setting sail for new lands, but in the end decided that this was a very cowardly thing to do. If the gods had granted him the power of sorcery, he thought, he should make the best use of it.

It was while he was reflecting on such matters that he passed by the fringes of Darkwood Forest, the wild mass of ancient woodland south of the Dwarf village of Stonebridge. It was the month of Hiding, and the cold weather was just beginning, but it was still pleasant to walk beneath the stars of dusk. As Yaztromo strolled on, his staff swinging in time with his steps, a warm mist suddenly closed in. All around him, the bizarre shapes of the trees loomed through the greyness, but Yaztromo was not afraid: he had his magic to protect him, which he would chance against any supernatural horrors the forest could set against him!

All of a sudden, however, he gave a start. Floating down the breeze came the sound of screaming – and something was burning. He ran through the tangled undergrowth of the forest for a few minutes, and came to a clearing in which a dozen or so Elven huts stood, all of which were ablaze. Dark shapes flitted between the trees, and although he had never seen them in the flesh before, he knew exactly what they were – Dark Elves! Needing no further goading into action, Yaztromo charged into the fray, fire blazing from his staff. That night he killed eight of the ghoulish Dark Elves, and won the immediate respect and admiration of the Wood Elves of Darkwood. In the days following the attack, the sorcerer stayed with the Elves, and learnt everything he could about life in the forest. Much of it seemed idyllic to Yaztromo, not unlike the Forest of Yore of his apprentice days, and he half-considered setting up his own magic school here.

But there were great problems and greater dangers lurking in parts of the forest. Despite its beauty, it was a perilous place for many of its inhabitants, and it really needed the protection of someone who could watch over it at all times. Yaztromo pondered upon the problems of Darkwood at length, and as his brief stay with the Wood Elves turned into six months, and then a year, he slowly came to the conclusion that he really wanted to stay there, and be the one to look after it.

As soon as he had had the honesty to admit this to himself, he felt much better, and immediately visited the Dwarfs of Stonebridge to ask them to help him build a tower near the southern end of the forest. King Gillibran and his subjects were very sceptical of Yaztromo's dealings with Elves, but they liked the wizard, and thought his staying close at hand was a great idea. Work was started, and soon completed with the help of a little magic, and Yaztromo moved into his tall, white tower within the year.

He still dwells there; indeed, he rarely leaves the tower any more, except when something very serious is brewing. News is brought to him by the birds and animals of the forest, who come and tell him all that they have seen throughout the day. He also has a pet crow, called Vermithrax after the Grand Wizard, who carries messages to and from the Dwarfs of Stonebridge or the Elves of the forest. Everyone in the forest knows him, and most respect him and the strength of his magic. The Darkside Elves, however, tend to think of him only as a harmless fool, so he has been able to keep a keen eye on their movements. Indeed, he keeps regular tabs on most of what goes on in this corner of Allansia, and exchanges messages with Nicodemus in Blacksand, and with many other informants besides.

He has restarted his business selling small magical items, in an attempt to gain money to satisfy his one major vice: the old wizard loves sugared cakes, which he orders from all over when he has the money to buy them, which is not as often as he would like!

Should you ever find yourself in the area and in need of assistance, you will find his tower set just off the path at the southernmost extent of Darkwood. It is an impressive affair, built in white stone with a massive oaken door. It has a great many chambers, including an observatory and several cellars designed for magical experiments, but eccentric old Yaztromo spends most of his time in the study-cum-library, which is always overflowing with books, papers, magical paraphernalia, animals, birds and much, much more – there is barely enough room for his favourite old oak armchair!

THE NEUTRAL FORCES

Between the Forces of Good, which are few in number but determined of purpose, and the Forces of Evil and Chaos, which are numerous but disorganized, there are the Neutral Forces. Well, they cannot really be termed Forces as such, for they have no real armies, and often prefer to use those of other people to do their work for them, if they wish it done at all, that is. For there are, in fact, two types of Neutral; the people you encounter may be one or the other. They may be followers of the Trickster gods, led by Logaan, the creator of man, who try to offset Good and Evil against each other, eventually to balance the two. Alternatively, they may have opted out of allegiance to either side, and prefer to remain aloof from the world and all its problems. This second type have no gods, no allies and few philosophies; they have simply turned their

backs on the world. Both factions may give you great help, or may hinder you terribly, almost according to their whims; as a result, you should be very wary of Neutral beings.

The basic philosophy of the Tricksters and their followers is simple, but it operates on a grand cosmic scale that is hard to grasp. Whatever happens, they say, the universe will survive only if the powers which pull it this way and that are balanced: too great a shift one way or the other will tear the fabric of the cosmos and the world will end. Therefore, whenever one side is in a very strong position, the Tricksters will either lend their aid to the opposing factions and hinder the stronger side, or they will live very dangerously by pushing the stronger side to even better positions, in the hope that the underdog will fight back and restore the balance. For all their apparently frivolous tricks and jokes, the followers of luck and chance are actually very serious followers of the balance of Good and Evil.

Lord Logaan the Trickster

As you know, Logaan the Trickster was one of the gods of the Celestial Court. Although different cultures call him by other names (which include Ranjan and Akolyra), and give him different forms (a woman or a mischievous cat seem to be the most common, though there are many others), all seem certain that it was he who first created intelligent beings when he made Man and Woman during the Godtime. Such universality is surprising, for it occurs in few other areas of mythology; such instances are usually taken to mean that the event described by the myths definitely did *not* happen.

Logaan is a strange god, for he has no recognized parents or relations among the hierarchy of the Celestial Court, whereas even Death has his brothers, Disease and Decay. One might have at least expected Logaan to be related to Sindla, the goddess of luck, for their domains overlap, but this is not so.

However, in the writings, statues and symbols of his devoted worshippers, he is joined by a pair of mysterious figures, known as Kata and Petros. These two are usually depicted as faceless, robed humans who stand flanking Logaan, pulling him this way and that – obviously symbolic of the way in which Logaan himself pulls the Forces of Good and Evil this way and that. Logaan is portrayed in many different guises, like all gods, but in his most common human form he is short and misshapen, like a clown, with bandy legs and a strange expression on his face. His hair is wild and his garments appear not to fit – but in his eyes there is always a look of extreme seriousness.

The other gods of Titan appear only in very serious mythological tales, but Logaan also crops up in many popular folktales. They are always set on the Earthly Plane, either just before or just after the other gods leave following the First Battle, and they always seem to end up with him playing tricks on someone who has been pompous, cruel or foolish. Many of the tales also explain how the Trickster discovered writing, or fire, or the wheel, or smoking-weed, or whatever. And although Logaan is always the hero of the tale, he often makes himself appear foolish too.

A typical folk-tale of this sort is *Logaan and the Troll*, which is a popular bedtime story told by farmers and woodsmen to their children in many different lands:

> *Logaan is wandering through the countryside when he comes to a village, where everyone is very sad. When he asks why, they tell him that a big, evil Troll comes down into the village every night and carries some of them off to eat. The Troll lives in a cave in the hills, where he hides during the day, because Trolls don't like the sun, which blinds them with its brilliance. Logaan climbs up into the hills, and finds the Troll's cave, which smells a great deal and is quite repulsive. Then he takes a rope, makes a lasso, and throws it into the air several times until it catches hold of Glantanka, the sun goddess, as she circles the sky. He pulls and pulls with all his might, until she is down on the ground, protesting like anything about being*

*dragged out of the sky and threatening all kinds of
punishments when she gets free. Logaan ignores her,
and sticks a large sack over her head. Immediately it is
night-time.*

*In his cave, the Troll stands up with a yawn,
muttering to himself about how quickly the day went
by. Gathering up his club, the Troll sets off for the
village, but no sooner is he out of his cave than
Logaan opens the sack and releases the rope from
Glantanka. The sun goddess shoots up into the sky
again, and the Troll howls in pain and drops his club
as he slaps his hands over his eyes. Logaan picks up
his club, and bashes the Troll's head in, before
dragging its carcass down to the village and its
cheering inhabitants.*

*As he walks away from the village early the next
morning, however, after a night of celebration,
Glantanka the sun goddess looks down on him from
the sky, and hurls a fireball at him, which singes him
all over, causing the villagers endless amusement . . .*

Servants of the Tricksters

Such folk-tales show up the frivolous side of the Tricksters, but
there are more serious sides, as can sometimes be seen in the
actions of their emissaries on the Earthly Plane. Those who
serve the Tricksters can be deadly adversaries, for they work
solely for the sake of balancing out Good and Evil – and if you
are working for the side of Good when you encounter them,
they may well react to you like servants of Evil!

The Netherworld Sorcerers of the Northlands of the Old World
are servants of Logaan and the other Tricksters; they are noted
both for their great powers at high magic and for their
seemingly arbitrary bestowal of gifts or curses. It was they, for
example, who created the powerful Ting Ring, which they
gave to the nobles of Gallantaria. The ring bestows all kinds of
special abilities on its wearer, depending upon the circum-

stances. If it is worn in battle, for example, it will protect its wearer from the effects of blows; if worn while hunting, it will instil the ability to track game; it can protect you from the effects of foul undead creatures, or tell you that there is poison in your cup!

Such magical artefacts are typical Trickster items, changing from one thing to another, depending on what is wanted. The Ting Ring is also imbued with a typical Trickster joke: it has a chameleon-like power which causes it to blend in with its background, and several emergencies have been caused in Royal Lendle by noblemen who thought they had lost the ring!

But it was also the Netherworld Sorcerers who conjured up the accursed Demon Fish which threatened the coast of the Onyx Sea for some years. It was a gigantic creature, larger than a warship, and would tear apart vessels and swallow fishermen whole. The fish was finally caught by the hero who solved Tantalon's tasks and became ruler of Gallantaria, but not before it had terrorized the coast and many fishermen had lost their lives. Why the Sorcerers inflicted such a beast on the coast we may never know.

We also know very little about the Sorcerers themselves. They are an ancient race, it is believed, who were dwelling in their remote towers in the Northlands for many centuries before man settled there; and they dwell there still. As to their numbers, or any further details about their life-styles, your guess is as good as anyone's, for they keep themselves hidden from the view of others. From their lofty homes, however, they obviously keep a vigilant watch over the whole of the western continent. When they see Evil or Good getting too much of an upper hand they interfere a little, to ensure that everything balances up in the end.

The Riddling Reaver is another unusual servant of the Tricksters. Legend says that he dwells somewhere amid the jungles of southern Allansia, in a place where all the normal rules have been disregarded – where water no longer flows downwards, where trees seem not to need soil, but float free in the air, and so on. Wherever he actually has his residence, however, he is

most often seen aboard his enormous ship, in which he sails around the world to carry out his tasks.

The Reaver is said to be a master of disguise, able to transform himself into just about anyone or anything in a matter of minutes; he often uses such disguises to get close to his 'victims'. He is also a very puzzling being, for he delights in leaving enigmatic rhymes behind him wherever he goes – hence his name. He seems to have almost limitless powers to draw on in his tasks of bringing confusion and balance to the world. Where he actually originates from is anyone's guess. He may be a human being blessed with peculiar powers by his equally peculiar gods, or he may be a supernatural being sent by the Tricksters to work special missions on the Earthly Plane, perhaps where a Genie – the usual Trickster emissary – would not be subtle enough.

Few non-human races worship Logaan the Trickster as avidly as some humans do, but there *are* races who seem to follow him. The peculiar Elvins of the Shamutanti Hills in Kakhabad (the small, Elf-like creatures, not the large sea monsters of the Inland Sea, which have the same name) certainly profess to worship the Trickster, who they see as a fun-loving god who likes nothing more than playing tricks on people all day. Elvins have a large repertoire of tricks themselves, which they spend most of their time perfecting – at the expense of some other poor creature, naturally!

Leprechauns, too, follow the mischievous path of the Tricksters – indeed, some folk call them Logaan's Children in honour of the fact that they are always playing practical jokes on people. Unlike Elvins, however, who only play tricks for amusement, Leprechauns use them to stay alive; they steal and cheat food or money out of their victims! Indeed, they can become quite violent if they badly need something from someone. This is not really true to the spirit of the Tricksters as such, however, and many now believe that the Leprechauns simply share many affinities with other servants of these gods, rather than being proper servants of them. It is true that Logaan's tricks are often violent, but their purpose is rarely to steal or cheat others – except when to do so is part of the joke, that is.

THE RUNES OF THE TRICKSTERS

The tricksters use two runes, which encapsulate the basic principles behind their alignment. One is an arrow point-

ing in both directions, symbolizing the balance of Good and Evil. The other is a star, which points in all directions – it means, quite simply, that absolutely *anything* can happen!

The Animal Court

For many centuries the knowledge that the many different creatures which roam the surface of Titan worshipped deities was conveniently forgotten. The animals, priests argued, were ignorant of the beauty of the gods and goddesses, and lived their lives completely unaware that there was more to existence than simply swimming about in the sea, soaring on thermals high above the land, or stalking the plains in search of prey. Such a view also 'proved', quite conclusively, that animals did not have souls, and therefore man was supreme, greater than any beast! The traditional response to such a pompous argument may well have been 'Man's not an animal? You haven't seen my husband!', but it blinded many cultures to the gods of the Animal Court.

Animals and their gods follow an alignment which is rather difficult to categorize, but which is sometimes known as 'True Neutral', which is why we are including a few details of it at this juncture. It is a blind belief, and an unintelligent one, for it seeks only to help the race of the particular animal, and disregards what happens to other beings. Every creature on Titan was made by a god during the Godtime, when the world was filled with the creations they made from the magic clay found by Throff in her garden. These gods did not simply disappear; they became the gods of the animals, and sit at the Animal Court, where they are indifferent to anything but the continued survival of their own species, no matter what the cost to Law or Chaos across the cosmos.

This attitude has been exploited on a few occasions, where creatures such as wolves and spiders have been persuaded to take part in weighty conflicts, because their gods were persuaded that to do so would be to the advantage of the species. However, being True Neutral, animals rarely feel regret if they have to double-cross their allies and change sides – for it is all justified by being good for the future of the species.

The gods of the animals are occasionally worshipped by men

and some of the inhuman races. Primitives such as Marsh Goblins and Neanderthals worship the gods of the Court simply because they are large, powerful monsters with the ability to cause great pain, suffering and destruction.

Others, however, desire to call upon the help of such creatures in a time of need, and to get closer to the animals with which they share their lives. The horse-nomads of the Flatlands, for example, are worshippers of Evil, but they also pay allegiance to Hunnynhaa, the stallion god, and pray that he will protect both his horses and their riders – for if the nomads were allowed to fall into the hands of their enemies the horses would suffer as well. If it ever came to a choice between whether a horse-nomad followed the side of Evil or the side of Hunnynhaa, he would always choose the latter. In a similar way, some Orcs give offerings to Almor, the wolf lord, especially in view of the help he was tricked into giving the Forces of Chaos at the First Battle, where he served alongside the champion of the Orcs.

There are even some sorcerers who are obsessed with the study and protection of animals to such an extent that they too begin to become entwined in the worship of the Animal Court. One hears many stories of Hurdagag Greenfinger, who made the study of moles his life's work. He would often be seen by intrigued passers-by, lying on the grassy forest floor, his head stuck inside a molehill, observing the fascinating little creatures at work! He learnt more and more about moles, of which he had at first intended to make only a very brief study. As he learnt more, he became more fascinated by them, for he had never realized that animals and other creatures had almost as sophisticated a culture as humans did! Eventually, the sorcerer's curiosity to know everything got the better of him, and he moved under the ground to live with the moles in their tunnels. Such is the danger of obsession and the quest for knowledge!

Rather than go into every animal cult in detail, which would be tedious in the extreme, we have simply devised the following table to show you the names and relations of all the members of the Animal Court.

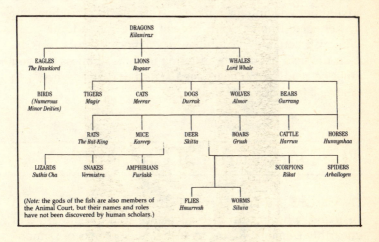

149

THE FORCES OF EVIL AND CHAOS

So, brave adventurer, you now know of the Forces of Good, who may offer you aid and friendship to lighten the burden of your quest. You also know of those factions undecided one way or another, the Neutral Forces, who may rattle a dagger in your ribs as easily as assist you. And you know of those allegiances that change with the wind, or so it seems – the Tricksters who will offer bread with one hand and take it away with the other, for ever playing their part in some almighty cosmic joke. All this you now know.

Let us turn our attention to the many horrific aspects of Evil and Chaos, from the blind, stupid hatred of the inhuman races – Orcs, Goblins, Trolls and Ogres – to the infinitely subtle schemings of the awesome Demon Princes. Know the weaknesses of your foe and your battle is half-won, they say in Analand; so study your adversaries carefully. Wherever he journeys in the wilderlands of this world, a pure-hearted adventurer will find the ranks of Evil arrayed against him, but by heroic and noble deeds he will win through to his goal. Wherever you find Evil or the warped mockeries of Chaos, be it on the field of battle or festering in some lightless pit, you must be ready, with sharpened sword and steady hand, to cleanse it from this world.

The Dark Lords of Chaos

The vile Orcs and Goblins are ruled over by their chieftains and shamans, who in turn give allegiance to a ghastly array of unearthly Demons. Ruling over the motley ranks of Demons are the Demon Princes, with their horrible perversions of courtly behaviour and chivalry. This you may know already, but few mortals have ever known much about the even more powerful deities who rule over Evil, even in the depths of Hell – the Dark Lords of Chaos.

Go far beyond Titan, beyond the Elemental Planes and the blasphemous Demonic Planes, beyond even space and time. There, at the heart of the Void, dwell the Dark Lords. They were imprisoned here at the Dawn of Time by the united might of the Forces of Good after the First Battle. Some are remembered in remote, savage corners of the world – such as Slangg, god of malice, still worshipped in the depraved city of Kharé – but most have passed from the short memories of mankind and are studied in secret only by the most ambitious of necromancers. It was once inferred by an insane seer that the Dark Lords numbered twenty-three in all, though this has never been verified.

The Dark Lords are thought, in their basic state, to be formless, shadowy beings, little more than hyper-intelligent manifestations of pure evil emotion. Some do take on more material forms for special visits to the various Planes of existence, but since their imprisonment it costs them dearly in energy, so that fortunately they can never reveal their true power on Titan. Others have had physical forms imposed on them by over-zealous worshippers who wished to build statues in what they believed to be their image. But there are thought to be some who never give any indication of their presence – though proving or disproving this will require the efforts of an eternity of seers and philosophers!

The First Lord of Chaos is Death, who holds the entire universe in his cruel grasp. It was he who imposed on the world of Titan the doom of Time and the decree that things may cease to exist, in direct opposition to the gods of Good, who can only create and mould, but never destroy. In different lands Death has many names and many forms. To the rugged warriors of Frostholm in the far north, he is known simply as the Closer or the Finisher, and takes the form (in their legends) of a mighty black Giant who wields an axe forged from the metal of night. To the nomads of the Scythera Desert of southern Khul he is Krsh, the sound of a man's last breath, and he comes as an

invisible hand to choke and strangle in the night. Every land has its own stories, traditions, names and images of Death, but all men fear his inescapable grip.

Other known Dark Lords include Disease, known as the Festering Lord in some far western lands. His brother is Decay, prince of insects and mould and all that rots, worshipped in southern Khul by the beggars and lepers of the foul city of Shakuru. They, in turn, are served by lesser nobles, who rank alongside the Demon Princes in the order of things, the various kings and lords of the insect races. These include Arhallogen, lord of spiders, worshipped by the degenerate primitives of the southern Allansian jungles; and Hmurresh, queen of the flies, who dwells on the Elemental Plane of Air, from where she dispatches her subjects to bring plague and pestilence to all corners of the world.

The deities worshipped in Kakhabad as Slangg, god of malice, and his sister Tanit, goddess of envy and jealousy, are thought to be related to many of the gods of Good; but it is said that because they sided with the Forces of Evil during the First Battle, they were exiled and fled to join the Dark Lords in the Void. The priests and scholars of other lands may dispute these beliefs, if they know of them at all, but in Kharé unlucky people are still said to suffer 'the grace of Slangg'. In the weird temples of the Cityport of Traps, spiteful citizens give offerings to Slangg and Tanit and implore them to bring their vengeance down upon others. The former is depicted as a grossly fat man with the forked tongue of a snake, typically posed whispering an aside behind his hand. His sister is more sinisterly portrayed as an astoundingly beautiful woman, dressed in a macabre hat, veil and long black robes, with a wicked curved dagger held behind her back and a cruel smile on her perfect lips.

The Dark Lords are served by the Demon Princes of the Pit, though somewhat reluctantly in some cases, since the Princes are arrogant beings – as all princes are – and do not serve others willingly. Some Lords use the Princes as their agents to work great Evil upon the Earthly Plane. Most, however, use subtler means, and work by suggestion and inspiration alone. Such is the influence of Death upon the Demon Princes. The First Lord sets perverted ideas to twist and writhe within their warped minds and affords them moments of extreme pleasure when they put another army, city or country to the sword. Death is the puppet-master who guides the scaly hand of Evil and Chaos, using its servants to bring about his ultimate aim – the enslavement or eradication of all life in the world.

Sith is rather ignorant of the fighting among her own troops, being far more concerned with the fortunes of her chosen servants on the Earthly Plane, the Caarth (the desert-dwelling Snake People). Despite her exhortations, the power of the vile reptilians is waning, and the various Lizard Man races who worship her princely rivals Ishtra and Myurr are on the ascendant. Sith's powers on Titan may be waning, but she still reigns in the Pit, though only through very careful manoeuvrings, diplomacy, intrigues and assassinations.

Although the three Snake Demons govern the Abyss from the

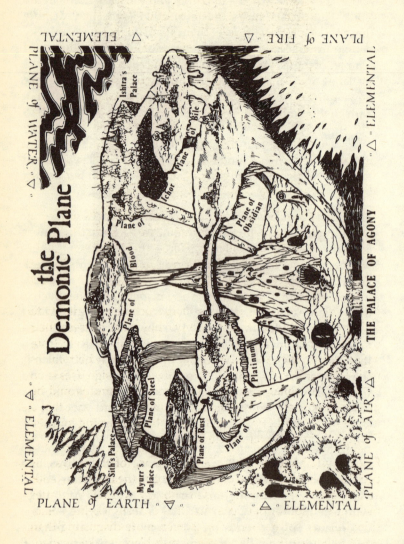

the Demonic Plane

PLANE of WATER

PLANE of EARTH

PLANE of FIRE

ELEMENTAL

Ishtra's Palace

Plane of Bile

Ichor Plane

Plane of Blood

Plane of Obsidian

Plane of

Plane of

THE PALACE OF AGONY

Plane of Platinum

Sith's Palace

Plane of Steel

Myurr's Palace

Plane of Rust

Plane of

STEVE 80

ELEMENTAL

ELEMENTAL

ELEMENTAL

154

ornate blood-diamond thrones of the echoing league-wide Ruling Hall of the Palace of Agony, they each possess their own retreats too. Sith dwells in a castle built entirely from snake scales, perched upon the edge of a seemingly bottomless ravine near the centre of the Plane of Steel. Its design uses such a strange, inhuman geometry that a mortal mind would be driven completely insane just by looking upon it – not that a mortal mind would have survived the brain-warping journey through the outer levels of the Pit to reach it!

Her Satanic Majesty, Sith, Demon Prince of the Abyss, is probably the most violent and sadistic of all the Demons – and, as any respected scholar of demonology will tell you after making the appropriate prayers, that is really saying something! In her natural form she is even more disgusting than when in her 'earthly' shape ('a greenish-black, snake-headed, four-armed, bat-winged, three-metre-tall monstrosity', as one erudite tome puts it). Perhaps four metres tall, maybe a metre wide, she takes on the body and tail of an immense snake, the torso of a beautiful Giant woman, six claw-tipped arms, and a hissing nightmare of a head which is half-way between a woman's and a viper's

Her unceasing lust for the violent death of other beings knows no bounds, and many poor souls have been slaughtered simply because she slithered out of the wrong side of her pit that morning. There is nothing she likes more than slowly stripping a living creature of its insides, through small punctures in its skin, by sucking and slurping until the husk is empty; though sometimes when she is in a hurry she will simply pull the arms off something and munch away. Like all Demons, she does not actually need to eat, but she loves to feel the waves of anguish and pain coming from a dying creature. Sith feels affection for only one thing – her pet python, Sussussurr. A truly awesome beast, Sussussurr is over twenty metres long and a metre thick; he is the immortal son of Vermistra, queen of snakes, who dwells in the thickest, most remote jungles of Titan.

THE PRIESTS OF SLANGG AND TANIT

The bizarre deities of Kharé in eastern Kakhabad are served by equally bizarre priests. Those who serve Slangg, the god of malice, dress in robes dyed bright orange and shave their heads. Unlike other holy men, they always carry a vast array of weapons and instruments of torture, for part of their ritual duties is the perpetuation of hate and violence against non-worshippers. To this end they burn down temples, put whole congregations to the torch and slaughter many innocent and not-so-innocent citizens – all in accordance with the rules preached by their deity. Tanit's priestesses are much subtler, working through delicate intrigues and carefully planned set pieces. When worshipping, they dress in the same robes as their goddess, but normally they work in the community, as it were, sowing the seeds of jealousy and envy among husbands, wives and lovers, always working to divide and frustrate, and subvert the work of the servants of Asrel, goddess of love and earthly happiness.

156

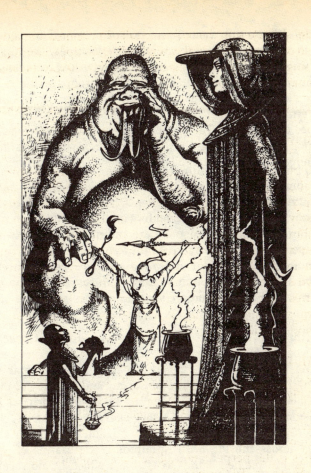

The Demon Princes, Masters of the Pit

Death is the most deadly of all masters and his chosen servants are dangerous in the extreme; the Demon Princes are his chosen servants. They are immortal monstrosities who rule over the Demonic Plane, using insanity, depravity and true Chaos to perpetuate their reign over the Forces of Evil and

Chaos. Where they came from, no one dares say for certain, but in the years before the War of the Wizards, the highest scholars believed that they were the captains and commanders of the evil armies in the First Battle. Many troops on both sides were slain when Death set foot on the world for the first time, but enough escaped, it seemed, and retreated to the outer Planes of existence. These are now known collectively as the Demonic Plane, though in truth there are many levels; their teeming inhabitants just call it the Pit.

The lords and masters of the Pit are the Demon Princes. Seven in number, they are the most evil, corrupt, depraved and Chaotic beings ever to have set foot on the Earthly Plane since the birth of Time. The seven are informally split into two groups: the trio of terrifying fiends known to some as 'Snake Demons', Ishtra, Myurr and Sith; and the 'Night Demons', Kalin, Relem, Shakor and Vradna. The former are the true rulers of the Abyss, and are served on occasion by the other four.

The three ruling Princes sit together in judgement over the souls of the damned, in the Palace of Agony at the very centre of the Demonic Plane. Ostensibly they rule by combined strength of will, but in truth they argue and disagree so often that it is only when two side together against the third that any decisions are actually made. Once every few centuries, their bickering and sniping gets out of hand, and a bloody civil war rages across the Pit, with hundreds of thousands of souls engaged in pitched battles to establish which Demon was in the right (or rather, in the wrong!). Each of the satanic trio is served, albeit very haphazardly, by one of the Night Demons, who captain their armies and act as right-hand demons for the duration of the civil war. Currently, however, Sith is being served by both Relem and Vradna. Several decades ago this was to Her Disgusting Majesty's benefit, as each led their half of her forces to greater and greater extremes to prove his superiority over the other. Now, however, the spark of unhealthy competition has dimmed, and they fight more against each other than against the armies of Kalin or Shakor.

Ishtra and Myurr are no match for Sith when it comes to pure cruelty, but each has his own special facets. Ishtra usually takes the modest form of a goat-headed, humanoid crocodile, though when he wishes to impress someone, or make a point during an argument, he reverts to a raging ball of energy, spitting streams of electrical sparks in all directions. His great love is fire, and the strange burning effect it has on contact with lesser life-forms! Of the three, Myurr is the subtlest (if such a term could ever be applied to the vilest beings in existence), and prefers to work through lies, rumours and other forms of deceit. He typically takes the form of an enormous toad, or sometimes appears as a sweet, innocent little boy, who just happens to have the oldest eyes ever opened upon the world. Myurr spends more of his time on the Earthly Plane than any of the Demon Princes, in disguise or inhabiting the mind of an influential leader or adviser, working as always to produce as much anarchy and destruction as he can.

DEMONIC ENTERTAINMENT AND THE WILD HUNT

Despite their perpetual differences, squabbles and cruel and violent wars, the Demon Princes and their favoured minions frequently gather together to take part in gigantic banquets. Here you might find several thousand undead beings, sprawled and slumped at tables covered by curious blood-red cloths with the texture of flayed skin, and piled high with all manner of dead, semi-dead and very-much-alive foodstuffs. The stomach-churning food frantically gibbers, squeals and scuttles until caught and eaten by the obnoxious revellers. Some diners get so excited that they start to feast upon their fellow guests!

For entertainment there are the merry antics of torturers, who gleefully flay new arrivals to produce the most exquisite music; the Demon-spawn jugglers who mutate endlessly and juggle with loose parts of their bodies; and the more traditional singers of naughty ballads. With the floor knee-deep in blood and slime, the air rent by the screams of the dying and the sounds of so many vile things chewing other vile things, the whole scene is how a pious man would imagine Hell – except that this *is* Hell and it is far worse than any mortal man could imagine.

At other times, however, the entertainment is much more serious. On cold, moonless nights in the middle of winter, when the crop of fresh souls is running low because it is too cold on the Earthly Plane for evil humans to go abroad and kill others, the Wild Hunt rides out across the world.

Usually led by one of the seven Princes – though more may come along if there is no war raging in the Pit – the Hunt is a motley collection of Lesser Demons, Demonic Servants, and Spirit Stalkers and other undead, all mounted on terrifying undead horses. These unearthly mounts are skeletal horses, with black skin stretched taut between their protruding bones. Their manes and tails crackle with a fire which is mirrored in their insane eyes. The dogs of the Wild Hunt are the Hellhounds. Howling like something out of your worst nightmares, the hounds sniff out living beings from the smell of fresh blood pumping in their veins! Sweeping out of the midnight sky, the Wild Hunt rampages across the countryside looking for isolated settlements and farmsteads where they can collect the souls they require, before moving on to continue their fun.

THE RUNES OF DEATH AND CHAOS

The death rune is derived from an inverted rune of life or man, and symbolizes the opposite force, that of death.

The Chaos rune shows a circle, meaning both nothingness and all things, the paradox at the heart of Chaos.

THE GENERALS OF THE LEGIONS OF THE DAMNED

The armies of Hell are commanded by the four Night Demons, Kalin, Relem, Shakor and Vradna. They sit in the war-room of the Palace of Agony, huddled in their carved thrones around a deep, misty pool set in the cold stone floor. The pool allows them to watch the results of their plans on the Earthly Plane. The Princes are devious tacticians, working subtly or blatantly, according to the situation, to further the evil ends of the Forces of Chaos on Titan.

By gazing down into their scrying pool, the unearthly generals can look in upon the secret construction of the dungeon complexes deep beneath the Moonstone Hills, where the foul necromancer Razaak assembles his terrible undead armies, preparing to sweep across Allansia and drive all before him. The unholy quartet look down as the swarming armies of the Lizard Man Empire continue to pound at the crumbling walls of the besieged city of Vymorna – at catapults throwing the heads of the city's young warriors back to their horrified countrymen, and two-headed high priests offering up the hearts of living sacrifices to the demonic generals, asking for just a little more aid finally to crush the city. As the mists weave, they watch with satisfaction the eldritch shapes stirring at the heart of the Wastes of Chaos, and the spirits of hundreds of undead warriors rising from the battlegrounds, brandishing notched and rusted weapons while they scream for vengeance upon the living with a single deathless voice.

Wherever the Demon Princes look, they see the smoke of battle, the glint of sunlight on armour, the flashing of swords and the splashing of blood. They see their demonic emissaries preparing Orcs and Goblins for battle. They see the dark shapes of Trolls and Ogres hiding in the mountains and the forests, waiting for their moment. They see ancient Dragons stirring in their sleep in chambers buried far beneath the surface of the world, knowing their time will soon come. And they see the new heroes, the adventurers and the warriors, defeating their forces in many lands; the sorcerers who still keep the lights of Goodness burning in the darkness closing all

around them; the ordinary folk who gather together to resist the incursions of Orcs or wolves or Trolls into their lands. The generals see all this, and continue to plot their strategies for the total domination of Evil over Titan, sure in their twisted minds that victory cannot be far away.

THE HIERARCHY OF THE PIT

Social standing is overwhelmingly important to the inhabitants of the Everlasting Abyss. Despite its apparent chaos, or perhaps because of it, there is a very rigid set of rules for etiquette when one Demon meets another, or some other inhabitant of the Infernal Domain who is lower or higher on the social scale. If the right gestures and greetings are not made, the slighted party has every right to rend the offender in two, if he is of a lower class, or at least challenge him to some ghastly duel if he is of the same or a higher group. For all their sickening atrocities, Demons can be boringly well mannered at times!

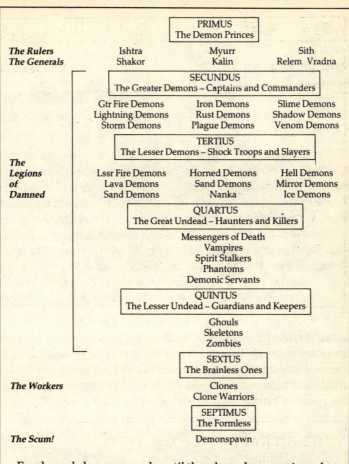

The Rulers

PRIMUS
The Demon Princes

Ishtra	Myurr	Sith
Shakor	Kalin	Relem Vradna

The Rulers
The Generals

SECUNDUS
The Greater Demons – Captains and Commanders

Gtr Fire Demons	Iron Demons	Slime Demons
Lightning Demons	Rust Demons	Shadow Demons
Storm Demons	Plague Demons	Venom Demons

TERTIUS
The Lesser Demons – Shock Troops and Slayers

The Legions of Damned

Lssr Fire Demons	Horned Demons	Hell Demons
Lava Demons	Sand Demons	Mirror Demons
Sand Demons	Nanka	Ice Demons

QUARTUS
The Great Undead – Haunters and Killers

Messengers of Death
Vampires
Spirit Stalkers
Phantoms
Demonic Servants

QUINTUS
The Lesser Undead – Guardians and Keepers

Ghouls
Skeletons
Zombies

SEXTUS
The Brainless Ones

The Workers

Clones
Clone Warriors

SEPTIMUS
The Formless

The Scum!

Demonspawn

Fresh souls have no rank until they have been assigned to a particular type. This task can only be carried out by a Greater Demon or Prince, though usually Demonic Servants will handle the assigning of 'job lots', fresh from a major battle, for instance.

163

Orcs – The Warriors of Evil

After the lords and masters, we come to the servants and the slaves of Evil. There are many inhuman races aligned with Chaos; we shall attempt to cover the main ones here, starting with the most numerous, the rank and file of the armies of Chaos – Orcs.

You will encounter Orcs wherever you travel, from the frozen wastes beyond the Icefinger Mountains to the idyllic desert islands of the Southern Seas. Wherever you go on Titan there is one thing of which you can be certain – Orcs will have been there before you, poking their snouts everywhere. They are tremendously curious beings, for all their lack of intelligence, and seem to enjoy exploring and discovering new things – though they never seem to take enjoyment in anything once they have control of it! It is this fact which keeps their armies marching ever onwards, and their miners digging ever deeper.

Orcs rarely keep records, except in the form of the oral histories passed from shaman to shaman, and they will kill and eat most humans as soon as they encounter them, so acquiring detailed information on Orcs for this book has proved quite difficult. At this point we would therefore like to acknowledge the great debt we owe to the sorcerer and mystic Enstaflis Anaren of Shabak, the renowned expert on Orcs, for much of the data we give here. Enstaflis recently spent two years in the mind of an Orc soldier from the Flatlands, gathering even more detailed knowledge of what it is like to be an Orc, but unfortunately he had to give his experiment up before he was finished after the Orc's battalion was ambushed and eaten by a pack of Tyrannosaurs. However, before he returned to his own body again, Enstaflis had the presence of mind to collect some amazing data about the digestive systems of a Tyrannosaurus Rex! The man is an inspiration to us all.

HASHAK THE CREATOR

Orcs say they are the children of a being called Hashak the Creator, who is believed by most modern-day scholars to have been a demigod in the service of the earth goddess, Throff – though Orcs believe him to have been far more important than her. Hashak is certainly not very handsome as demigods go: he is usually depicted as a stunted, brown-skinned Hill Giant. Hashak was ambitious and curious about the new 'creations' of the gods, and was especially jealous of the beings called 'Dwarfs', whom Throff was spending so much of her time peering at from the heavens. So in a fit of pique and jealousy, Hashak slunk away to a quiet corner, with a good-sized lump of the magic clay which his mistress had used to create those annoying Dwarf-things, and began to fashion his own creations.

Hashak was astounded by the little things he had made, which wriggled and kicked as he held them in his fingers. He called them 'Trolls', and played with them for a while. But they were stupid creatures, and very ugly, and Hashak soon became bored with them. He took his Trolls and put them down on Titan, hiding them away in the mountains where no one would see them, for he felt embarrassed at having made such ugly things. But Hashak missed his creations, and resolved to make some more the next day. This time he took more care, and created a smaller, more finely detailed set of models, which could think and talk a little. The word the little creatures said most of all was 'Urk! Urk!' and Hashak decided they would be called 'Urks'.

But that day Throff came back early, and found Hashak in the corner playing with his creations. She was livid, and ordered him to destroy them at once! Hashak wailed and cried, but it was no use: he had taken her magical clay and made some nasty little creatures out of it, and now he must pay the consequences. Hashak looked at the marbled floor, and asked sheepishly if he could just take his creations outside and say goodbye, on his own, before scrunching them up into a ball again. Throff was a kindly soul underneath (she must have been to have taken in the simple-minded Hashak in the first place, human scholars generally point out at this point), and she gave in and said he could.

Crafty Hashak had a plan. Scooping up his 'Urks', he went outside, but rather than saying goodbye he hid most of them in a dark corner, and only scrunched up a few. Before returning the ball of clay, he mixed in some ordinary soil from the garden of Galana, the goddess of plants, so that Throff would not notice. That night, Hashak crept out and retrieved his 'Urks', and hid them away in all the dark corners of Titan alongside his Trolls, before sneaking back to his bed.

What Hashak did not know, however, was that he had been observed by several of the Dark Lords, who were awake that night plotting against the other gods. They followed him, and saw where he hid them. After Hashak had gone, they took each 'Urk' in turn, and breathed their Evil over it. To this day, Orcs are tainted with the curse of Chaos, with the result that they are bound to serve the Forces of Evil, and also Chaotic mutations are common among their offspring.

SHAMANS, THE TRIBAL SORCERERS

Ultimate power over the Orcs rests with the shamans, the tribal witch-doctors and magicians who govern all spiritual matters and provide direct links with the supernatural commanders of the armies of Evil and Chaos. The tribes each have their own kings and chiefs as well, but these are more concerned with the day to day business of ruling over the Orcs. Tribal chiefs always get caught up in issues such as whether an Orc was wrong to eat his brother-in-law for spilling his ale, or whether a captured Dwarf should be eaten immediately or fattened up for later consumption.

But shamans have far more important matters to worry about. They must consult with their horrific patrons, usually by means of ritual dance and blood-sacrifice, and question them about the immediate future. They dress scantily, usually in little more than a loincloth and a good deal of garish paint and blood, and they are always waving bones and skulls around,

for they consider themselves to be Death's representatives on the Earthly Plane. Orc shamans have developed a great variety of means of divining the messages sent by their demonic masters. A common one features a rat allowed to run free inside a cage around which are painted the fourteen letters of the Orc alphabet; as it runs to and fro it is meant to spell out the message from beyond. Other methods include slicing open a freshly captured Elf and examining the entrails for signs (a technique known as 'elfomancy'); or throwing into the air fourteen cockroaches, each marked with a rune, to see what message they spell when they come back down to earth.

Ordinary Orcs know little about religion, for they care little for anything beyond the end of today. Indeed, all Orcs are notoriously unconcerned about the future. Most dream of the 'some day' when Orcs shall rule the world, but none anticipate it. Perhaps this attitude has developed because they have enough trouble surviving from one day to the next without having to worry about the day after as well (or perhaps it is just because they are stupid!). To the common Orc, shamans are good for a few heartening spells before battle and for making the subsequent celebrations fun, what with all their sacrificing and blood-letting; and they always tell a good tale. But beyond that they mean very little.

ORCS AND THEIR SIMPLE PLEASURES

Orcs are creatures of simple tastes. They like to eat, they like to drink, and they like to fight. The first of these three essentials to Orc happiness is always easy to come by, for Orcs will eat just about anything they can get their hands on and their jaws around. Their favourite food is the flesh of their enemies, and they are noted for the many unsavoury meals they can cook out of the corpses of Dwarfs and Elves. The legendary 'Elf Intestines in Gnome's-blood Sauce', for example, is a speciality of the Severed Arm tribe of Xamen and the Zanzunu Peaks in northern Kakhabad, though owing to the very rich nature of its ingredients it is considered a special delicacy, and is only eaten on very important occasions (generally, it must be said, to celebrate the death in battle of a large number of Elves and Gnomes).

If they cannot get fresh meat, Orcs will resort to other food-stuffs, including vegetables, wood, metal, rocks and dirt! They have a special second stomach, which allows them to digest all kinds of hard or sharp objects. For this reason, it is often very difficult to imprison an Orc for long, for in the end he will just eat his way to freedom. However, after very heavy meals Orcs do get drowsy, and often need to sleep after the exertions involved in stuffing their voluminous gullets. Orcs who have escaped from a dungeon by chewing their way out may sometimes be found close by, fast asleep and oblivious to any need to flee the immediate area of their prison!

Orcs are not cannibals, however, and they consider it gravely offensive to eat other Orcs, except in the direst circumstances. However, they seem to believe that once an Orc dies, he is no longer an Orc, and is therefore to be regarded like any other tasty snack! At Orc funerals, indeed, the guests are supposed to show respect and reverence for the deceased by taking a large bite or two out of them, before the dear departed are consigned to the ground or the cleansing fires of the funeral pyre! Orcs also will not eat undead creatures, even if they are warmed up, for they do not find them at all filling. Apart from these two exceptions, however, there are very few things Orcs will not at least *attempt* to eat.

As far as drink is concerned, Orcs consider themselves to be the finest brewers around. Orc ale is extremely potent, often to the extent of being deadly poison to a human being. Orcs' favourite drink is a truly vile concoction called 'Guursh', though some also call it 'Hweagh' – the only reason for these names that we can think of is that they represent the sorts of noise one would hear after drinking too much of it, though perhaps there is some more tasteful explanation really. It apparently tastes to humans like licking the inside of a mossy cave with several cockroaches jammed in your nose or so we have been informed by someone who knew someone who once claimed to have tried some. What is certain is that it is greeny-pink in colour, and is kept in lead-lined barrels to stop it eating through the wood. Orcs consider it a rather light, delicate drink, and are even supposed to have vintage years when the Guursh was better than ever: it apparently must have large lumps floating in it to be declared vintage – large lumps of what, though, our informant did not say.

Orcs get drunk fairly easily, which is not surprising considering the potency of their drinks, and in such a state they tend to perform all kinds of outrageous acts. Every tribal shaman has a vast repertoire of cautionary tales to do with drunkenness, such as the one concerning foolish King Morgag Knuckle-breaker, who bought a puddle off a passing Goblin because he saw the reflection of the moon in it and thought it was a large silver plate. Then there was Uglar Goblin-Face, who ate a whole camel for a bet while under the influence and then burst in a most unsavoury manner. Or . . . the list is endless. Orcs seem to take great delight in hearing about the misfortunes of others, including other Orcs, though, of course, they never realize that they just might be that stupid too!

THE BONERAT CAVES
An Orc Settlement

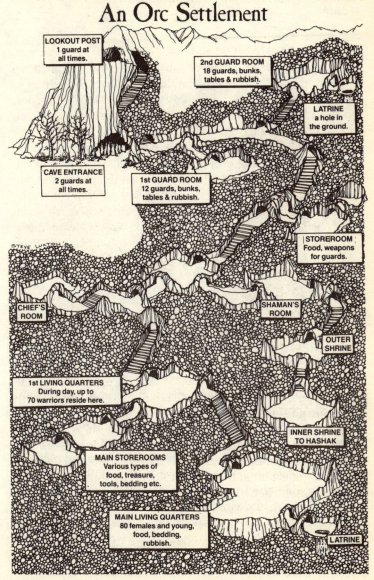

LOOKOUT POST
1 guard at all times.

2nd GUARD ROOM
18 guards, bunks, tables & rubbish.

LATRINE
a hole in the ground.

CAVE ENTRANCE
2 guards at all times.

1st GUARD ROOM
12 guards, bunks, tables & rubbish.

STEVE LUXTON '86

STOREROOM
Food, weapons for guards.

CHIEF'S ROOM

SHAMAN'S ROOM

OUTER SHRINE

1st LIVING QUARTERS
During day, up to 70 warriors reside here.

INNER SHRINE TO HASHAK

MAIN STOREROOMS
Various types of food, treasure, tools, bedding etc.

MAIN LIVING QUARTERS
80 females and young, food, bedding, rubbish.

LATRINE

Their third basic need, that of fighting, is catered for in their armies, and also by an increasingly large number of very violent field-sports which have become popular in recent decades.

The most widely known of their games is 'Orc Knees', a peculiar game played by two teams, each with four members, who are chosen from a reserve squad of twenty. The pitch is a large circle, divided across the middle by a length of netting or rope. It is played using an inflated pig's or Troll's bladder, though cabbages, melons and Dwarf heads have all been known to suffice on occasion. The first Orc starts the game by punting it over the net to a member of the opposing team, who has to return it using only his knees or his head and so on. If the ball goes outside the circle, the side which did not hit it gains a point; if it lands on the floor within the circle, the side which did gains a point. The first team to reach seven points is allowed to eat one of the opposing team members, and the game is won when there is only one team left. Orc-knee players are very highly paid, to compensate for the fact that their careers as sportsmen are often over very quickly.

Even more violent is the game of 'Pass the Slave', where a human or Dwarf captive is tied up in a bundle, and then kicked, thrown, bounced and pushed up and down a field by up to eight or ten opposing teams from different tribes, who are each trying to keep the slave alive long enough for them to get it into one of the small pits at either end which count as goals. Apart from the basic rule that the slave must be alive and in one piece when it goes into the goal-pit, and that players should try to remain within the boundaries of the field if they possibly can, there are no restrictions on play. As a result, the game usually turns into a blood-bath, albeit a very enjoyable one to Orcs. All Orc sports involve a certain amount of death and violence, because they are crude, blood-thirsty creatures. But their sports will never take the place of war . . .

FAMOUS ORC TRIBES

Orcs are sociable creatures, who band together in large, shambolic tribes, each with their own special signs and customs. You can always tell to which tribe an Orc belongs by looking at his ears, for they decorate them with the symbols of the tribe.

The Throttled Skull: Live in large system of well-protected caves in the mountains of southern Lendleland; number about 2,500; led by King Yargaas Skull-splitter, who got his name from a titanic wrestling-match with three Cave Giants; tribal symbol is, naturally, a throttled skull.

The Clawed Eye: From the central Moonstone Hills in northern Allansia; number around 1,700; led by the ageing Chief Urgari Grinning-Teeth and his twenty-three sons; named after a famous, one-eyed tribal hero.

The Iron Fist: Dwell in small villages in forests near Pikestaff Plain in north-eastern Khul; number only a few hundred; have a peculiar habit of binding iron around their hands with leather thongs, in the belief that eventually their hands will turn to iron too; led by Chief Uzgreg Sour-shriek.

The Curse of Vashanki: A nomadic tribe from the Flatlands, led by King Argar Kin-Slayer, the only surviving member of a famous family of forty-two Orcs; number around 3,000, split into many wandering families.

ORC ARMIES

To put things very bluntly, Orcs hate physical work, but love fighting. They do not really care who the enemy is – and if there is no enemy, then members of another tribe or family will do – as long as they are weaker, so that the Orcs can capture lots of slaves, who provide much of their wealth and free them from the burden of having to work. When there is some special prize to be fought for, however, such as the plundering of a rich city, Orcs will work *and* fight until they drop. Orcs love treasure almost as much as they love the fighting by which they obtain it.

Orcs are cowards, however, and morale and organization on the battlefield are often a problem, unless they are led from behind by someone with a long whip and a loud voice! This helps explain why Orcs fight for the armies of Chaos, which are invariably led by very charismatic sorcerers and evil, but forceful, warriors.

Scouts   Troops   Troops   Chiefs
Banner-bearer   Banner-bearer   Heralds   Rearguard

In any battle, the strongest and largest Orcs will push the smaller ones ahead of them, and if they have had enough time, the smaller Orcs will have cajoled Goblins or Trolls to fight ahead of *them*.

Orcs have a lot of stamina, and can march surprisingly fast if kept in tight formation by their commanders. They have been forced to learn this, mostly because many creatures cannot stand to be near them. Only wolves will allow themselves to be ridden by Orcs, and even they will turn on their riders if the pickings are not plentiful enough to satisfy their powerful appetites. Orc columns tend to use the same formation when they are on a forced march.

The scouts keep about an hour's march ahead of the main force; their job is to make sure that the road is clear of the enemy, and to keep the chiefs informed of what lies ahead. Behind them come the rank and file, divided into battalions, each led by a banner-bearer. (Orc banners are grisly affairs, and are often decorated with skulls and other parts of their enemies, but they give the troops a rallying point if they get lost during a battle.) Behind the troops come the chiefs, sometimes being carried in chairs held aloft by slaves or less fortunate Orc soldiers. The whole entourage is rounded off with half a battalion as the rearguard, who spend some of their time watching for pursuing forces, and the rest picking up stragglers from the main army.

Wherever they march, Orc armies bring fear and death to all humans, Dwarfs and Elves. It is not hard to see why Orcs are despised so much, for they are vile, bloodthirsty creatures, intent on killing as many of their enemies as possible, and ultimately establishing themselves as sole rulers and masters of all of Titan. But a nagging question still remains over how Man-Orcs and other foul creatures came into being. We can only shudder and say that it must be a real nightmare being a slave to Orcs . . .

Goblins – The Children of Evil

Compared to Orcs and their ilk, Goblins are indeed children, but what nasty, vicious, violent children they are! Like Orcs, you will find them almost everywhere you travel, and they will always be causing trouble for some poor souls. Unlike their inhuman relations, however, they are not usually organized into armies, and many live quite pleasant lives as farmers or scavenging hunters, though there has not been a Goblin born who would not exchange his plough for the chance to rob a traveller, if he could get the drop on him! In times gone by, it is said, they did indeed serve with the great Orc armies, but the habit the Orcs had of putting Goblins in the front line of any attack quickly changed that! Nowadays, whenever Goblins do serve with Orc armies, they tend to make up separate regiments, such as the legendary Skallagrim's Lifestealing Crusade, and the Blood of Heaven's Deliverers (Goblins are well known for the overblown names of their regiments!).

Where Goblins actually came from is not known for certain, and every scholar who has studied them has his or her own theory. Problems come when you actually ask Goblins where *they* think they come from, for every tribe has its own, usually very different, story. Despite the efforts of many great scholars and sages through the years, there has never been a unified theory of their origins. This sort of thing is very frustrating for us scholars, for it means we can never be sure of the truth of what we write. However, the various stories can be very interesting, and they do allow us to indulge in one of our favourite pastimes – arguing with one another!

The Children of Hashak. One legend states that Goblins were made by the legendary creator of Orcs, Hashak, after he had made such a bad job with Orcs and Trolls. He took one look at his ugly, stupid, violent creations, and decided to start again, and eventually came up with the far superior Goblins! This is not as strange as it sounds, for Goblins are much better than Orcs at many things, though they are also much weaker and less warlike. Goblins who believe this legend tend to keep very quiet about it when Orcs are around, for this story can drive the latter to extremes of violence!

Brothers to the Woodlings. Another legend (not widely believed by the Goblins themselves) states that there was once a single race of woodland creatures, related to Elves and Gnomes. Over the centuries they slowly divided into many different groups. Some turned into Woodlings, the shy forest-dwellers; others became the mischievous Pixies; and some were tainted with a streak of Evil, and developed into Goblins. This legend also has a ring of truth to it, for some Goblins do still live quiet lives in the forests and hills of wilder lands, and they do bear a superficial resemblance to their supposed relations. But no one, surely, believes that Goblins are in any way related to Elves? It is interesting to note that if you told a Goblin he was related to an Elf, he would probably run you through there and then!

Interbreeding. It is widely known that Orcs have bred with many other races, both good and evil, over the centuries, creating many peculiar offspring, including Doragar and Hob-goblins. It is, therefore, not inconceivable that Goblins are simply the result of earlier crossbreeding between Orcs and other creatures – maybe even human – and then developed as a race in themselves. Goblins certainly appear to be related to Orcs in many ways that even closer relations – such as Doragar – are not. Both species are wary of sunlight and can see in the dark better than they can in daylight, and they have similar body structures (though Goblins are smaller and lither), and many of their tribes are organized in the same way. On the other hand, Goblins are much cleverer than the average Orc, especially at making nasty little mechanical traps and instruments of torture. They also have this inclination towards the natural life, as we have said, which no self-respecting Orc would ever share!

GOBLINS EVERYWHERE!

However they first came to walk the face of the world, it is certain that Goblins are here to stay, for they infest just about everywhere. Not only do tribes of the creatures lurk in every range of hills and every thick forest, but they are also found much further afield, in places where you would not expect them. In the sweltering heat of the southern Khulian wastelands, for example. Goblins still live around Lake Mlubz and the ancient ruins of Zagoula. There are Goblin settlements on some of the islands in the Black Ocean. And even on the fringes of the Desert of Skulls, a few Goblin tribes try to scratch a living out of the parched land – as well as regularly raiding passing merchants. Marsh Goblins, the Uggluk-jai, are very well known, for they are even crueller and nastier than their land-based cousins. Everywhere you look, from Allansia to Kakhabad, from Lendleland to Khul, Goblins are thriving and multiplying.

TRIBAL LIFE

Goblins occasionally refer to themselves as 'the Goblin nation', or 'Harajan-jai' in their own guttural language, but in truth there is no such thing. Certainly, they live in tribes, and are recognizable by members of other tribes when they meet them, and they share customs and legends and the like, but it is not true to regard them as one nation, as one would the Elves, for example. Most Goblins could not care what happened to other tribes, as long as the survival of their own was guaranteed.

Each Goblin tribe has its own territory, within which various families may live wherever they please. Tribes are ruled over by a chief and a shaman, who dwell near to the tribe's recognized 'meeting-place', which is usually at the very centre of the Goblins' territory. Every so often, all the members of the tribe gather at the meeting-place – a clearing marked by totem poles and standing stones carved with tribal history – for a very rowdy celebration, during which much potent Goblin ale will be drunk, ancient Goblin legends will be told yet again, and everyone will eat until they are sick.

The chief of any tribe is elected, quite simply, because he is the strongest and most heroic of them all. When a chief dies, if there is no obvious hero to take his place, all eligible Goblins are sent away to prove their courage by performing such deeds as killing a Mountain Giant in single combat, or skinning a Manticore. The Goblin who brings back the best trophy at the end of five days is declared chief, and his trophy is placed on one of the totem poles in the tribal meeting-place.

Goblins are quite religious creatures, and their shaman is regarded as the earthly link with their many gods and demi-gods. All Goblins worship Hashak, obviously, but they also spend a great deal of time worshipping past heroes of the Goblin race, such as One-Eyed Urm, Jorun Dwarf-Boiler and Klarn Ugbar the Three-Fingered. They fully believe that heroic Goblin warriors are elevated to sit beside Hashak when they die, from where they can watch over the fortunes of the Goblin race. The shamans themselves are quite peculiar creatures, who often run around completely naked, their scrawny bodies painted with religious symbols and runes, and with bones woven into their hair and stuck through their ears and noses. They are quite frightening to look at if you have seen nothing like them before, for when they want to scare someone they can rant, rave and gibber so impressively that you would

179

swear they were possessed by Demons! Most shamans are able to do a little magic, and on rare occasions they can even summon up the spirit of some past hero to put a curse on their enemies.

The shamans are also responsible for the upkeep of the totems, which usually hang on poles made from the trunks of small trees and carved with images from the tribe's history. The trophies of all the chiefs are fixed to the poles or impaled on the top, and depending on how old the tribe is there may be upwards of half a dozen such poles. Every sunset, the shaman will perform a ritual dance around the poles, and on very special days he may ask the warriors of the tribe to procure him a human or an Elf for a blood-sacrifice.

Ordinary Goblins live fairly unremarkable lives, farming or hunting for the most part. For relaxation, however, Goblins do like to raid other cultures, or perhaps perform a little highway robbery on some unsuspecting travellers. They take great delight in traps and mechanisms of all kinds, and they seem to

find entertaining such thoughts as people falling down pits on to poisoned spikes, or having their ears sliced by hidden blades, or having sharp needles stuck in their feet by springs. Their caves are often protected by very sophisticated traps, which are usually enough to dissuade even the bravest or most stupid intruders.

GOBLIN ARMIES

As we have already said, Goblins now form their own regiments in the armies of Chaos rather than simply serving alongside their inhuman brethren. They perform many different roles, but they are most often used as light infantry, to slip deep into enemy country to leave booby-traps and sabotage bridges and roads, or as sappers and engineers at sieges. They are hardy warriors, despite their size, and they are much less prone to cowardice than their larger companions.

In Goblin lands, many tribes organize their warriors into bands which patrol the territory, watching out for hostile intruders and large animals. Goblins tend to share their lands with enemy races such as Dwarfs or Elves, and they have to be very careful to avoid them, and also to hide their villages away from them.

MARSH GOBLINS

One peculiar strain of Goblins are the Uggluk-jai, the Marsh Goblins. They differ from their more familiar relations in that they are even scrawnier, and have green-tinted skin and webbed hands and feet. They make their homes, obviously, in the middle of large areas of marsh and swampland, where they live on small creatures like water-rats and marsh-voles. They are nasty, spiteful things, even more than normal Goblins, and they delight in leaving snares and traps everywhere, perfectly placed for unwary creatures (and occasionally adventurers) to step into.

They usually live in strange communal huts, which are built out of mud and reeds on raft-like platforms floating on the surface of the swamp. Part of them, including the only entrance, is hidden underwater for protection, and to anyone

who does not know better, they look like tangled clumps of reeds, though a trickle of smoke seeping from a hole in the top may give them away. Inside the buildings, there is usually little light and the atmosphere is very damp and rotten, with lots of Goblin families sharing the same small space.

The favourite pastime of many Marsh Goblins is to tie some tasty morsel (such as a plump human adventurer, for example) to something solid, leave it in the middle of the swamp, and watch what happens when larger swamp monsters pick up the scent and come to feed. They also use live bait to attract large creatures when they are hunting. Marsh Goblins do not have tribal leaders, but their shamans are very similar to those of land-dwelling Goblins. They worship Hashak, like all Goblins, but also a peculiar number of disgusting marsh deities, including Sluurm, an immortal giant slug, and Vurrk, Lord of the Marsh Wraiths.

Marsh Goblins speak a weird language which sounds more like gargling than speech, even to other Goblins. They are violent and cruel, which is hardly strange for Goblins, but they are so to one another as well as to other races. Their various tribes are often caught up in pointless, bloody wars against one another, perhaps for possession of only a few square metres of swamp. Marsh Goblins do not like normal Goblins either, and will attack them unless the latter are very careful. They also hate Kokomokoa and the other races who share their swamp-land domains; indeed, it seems that Marsh Goblins are always fighting someone!

FIVE MISCONCEPTIONS ABOUT GOBLINS

1. They do not eat rocks and dirt. Orcs do, which is where the confusion arises. Goblins eat roots, berries and quite a lot of fresh meat.

2. Despite the jokes, Goblins are not stupid. They may not be intellectuals, but they can be cunning and conniving. Try telling a 'Goblin joke' to one, and you may find out!

3. Goblins do not worship trees and boulders. This misconception arose because someone saw a shaman bowing down before a wooden totem pole and a rock on which Goblin legends had been carved.

4. Goblins do not eat their children by mistake. They only do it when they are *very* hungry, and then it is quite deliberate.

5. Goblins are not afraid of the sky falling on their heads, although it is true that they do not like all that big sky up there, and that they do not like bright sunlight. If you see a Goblin running around clutching his head and wailing it is just that someone has hit him, that is all!

Troglodytes

Troglodytes are thought to be distantly related to Goblins. Certainly, they share many physical characteristics, for Troglodytes look very much like short, big-eared Goblins. It is quite possible that they evolved from Goblins who started to dwell deep underground in caves and dungeon complexes away from their surface-loving fellows. In time, perhaps, the low ceilings of their cramped domain caused them to produce shorter and shorter offspring, and at the same time their ears and noses grew larger to cope with the lightless conditions down there. Although Goblins can see in the dark, their eyes are like those of cats, and require at least some light to be able to see far. Troglodytes, however, developed a system like that used by bats; echoes tell them where the walls and ceiling are, and help them pinpoint their prey with deadly accuracy even in the darkest of situations.

LIFE UNDERGROUND

Troglodytes live a fairly pleasant life underground, though it is not without its hardships. They feed mostly on beetles, moss and fungus, which they grow in large caverns, tending them carefully under the light of phosphorescent plants. Occasionally, however, they will hunt out a tastier morsel, such as a lone adventurer, Dwarf or even a Dark Elf (though the latter are a very rare, and quite perilous, delicacy, normally reserved for *very* special occasions). They are as skilful as Goblins at setting up traps – though they know little of more sophisticated mechanical ones – and they often capture their prey with a well-placed tripwire or a false floor which tilts its victim into a pit. Troglodytes are great burrowers, and their tiny tunnels will often riddle larger Dwarf or Orc dungeon complexes, which from time to time they will enter to hunt prey.

Some tribes of Troglodytes have managed to tame giant beetles, centipedes and rock grubs, which they use as mounts. They have even trained them to stay in line like cavalry horses, and they use the armoured creatures in their occasional battles against the larger denizens of the underground world. Troglodytes are very possessive about their caverns and tunnels, and will fight against overwhelming odds to keep larger creatures from taking over their areas. Favourite Troglodyte weapons include small throwing-axes and daggers, as well as bows which fire flint-tipped arrows with great accuracy.

THE RUN OF THE ARROW

In fact, it is their skill with their small bows which provides the one aspect of Troglodyte culture for which they are famous – the Run of the Arrow. This bizarre game is played when Troglodytes have captured a large being such as a human or a Dwarf (they never play it with Dark Elves – why waste all that succulent flesh?). Their captive is freed, an arrow is fired into the distance, and he is allowed to walk safely as far as that point before the Troglodytes will try to hunt and shoot him down. One recent Troglodyte, captured and interrogated by Dwarfs, revealed that Troglodytes always fire short with their first arrow, just in case their aim is a bit off that day! Even worse, the creature also told of a new variant which was being practised by the Uurgag tribe. Just beyond the point where the first arrow lands, there may be a hole in the ground, which, the Troglodytes tell their captive, leads to freedom. The captive is allowed to get as far as the mark as usual, but when he leaps into the hole he finds that it is actually full of sharpened spikes! The Troglodyte seemed to think that this was an excellent new addition to the game, until the Dwarfs 'persuaded' it otherwise.

SHAMANS AND IDOLS

Like Goblins, Troglodytes are led by high chiefs and shamans, who organize the tribal worship of their many peculiar gods. Troglodytes seem to worship just about anything they can, from Hashak to 'the All-consuming Blindness' (the sun), and from Scratta Many-legged (a giant centipede of awesome proportions) to something called Shreech, the rat king. Indeed, it is quite possible that any adventurer who managed to impress them with his or her prowess would become one of their deities too – though he or she might have to die first. They erect large statues, made from gold they dig out of the rock around them, in caverns at the heart of their territory, around which they dance wildly at the least excuse, while their naked shamans chant and shriek and scream, just as all shamans do!

Trolls and Ogres

The real heavyweights of the armies of Evil are Trolls and Ogres, large, brutish creatures who lack even the small amounts of intelligence and subtlety which Goblins and their ilk possess. Both are related to other inhuman races, but like them they have gradually developed their own particular 'culture'.

IT'S A TROLL'S LIFE

As with Goblins, the origin of Trolls is notoriously difficult to be certain about. However, two views prevail among scholars who have made a study of such things: either they developed from early crossbreeding of Orcs with Giants, or they were in fact created alongside Orcs by Hashak. (Indeed, when a Troll wishes to pick a fight with an Orc – which is quite ᵗᵉn – he needs simply to say, 'Ha! You're just jealous 'cos you got made second!' Orcs are very irritable when their supremacy is called into question, especially by something as obviously inferior as a Troll!)

However they came to be on Titan, Trolls quickly spread across its entire face, from the tops of mountains to the bottom of the sea. Despite their wide range of habitats, however, Trolls are not very populous, for they breed only rarely. Why this should be is not known, though some scholars have theorized that it may have something to do with the extreme repulsiveness of female Trolls, which also explains why so many male Trolls join up as soldiers.

All Trolls are disliked by those races aligned to the side of Good, but especially by Dwarfs, who suffer from a berserk rage whenever they encounter a Hill Troll. This stems from an incident over seven hundred years before the War of the Wizards, when the great Dwarf hero Harlak Vanagrimsson was killed by a tribe of Hill Trolls while trying to force a passage through the Kalakûr (known to humans as the Freezeblood Mountains). Even previously, a Dwarf knew he could expect no mercy at the hands of a Troll – sudden death would be the end of the matter. On this occasion, however, a vile Hill Troll shaman managed to bring Vanagrimsson back to life as a zombie under his command. For three years afterwards, the Dwarfs of Fangthane found themselves under attack from their beloved hero, who was made to lead the Hill Troll armies, until a raiding party found the Troll shaman and killed him. Now, when a Dwarf meets a Hill Troll, he fights to the death, praying that if he does fall, his body will be so injured that it can never rise again.

Trolls do not organize themselves into nations, and only Hill Trolls gather into tribes. It is only in the armies of Evil that you will find Trolls working and fighting together, though their

temperament is such that they often end up fighting among themselves instead of with the enemy. They are rough, unruly creatures, who enjoy Orc ale and violence, and they are not cowardly in battle. Owing to their extreme stupidity, however, they tend to be exploited by Orcs. Now that Goblins have their own regiments, it seems Trolls are the favourites for leading the armies of Evil into battle, though the Orcs try to disguise the situation by giving the Trolls grand titles and allowing them special privileges, such as eating the dead after the battle is over. Of course, what the Orc commanders fail to tell the Trolls is that they are unlikely to survive to the end of the battle if they go in the front lines! Such is the way of Chaos, with the strong exploiting the stupid, and death cheating them all.

TROLL HUMOUR

Trolls are known in many lands for their sense of humour, which is highly developed, but rather unsophisticated, to say the least. Repetitive in nature and brutal in content, it provides great insights into the workings of the Troll mind. The greatest Troll comedian of all time is widely recognized to have been one Zark the Violent, who used to wander the Flatlands of Allansia with his travelling show, until he was unfortunately killed after playing to an audience of Dwarfs by mistake while drunk on cheap Orc ale. Here are a few chestnuts from his vast repertoire of the very best in Troll humour:

'Why did the Dwarf cross the road? Because I said if he didn't I'd cut off his feet and stick them up his nose! Ugh! Ugh!'

'What do you get if you hit a Dwarf with a very large rock? A big laugh! Ugh! Ugh!'

'What would you say to a Dwarf with twelve helmets on? Nothin', you just hit him in the stomach instead! Ugh! Ugh!'

'How do you get six Dwarfs into an ox-cart? Well, first you take a big axe and you cut them up into little pieces, then you eat them, and then *you* get in the ox-cart! Ugh! Ugh!'

OGRES AND THE TAINT OF CHAOS

Orc shamans tell the following story about the creation of Ogres; it is not known where it originated, but it has been around for many centuries.

At the end of the Godtime, when Death and his fellow Dark Lords had been banished into the Void for releasing Time into the world, there were still many places on Titan where the power of Chaos was strong. In one such area, now thankfully sunk beneath the sea after the continents shifted, Hashak, the creator of the Orcs, placed some of his new-born Orcs. It was a dark place, like all the others in which Hashak had left his creations to grow, and Hashak did not look into it too carefully. He had a great many of his Orcs to hide before the sun rose again, and he was in a hurry to finish his task.

In the darkness, the new-born Orcs grew quickly, but they grew with the taint of Chaos in their flesh, not knowing it was changing them. By the time they were strong enough to set foot outside in the light, they had been warped by it, and they were different from the other Orcs – they were now Ogres, the Warped Ones. Since that time, long, long ago, the other races aligned with Evil have become touched with the taint of Chaos, and mutations are common, but no other race has Chaos at its core. There are still many Orcs who are normal in shape and mind, but no two Ogres are ever the same.

During the War of the Wizards, when Chaos returned to the world in great strength, Ogres formed a large part of the evil armies. They would lead mutating troops into battle, marching ahead of nameless beings which writhed and formed new shapes even as they wriggled and crawled towards the enemy! The armies of Chaos were ultimately defeated, however, and the few remaining Ogres were scattered across the face of the world again.

Many Ogres live pitiful lives away from civilization, which spurns them as it would any other mutant, though most Ogres look almost normal on the outside. They lurk in caves in the wasteland, and live by hunting whatever they can catch. They have little or no tribal organization, no leaders and no shamans. However, in the mountains south of Lendleland known as the Anvils of the Gods, there is talk of 'the Three', a trio of Ogres who have somehow learnt the ways of sorcerers and shamans, and who practise magic! While it is conceivable that a Chaotic creature could be spawned with some innate magical powers, it is quite ludicrous to suggest that *three* such creatures could have the powers of master sorcerers simply by chance. Until we know more about 'the Three' we cannot give any more accurate details, though it certainly seems to most learned people that some great sorcerer or unearthly being must have been involved in granting such powers to three Ogres. However, from the rumours we have heard, their powers are very great, which makes them incredibly dangerous. They seem to provide yet more evidence of the resurgence of Chaos in the forgotten corners of our world.

Some Ogres are beginning to find service in the armies of insane servants of Evil such as the necromancer Razaak, where they are proving themselves strong and reliable. These days, their Chaotic nature more often than not results in nothing more than some small mutation, such as scaly skin, boils, horns or a third eye. They are proving to be very valuable troops, if given sufficient training to cope with such incredibly complicated weapons as bows and slings! One very famous Ogre was Naggamanteh, the brutal Master Torturer of the evil Archmage of Mampang in Kakhabad. Grossly deformed, with only one eye and a face that made milk turn sour and even grown Trolls feel ill, Naggamanteh was very successful at his job, and turned it almost into an art – though a very sick, depraved one! Many of his specialities have passed into the lore of other torturers, who swear by 'Naggamanteh's rusting thumbscrews!' and 'the Ogre's crushing clamps!' In fact, Naggamanteh even penned *Naggamanteh's Book of Tortures* (he was not very good on titles), which has long been recognized as a masterpiece by torturers across Titan – and although the spelling is atrocious, it shows just how successful an Ogre can become if given the right outlets for his 'talents'.

The Snake People

The races we have discussed up to now have been crude, barbaric and not too gifted with intelligence. But now we come to three races which are far more sophisticated in their service of Evil and Chaos. We shall shortly discuss the accursed Lizard Men of the southern jungles and the demonic Dark Elves of

Tiranduil Kelthas, deep beneath the surface of the world. But let us start in the baking deserts of Titan, with the Snake People.

SOME LIKE IT HOT

The Snake People of Allansia and Khul dwell only in the very hottest parts of the Desert of Skulls and the Scythera Desert, for they are cold-blooded creatures who need warmth to survive. It is this basic need which has kept them from encroaching on more temperate lands and spreading their cruel dominion to more populated areas of the world. As it is, they control vast areas of the two continents, bringing their own peculiar forms of death to many peoples.

The Caarth, who are the major race of all those known collectively as the Snake People, have long been creatures of legend, and subject to all kinds of myths and conceptions. Many past writers of bestiaries and myths have described the Caarth as bald, snake-tailed monstrosities, for they had to use hearsay, in the absence of any first-hand accounts of meetings with such creatures. In fact, however, they are more like snake-headed humans, similar in form to the Lizard Men of the

southern jungles, and with a similar attitude to the other races of Titan: they simply wish to kill every last member of every last one!

From their stone cities deep in the desert wastelands, they send forth their warriors to conquer and enslave all lands around them. During one such raid, about thirty years ago, a band of Caarth warriors captured a travelling merchant, Voloidon Carsak by name. Fearing for his life, the man fainted clean away when the serpent warriors came over the ridge in front of his caravan, but woke to find himself strapped upside down across the back of a Giant Lizard, just behind its scaly-skinned rider. He was taken as a slave to a small encampment by a desert oasis, before being moved on to a massive stone citadel on the edge of some low, rocky foothills. Here he was put into service, first as a litter-bearer for a high-ranking Caarth priest, and later as a trusted slave to a captain of the serpent warriors' armies. Eventually, after twelve years, he worked himself into such a position that he was left alone for a good part of the day, and Carsak gradually secreted away enough food and water to attempt to escape from his captors, though he knew that if he was caught he would be skinned alive and his body offered to the desert scorpions.

He chose his moment well. His master, along with many other Caarth warriors, was called away to the southern frontier in the Snakelands, where a Lizard Man expeditionary force was scouting for suitable settlement sites. Carsak had memorized the exact position of the citadel from maps he had seen while in the service of the Caarth priest, and his extensive knowledge of the trade-routes helped the rest of the way. Eventually, painfully thin and dehydrated but still alive, Voloidon Carsak staggered into the camp of a trader from Warpstone, who was bound for Salamonis in the southern part of settled Allansia. Carsak reached Salamonis and revealed the previously un-known world of the Snake People. Most of the information we present here is based upon Carsak's own recollections of his life among the Snake People; although it is more than fifteen years old, much of it still applies, and we have managed to add more recent details by the careful use of divinatory magic.

SITH'S REVENGE

When the Dark Lords of Chaos were banished from the Earthly Plane and imprisoned in the Void, their generals, the Demon Princes, fled into the darkest corners of what became known as the Demonic Planes, where they quietly rebuilt their strengths. The most dominant of all Princes was the Snake Demon Sith, who quickly established herself as the most worthy servant of the Dark Lords with the grossest acts against her fellow Demons, and later against earthly beings. Sith's great love is for snakes (the title given to her by scholars on the Earthly Plane, Snake Demon, stems from this), and she wanted to find some way of increasing their power on Titan, to carry out her revenge on the Forces of Good which had banished her masters and caused her to hide away in fear in the outer reaches of the multiverse for so long.

Inspired by the Orcs and the other inhuman races, which were by now teeming everywhere across the surface of Titan, she gathered together several fine human specimens, and several

of the finest snakes, and blended them in a vast spawning vat. After a great many horrific mistakes, on which it is better not to dwell, Sith created the creature known to the Caarth as S'hghkull, which means 'Sacred Father of All' – the first of the Snake People.

S'hghkull was eight feet tall, with four arms and the head of a cobra, but little in the way of human intelligence. But Sith was not deterred, and she soon spawned him a mate, known to the Caarth as H'ssghkull ('Sacred Mother of All'). She was smaller, with only two arms and the head of a viper, but much cleverer, with both the natural cunning of a snake and the reasoning powers of a human. Between them, S'hghkull and H'ssghkull quickly produced several dozen offspring, and the Caarth as a race were born. Sith transported the offspring to the Earthly Plane, secreted them away in the hottest parts of what were later to be called the Desert of Skulls and the Scythera Desert, and left them to thrive.

THE CITIES OF THE SNAKE PEOPLE

More than a millennium later now, the Caarth have constructed their own citadels, carved from the solid stone of desert rock-formations, and established their dominance over a wide area of the surface world. Indeed, there are not just Caarth any more either. They have been joined by the fearsome Justrali, the snake-tailed serpent guard, who patrol the very edges of their domain, bringing slow, painful death to any who dare trespass on the land of the Snake People.

In Allansia, the Snake People (a generic term for Caarth, Justrali and other assorted snake-mutations) dwell for the most part in large stone citadels, though every oasis in the heart of the desert has its own small settlement of Caarth, who usually dwell under canvas in a manner learnt from the human nomads who dwell on the fringes of the Snake People's territory. In Khul, all Caarth live in this way, for their power on that continent is very small. It is their cities, however, which most interest those who study the Snake People.

Their main settlements are the citadels of K'rrstal ('Heart of Glimmering Stone'), S'turrak ('Cool Providence of Shadows') and the Caarth capital, S'hchtiss ('Jewelled Oasis of Sighing Worship'). There are also about a dozen small fortifications in a wide ellipse around these three citadels, each of which houses a garrison of Caarth and Justrali warriors and little else. The merchant Voloidon Carsak lived in the citadel of S'turrak, but believed that the other two were much the same.

THE CITIES OF THE SNAKE PEOPLE
This map is based upon one drawn from memory by the merchant Voloidon Carsak, and is only approximate, but it is the best anyone has ever been able to manage.

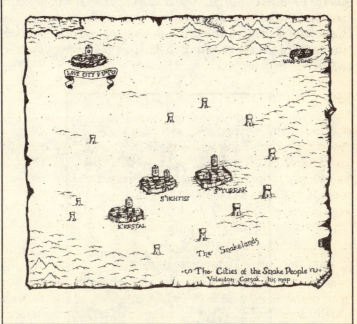

The Cities of the Snake People
Voloidon Carsak, his map

S'turrak is built into the side of a large mesa, a massive block of stone several leagues across which rises several hundred metres above the level of the desert. From its highest towers it was said that one could see those of S'hchtiss glimmering in the sunlight, many, many leagues away. Indeed, the Caarth used to communicate with heliographs, mirrors which they would flash in the sunlight according to specific codes, relaying messages via the watchtowers and oases between the cities.

The citadel of S'turrak is a bizarrely designed place, with dozens of towers and walls, around which run many spiralling staircases and ramps. At its base, on the desert floor, its inhuman builders constructed a series of walls and gates thick enough to withstand the assaults of the most determined enemy – though none has ever attacked it. The Caarth builders had previously bored deep into the rock behind the citadel, to create a warren of large, cool chambers in which their young were able to hatch in complete safety, and where many slaves were kept when not being put to work elsewhere. Although they are not always good designers, their skills at working rock are nearly a match for those of Dwarfs or Skorn.

At the top of the mesa, the Caarth scraped away a smooth expanse of rock, to form a wide avenue, which is lined on either side with disconcerting statues of warriors, priests and Demons, and ends in a small stepped platform on which many sacrifices are made. Behind the platform is the main temple to Sith, a monstrous, pyramid-shaped place of shadows where the whole floor perpetually slithers with snakes of all types and sizes. Indeed, much of the citadel is infested with the scaly reptilian creatures, who are regarded as pure and sacred by all Snake People. The snakes occasionally bite slaves and one another, but never attack a Caarth or Justrali.

FORBIDDEN KNOWLEDGE

Casting their shadows down over the top of the mesa are the tallest of the towers of S'turrak, which house the high priests and the mystic library and observatory of the Caarth sorcerers. The Snake People have not been on Titan as long as some races, but they have collected a great deal of knowledge from every source they can. Prisoners are thoroughly questioned, and hypnotism or mind-loosening potions are used to extract every last scrap of knowledge from their frightened minds before they are turned over to the slave-masters. Caarth sorcerers apparently excavate ancient desert cities, in their constant search for new learning. In their libraries they keep records of all their knowledge, written in their indecipherable script on thin slivers of metal and stone, which will not suffer the ravages of time as badly as parchment.

In their observatories, Caarth use telescopes of prodigious size, with lenses and mirrors made, by obscure magical techniques, from massive discs of highly polished quartz; with these they observe the stars and gradually map out the universe. It is widely believed that the Caarth have discovered other planets near to Titan, something which human scholars have long suspected but have never been able to prove.

The Snake People know much of other topics too. Their knowledge of poisons and venoms is unequalled. They have poisons, extracted from snakes, spiders and desert scorpions, for all purposes – to make an enemy sleep or die, to turn him

insane or make his body break out in reptilian scales in preparation for another ghastly Caarth experiment. Most Caarth and Justrali weapons are coated with poison of one sort or another, which invariably makes them fatal, even if they only graze an opponent.

The knowledge Caarth sorcerers have of mutations and interbreeding is also vast, for they have been creating new species for many centuries in unholy attempts to continue the work of their snake forefathers by creating the most powerful combination of humans and snakes possible. This is how the Justrali were created, along with many other less successful mutations which lurk in the desert, abandoned by their creators. The priests of S'turrak also attempt to resurrect their forefathers by reshaping slaves' bodies into vehicles for their souls to return to life, but these experiments have been notoriously unsuccessful, as the case of the nearly legendary Serpent Queen of Port Blacksand shows.

SITH'S REPRESENTATIVES ON THE EARTHLY PLANE

The Snake People are ruled over by their high priests, who act both as commanders of their armies, and as the direct representatives of their beloved Sith on the Earthly Plane. The high priest of S'turrak at the time when Carsak was there was known as H'kchktaress (which means, according to Carsak, 'Venom Drips Like Honey from His Blade' in the language of the Caarth), and he was a pure embodiment of evil. His duties included the ritual sacrificing of slaves to Sith, and the conjuring of Sith's demonic servants in the mesa-top temple for consultations.

He was also the head of the city's Caarth and Justrali warriors, and one of the trio of leaders of the Caarth nation. The power of the Snake People has been on the wane in recent years, for they have been penned into the desert regions by the colder climates of the northern and southern lands, and they have had little new territory to overwhelm. They are also using up their supply of slaves from the subhumans who live on the fringes of the Desert of Skulls, and cannot roam further afield for them. Sith has not been able to concentrate on their problems, as she has been distracted by another civil war with her fellow Demon Princes. In the meantime, in Allansia, Ishtra's Lizard Men have been creeping ever closer to the edge of the temperate wastes known as the Snakelands, which divide the Desert of Skulls from Vymorna on the edge of the southern jungles. The Lizard Men may have been held at the Siege of Vymorna for a short while, but it can only be a matter of time before they push towards the territory of the Snake People. When this time comes the fighting will be fierce and bloody, as the whole of the southern lands will be plunged into war.

The Lizard Men of the Southern Jungles

The gruesome Snake People are common to both Allansia and Khul, though it is in the former that they are really powerful. This is also true for the Lizard Men, though their successes far overshadow those of the Caarth. It is looking increasingly likely, to sages and scholars who know of such things, that the main threat to humanity on Allansia will soon be the Lizard Man Empire, which already covers an area larger than all the settled parts of Allansia put together. Until fairly recently, however, few learned men were able to glean much information about the Lizard Men, for they would try to kill any human they came across, whether he was a heavily armed warrior or a poor defenceless sage. But only four years ago, the great mystic Ar-Kalagôn of Kaynlesh-Ma managed to capture a Lizard Man warrior, and subject his mind to a form of magical interrogation. He cast several hypnotic enchantments on the gross, leathery being, and then magically read the contents of his mind in a scrying pool. Ar-Kalagôn learnt much about the Lizard Man culture . . .

IN THE BEGINNING

During the Godtime, there were many lesser deities, including gods of all the animals. Among these was a very sly and ambitious god, who is known to those on the Earthly Plane as Suthis Cha. When the greater gods began fashioning human-shaped creatures to people the world, Suthis Cha became very jealous of them, for he considered his own lizard form to be the most beautiful of all shapes (he was arrogant and conceited, as well as sly and ambitious). So whenever the gods were working on their creations, Suthis Cha ensured that he was close at hand, quietly watching and remembering how creatures were shaped, in preparation for the time when he would create his own beings, to bring *his* image to the face of the world.

The First Battle began, with the evil powers fighting to overcome the Forces of Good and wrest control of the universe

202

from them. All the gods and lesser deities were drawn into the conflict – all, that is, save Suthis Cha. Being blessed with some slight powers of divination, the scaly god had foreseen the coming battle, and seized his chance to slip away unnoticed. So when the battle was at its height, Suthis Cha was on the Earthly Plane, carving and moulding the first Lizard Men from swamp mud and lizard skins. He hid his creations away in the swamplands of Titan, knowing they would be safe there, out of sight of the other gods and their own creations, and returned to the Outer Planes. Upon returning he encountered the tiny mouse god, Karreep, cowering with fright in a quiet corner of the Halls of the Gods. There was no one else around, so Suthis Cha gave in to temptation and did something he had been desperately wanting to do for many a long aeon – he ate Karreep. The mouse god was, however, a god, and fought back with all his might. Suthis Cha choked to death (in so far as a god can die – he transmuted), as the small furry thing grew and stuck in his throat, before hopping out as the scaly deity crashed to the marble floor of the Halls of the Gods.

The Lizard Men thrived in the swamplands, and quickly became even more cunning than their four-legged relations. Without a god, however, they were disorganized and unambitious, preferring simply to swim about their marshy domains, hunt smaller beings, climb trees, sun themselves and generally have a lazy time of it. As the Dark Lords recovered from their exile in the aftermath of the First Battle, however, one noticed the scaly little things which ran around in the swamps and jungles of Titan, and asked the Snake Demon Ishtra to investigate. The crafty Demon Prince did more than that – he appeared to the Lizard Men while they were gathering for their regular midsummer's eve spawning, as a gigantic Lizard Man, spitting fire and wielding a flaming sword against the setting sun. The Lizard Men abased themselves before him, and they have worshipped his unholy form from that moment on. In time, various other gods and deities were introduced into Lizard Man culture by their powerful priests, including Myurr, another Demon Prince, and numerous lesser Demons and reptilian gods. Ishtra also brought the taint of Chaos to the race, initially to create the powerful two-headed priests who would act as his focus for ruling over the Lizard Man race – but this also brought the curse of mutation to ordinary Lizard Men.

THE LIASH CHA
Not all two-headed Lizard Men are priests, but all Lizard Man priests have two heads. They are an élite class among the Lizard Men, known properly as the Liash Cha, and they have the power to do almost anything they wish. They dress in particular ways (they are the only Lizard Men allowed to wear the sacred colour red, for example), have their own language and are the only Lizard Men able to write. The centre for the

priesthood is the Temple to Ishtra, in the centre of the Silur Cha swamplands, about fifteen leagues away from the capital city, Silur Cha. Part monastery and part astronomical observatory, it is home to several thousand two-headed priests and their servants, who spend all their time in performing rituals, sacrifices, prayers and other unholy duties. The priests have collected a great store of knowledge over the centuries, much of it unknown to civilized man, for they have peculiarly logical, unemotional minds which seem able to grasp some philosophical questions much better than men or Elves can. Their observatories are sophisticated to a degree unheard of in civilized lands, and they have learnt much about the universe and its workings.

On the other hand, their cold, calculating, unemotional natures make them cruel and violent, for they have no feelings for other creatures, or even other members of their own race. The Liash Cha believe, above all things, in the purity of their race, which they have been taught (by Ishtra) to consider the high point of all of Nature's creations. They despise the mutant Lizard Men as a result, and sacrifice many to the gods to appease them, and to try to persuade them to stop the curse of Chaos. Living sacrifices are common, and many of their captives suffer this fate.

THE LIZARD KINGS

Although the priests run the religious side of the Lizard Men's life, the politics are cared for by the Lizard Kings. Each tribe is ruled over by a Lizard King, and they in turn pay fealty to the Council of Thirteen, who sit in Silur Cha, the Lizard Men's capital in the southern swamplands of Allansia. The Lizard Kings may once have belonged to the same species, but now they are a distinct race, being much larger and stronger, and with greater mental powers – though they will never match those of the Liash Cha. It is believed that they are telepathic, able to keep in touch with all other members of their race by thought alone, though the extent of this communication is not known. Lizard Kings also seem to have some form of empathic hold over their people, for when a Lizard King is killed on the field of battle, his troops immediately become confused and

disorientated, as if they were suddenly being released from hypnosis in a strange, unfamiliar place. Whatever the truth of this, the Lizard Kings do hold the ordinary Lizard Men in their scaly grip, and have the power of life and death over the entire Lizard Man Empire.

The Council of Thirteen is led by the High King, the Luk Ten Cha, who is widely believed to be a physical embodiment of their gods, sent to the Earthly Plane to watch over the Lizard Men. When he dies (Lizard Kings live to around 130 years, almost twice the span of normal Lizard Men), it is believed that he is reborn that same instant, as his life-force passes into a new-born Lizard Man freshly hatched in the egg chambers of the palace. When the new child reaches thirteen years old, he is brought before the Liash Cha, who perform the Ritual of Remembering, during the course of which the Luk Ten Cha slowly begins to remember all his past lives, and all his past knowledge, and is then ready to take his place as ruler of the Lizard Man Empire once more. In the intervening thirteen years, each member of the Council in turn rules the land for a year.

SILUR CHA, THE LIZARD MAN CITY

The High King, the Luk Ten Cha, dwells in a gigantic towering palace at the very centre of the bizarre city of Silur Cha, which itself is right at the centre of the Lizard Man Empire, in the

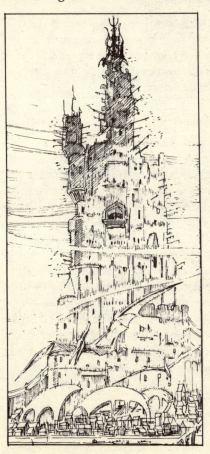

southern swamplands of Allansia. Silur Cha has been built out over the swamps, and much of it rests upon wooden platforms, with only the most important buildings having stone foundations (usually created by magically transmuting the mud of the quagmire into solid rock, a process which requires a great many spells and innumerable sacrifices). The Lizard Men have other fortifications and other cities dotted around their Empire, but Silur Cha is the crowning glory of all of them. It has taken several thousand years to reach its present form, and it is being added to all the time, as the Lizard Men's power grows ever stronger.

LIZARD MAN LANGUAGE

Lizard Men use a very strange language, where every slight inflection of the voice, wave of a hand, or position of a tail means something completely different. The word 'Cha', for example, can mean 'us', 'we', 'him', 'I', 'Lizard Men', 'religious', 'good', 'beautiful', 'swampy', 'delicious' and 'to give orders'. Owing to their swampland habitat, Lizard Men have over a hundred names for different conditions of the swamp, and they can recognize a great many different types of grass and tree which all look identical to us humans.

The Liash Cha have their own language, which deals almost exclusively with high-powered religious and philosophical arguments. They are almost unable to carry on a normal conversation in it, though they rarely indulge in everyday small talk anyway.

Silur Cha is a maze of temples, dwellings, open wooden walkways (both on the surface and way up in the sky), towers, barracks, wide squares, pools and streams, all cut out of the swampland itself. Everywhere is decorated with carvings of Lizard Men, their gods, history and battles. Silur Cha is situated on a great U-shaped curve in the nameless river which waters the swamplands. The Lizard Men are not used to being sailors, but their strangely proportioned and bizarrely decorated boats regularly ply up and down the jungle and swampland rivers which they control, and can occasionally be seen out at sea, ferrying supplies to one of their outlying colonies. On a few occasions, way back before the War of the Wizards, the Lizard Men actually fought sea-battles against other nations, though there are now few nations with fleets strong enough to fight such battles.

LIZARD MAN SOCIETY

At the top of Lizard Man society, we know there are the Lizard Kings and the Liash Cha, the two-headed priests. But what of the regular Lizard Men? Most dwell in tribes, which are subdivided into families. Each tribe has its own area, as well as its own peculiarities of dress, language, weapons and so on. Lizard Men often paint their bodies with markings which distinguish them from other tribes, and they also use scars and cuts on their bodies for the same purpose. The tribes are each ruled by a Lizard King, who usually lives in some splendour at the heart of the tribal territory, taking tributes in the form of servants, food and goods from his people.

A typical Lizard Man family is made up of between ten and thirty creatures, who all dwell in the same area of the swamp. Their houses come in many different shapes and constructions. In the heart of the swamps, they may be wooden cabins perched on legs sunk deep into the sludge, or tree-houses with carefully woven rope bridges linking wooden platforms. On more solid land, Lizard Men are likely to live in huts, which are made of mud and branches, and are huddled against one another to create a low, sprawling building with lots of small rooms.

Many Lizard Men (especially females and adolescents) spend their days hunting for food in the swamplands, using snares, spears and even their teeth and brute strength to catch food for the family. Some pursue crafts, such as vine-weaving, carpentry or weapon-making, while others teach the younger members of the tribe the rudiments of hunting and other skills. In the cities and towns, and especially in Silur Cha, there are traders, slave-masters, metal-workers and other craftsmen, just as in a human city, though there are differences. Lizard Men have little need for fire – they live in very warm climates, eat all their food without cooking it, and can see in the dark – and it is only really used for smelting metal and at ceremonial occasions. The priests, however, delight in using fire, for they know the effect it has on others.

Many Lizard Men are enlisted into the armies of the Lizard Man Empire, serving their kings for the greater glory of the Lizard Man race in many parts of the southern lands. Indeed, for mutated Lizard Men, the army is the only choice open for them, for they are not allowed to join tribes and are never allowed into a city like Silur Cha without special permission or as part of a serving battalion. They are outcasts from the whole of society, and are 'encouraged' to serve in the army, where good use is made of their prodigious strength.

ARMY AND EMPIRE
A Lizard Man fighting unit may consist of between six and thirty soldiers. Each unit belongs to an informal regiment of up to a thousand warriors, commanded ultimately by a Lizard King through a succession of captains. There are always a dozen or so Liash Cha assigned to a regiment too, for the spiritual welfare of the troops is an important factor in driving them to victory against the unclean humans.

Different units are assigned different tasks in battle. There might be a death-squad of mutants, who will lead the force into the fray, driven by an insane frenzy which is itself sometimes enough to rout their opponents and send them fleeing from the field of combat. The 'sappers' are adept at destroying city walls and gates by using battering-rams, catapults and the pulling power of Giant Lizards, and sometimes very delicate magical explosives are administered by a priest. There are also cavalry units, mounted on Giant Lizards and semi-tame Dinosaurs like Styracosaurs. There have been reports from the Siege of Vymorna that some Lizard Man units have managed to tame Pterodactyls and Pteranodons, to create terrifying units! Even if this is not true, it is surely only a matter of time before they do develop such tactics. The Lizard Man armies are strong and well trained, and are easily a match for any human army.

The Lizard Man which Ar-Kalagôn of Kaynlesh-Ma captured was a soldier, serving with a regiment called the Kreashian Kux Cha, or 'the Divine Gougers of Whiteskin's Eyes'. He saw service at various battles, including the Siege of Vymorna, which is still continuing. The regiment was made up as follows:

Commander:	The Divine Lizard King, Yurnik Eerin Cha
Royal guard:	26 Lizard Men, the Divine Slaughterers, together with 8 standard-bearers, heralds and messengers

War-priests:	13 two-headed priests, the Divine Vengeance of Ishtra
Shock troops:	266 mutant Lizard Men, the Divine Scar of Chaos
Cavalry:	130 mounted Lizard Men, half on Giant Lizards, half on Styracosaurs, the Divine Mounted Death-bringers
Regulars:	1,326 Lizard Men, divided into 58 units of between 7 and 28 troops, known by many names but collectively as the Divine Gougers Who Shall Bring Death to All
Sappers:	125 Lizard Men, the Divine Cataclysm of Stone
Others:	138 servants, baggage-handlers, food-foragers, etc.

The Lizard Man Empire stretches over much of the southern lands of Allansia, from the edges of the (thankfully impassable) Mountains of Grief in the far south, across the whole of the immense swamplands as far as the edges of the Plain of Bones, and north as far as the Vymorn River and the city of Vymorna, which is still – just – held by humans. Across the other side of the Gulf of Shamuz, the Lizard Men control all the jungle lands from the Snakelands to the edges of Arantis. They have outposts as far north as Fire Island (though this is thought to have fallen recently, as no word has been sent by its commander for some time now), as well as dotted along the Skull Coast and the wastelands north of the Pirate Coast. There are also outposts on Khul, though they are much less important to the Empire, being smaller and less organized, and situated in rather desolate areas such as the Scythera Desert and the jungles beyond Marad across the Inland Sea.

THE SIEGE OF VYMORNA

For six years now, the combined forces of magic, explosives, battering-rams and sheer weight of numbers have been slamming against the walls of the ancient city on the mouth of the Vymorn River. It was once an important focus at the northern end of the Gulf of Shamuz, with traders coming from as far away as Salamonis in the far north. It used to have a population approaching 100,000 people, but they have been reduced to little more than a twentieth of that over the six years that the siege has lasted. The king of Vymorna, Alexandros II, died in a massive assault which breached the penultimate wall last year, and the troops are now led by his wife, Queen Perriel, who fights on the walls with the troops. The people know Vymorna must fall, but they fight on, hoping in their hearts that they will buy time for the other cities to prepare their own defences against the sieges to come.

Dark Elves – Servants of the Night

You know, adventurer, of the great friendship which Elves can give you on your travels around Titan. But not all Elves, it must be said, are on the same side. We made slight reference to the Dark Elves earlier; now we will examine them more closely. Information on the Dark Elves is limited, for they are a proud, secretive and above all very perilous race, and are not prone to allowing sages and scholars to wander around their underground domains, even for academic research! What little we know of the ways of the Dark Elves has been gleaned from human and Dwarf slaves who have escaped from their subterranean prisons.

THE PARTING OF THE WAYS

Way, way back at the beginning of the first age of life on Titan, after the First Battle, when the gods departed to take their places in the heavens, the world was populated by several major races. There were the short-lived, youthful humans, the stout, inquisitive Dwarfs and the graceful, spiritual Elves. As you learnt from our previous treatise on the good Elves, the race grew in power and learning, bringing unity and lore to many parts of Titan. Elves were the elders of the world, the wise rulers and the advisers. They kept themselves pretty much to themselves, living in their forest villages and palaces, but occasionally ventured out into the world to give aid where it was needed. Their numbers were never very great, for their near-immortality is balanced by a lack of children, but their race thrived far more than any other at that time.

Some Elves, however, became disenchanted by the neutral attitude of the Elven peoples. They believed that since the Elves were the wisest, the longest-lived, the most skilled and the strongest of all races, they were natural candidates for being the lords and masters of all the other races. In the unceasing conflicts with Orcs, Goblins and other servants of Chaos, they felt that they should be the leaders, the generals and commanders of an army which could then be organized to cleanse the vileness from the face of the land. The Elven Council did not agree to such demands, however, and persisted in upholding the non-committal stance taken by all Elves since long before the rise of Orcs and their ilk.

The leader of one of the Elven clans, Prince Viridel Kerithrion, was the most vociferous of all those arguing for greater power and strength. A brave and noble warrior, he had proved himself a hero in many engagements against the Forces of Evil. As a result, he was respected by the majority of the Council, though some feared his rather active nature; it is not normally the way of Elves to get physically involved in the petty struggles of lesser mortals, except by offering advice and some token assitance. Elves know that they will still be walking the world when all wars have been forgotten, and it makes them wary of offering physical aid in the manner adopted by Prince Kerithrion.

Unknown to Elves outside his own clan, however, Viridel was an acolyte of Slangg, god of malice, who was known to the Elves as Ar Anwar Gerithan, 'Grey Whisperer of Shadows'. The god had been worshipped since the Time of Legends by Elves who wished to learn more about the transient ways of humans and other short-lived races. Ar Anwar Gerithan was considered, by those Elves who studied him, to be the embodiment of the human spirit – malicious, petty, vengeful and violent. As an acolyte of Ar Anwar Gerithan, it is not surprising that Prince Kerithrion had as much interest in the affairs of humans as in those of the Elves.

Finally the Elven prince could no longer stand back and condone the non-committal stance taken by the Elves. Gathering together all the warriors of his clan, and of the other clans who thought much the same as he did, Kerithrion marched on the Elven Council, which at the time was based in a large citadel on the edge of what is now the Flatlands, and after slaughtering over two dozen other clan leaders he and his rebels seized power over the Elven nations.

Unluckily, he had missed the Council's leaders, including King Glorien Thelemas and his sons, and most of the stronger clan princes too. Thelemas's queen, Ariel Aurlindol, had the power of divining the future, and in a dream the night before, she had seen Kerithrion's forces marching on the Council. There was no time to warn the rest, but she persuaded the king and his family to be absent on that fateful day.

Reaction to Kerithrion's take-over was not long in coming, and within three days a massive Elven army was camped around the palace of the Council. For nineteen days they fought with the rebels, pounding the walls to dust with catapults and powerful sorcery, but on the twentieth a trio of Viridel's captains marched out of the ruins waving the green banners of truce, and asking to talk terms. They were accepted, and were brought before King Thelemas. While the peace talks were

continuing in the king's tent, however, the rest of the rebel forces slipped away through tunnels they had been building for the last seventeen days (for they had quickly realized they could not hope to win against the united Elven armies, regardless of how long they held on to their well-defended position). The parleying captains dragged out the talks until after sunset, before agreeing to return to their own side and deliver Thelemas's orders for the surrender and then lead out all the rebels. The captains returned to the palace, their way picked out by hundreds of blazing torches which the defenders appeared to have lit for them. The king's forces waited until dawn, but neither the captains nor Kerithrion and the rest of the rebels appeared. Attacks recommenced, but it was soon obvious that the rebels had fled.

THE MAJOR CLANS OF TÌRANDUIL KELTHAS

Tesarath. Symbol:
black beetle's head on silver diamond. Main areas of control: insect-farming, food-preparation, clearance of land for farming, food-transportation.

Mirisgroth. Symbol:
green gemstone on narrow black bar. Main areas of control: mining, metal-working and smelting.

Camcarneyar. Symbol:
octagon-shaped white skull. Main areas of control: slave-procurement (surface raids), security, assassination, the royal guard.

Kerithrion. Symbol:
silver dagger and crown. Main areas of control: the ruling family.

They retreated only as far as Kerithrion's native lands, however, where they attempted to declare an independent nation. In an unusually swift move for an Elf, Thelemas ordered his armies into Kerithrion's lands. Many battles and skirmishes followed, before the rebel Elves retreated into the mountains (in a western area of the highlands now known as the Moonstone Hills), and from there underground, taking over an all-but-abandoned Dwarf city which Kerithrion had earmarked as a final bolt-hole in case all his plans came to naught. The rebel Elves sealed the way behind them, and the king gave up the chase. The Council palace was pulled down stone by stone, and a new one constructed many leagues distant. The rebels passed quickly from the memories of the Elves, their actions were never recorded in the histories, and with the start of the first of the Orc Wars soon after, the Elven nations were far too occupied in defending their precious forests.

THE UNDERGROUND CITIES
In the darkness underground, the rebels thrived far better than

anyone could have known. They explored every inch of their lightless domain, and began to adapt to life without sunlight. Necessity made them learn quickly: they discovered how to grow fungus and moss for food, and how to breed lizards and giant insects. They learnt how to work rock, and expanded westward until they chanced upon a series of natural caverns deep under Darkwood Forest in what is now north-western Allansia. Over the centuries they grew strong again, but they changed too, slowly turning in their isolation into true creatures of darkness. Their worship of Ar Anwar Gerithan grew stronger still, but they also picked up other deities – perilous beings such as the Demon Prince Myurr, and many others. They changed from creatures of light and truth and beauty into a sickeningly decadent race of ghoulish Demon-worshippers – the Dark Elves.

Now they dwell under Darkwood, and there are small underground colonies in other parts of Allansia as well. Recent rumours tell of a Dark Elf scouting party being seen in north-eastern Khul, though what they were doing there, so far from home, is anyone's guess. The Wood Elves know of them again now, for the Darkside Elves continue to send small raiding parties against their surface-dwelling brethren, whom they hate with every fibre of their being. To the Wood Elves, they are no better than Orcs or other trash, and they give no quarter to any they encounter.

Their city is called Darkside, known as Tìranduil Kelthas to its inhabitants, and it is a wondrous place. It is built in an enormous natural cavern, lit only by the dim glow of phosphorescent plants and fungus and glimmering lanterns. When the Dark Elves first started to construct it, they began by using traditional Elven architecture, but gradually the styles changed, and it is now a bizarre, twisted place, with towers and walls jutting out at many different levels, and decorated everywhere with insane carvings of the city's adopted demonic patrons. Linked to the outside world by a succession of maze-like passages, each blocked by gigantic carved stone doors and guarded by many Dark Elves of the sinister Clan Camcarneyar, it is a fascinating and terrible place, a city of

shadows and Demons, of slaves and dark magic. Alleys twist and wind between the weirdly shaped houses; squares may be surrounded by walls so that no one can enter them; nightmarish parks and gardens glimmer in the light of caged fireflies, while giant beetles scuttle in the mossy undergrowth. At the very centre of Tìranduil Kelthas there is the Palace of Kerithrion, the Aiù Lindàlé Kerithrion, named after the city's founder, and after the clan which still rules over the city. Built out of black crystal, it towers over the city like the Grim Reaper, as if watching its citizens like a vulture waiting for a dying creature to breathe its last.

Life in Darkside is very different from that of the Wood Elves in the forests above ground. In their subterranean city the Dark Elves have developed their own, highly intricate society, based on the original rebel clans, which are now led by sorcerer-kings and witch-queens rather than by warrior-princes. All Dark Elves belong to a particular clan, which acts as an extended family. Each clan has its own name, symbols, badges of office, headquarters, and area of the city, where its

219

rules are law, and where members of other clans require specific permission to walk. Many have their own special languages and signs, which allow members to recognize one another without the need for symbols; all worship their own special demonic patrons. Clan rivalries are great, and there are always intrigues afoot at the highest levels of Dark Elf society as each clan tries to wrest some small fraction of power from the others. Rivalries between the clans regularly lead to assassinations, arson and in some cases full-scale slaughter, which usually only stops when the terrifying Clan Camcarneyar step in. They are never allied to anyone, for all fear them; they are ultimately loyal only to the continuation of the Dark Elf race, and the city of Tìranduil Kelthas.

Tìranduil Kelthas – the Dark Elf City

A RACE OF PRINCES

While there are some paupers among the citizens of Tìranduil Kelthas, as there are in all cities, most Dark Elves live very comfortable lives. The great wealth extracted from the earth by the slaves in the silver and copper mines has meant that money means little to Dark Elves, and all but the very poorest of them are weighed down with masses of silver – around their necks, wrists and ankles, wound into their hair, woven into their clothes, engraved into their weapons, painted in traceries on their skin and so on. Every Elf in Darkside is related to the nobility in some way, and all Dark Elves have a regal air, especially the women. Dark Elf women have an unearthly beauty, far greater than that of any human, with their velvet black skin, white or silver hair and totally green eyes; and their beauty is greatly enhanced by the bizarre fashions in clothing and decoration which have developed over centuries in complete isolation from those of the outside world. The whole atmosphere of Darkside and its citizens is simultaneously similar and dissimilar to the world above ground, with the result that it is faintly disorientating and disturbing, to anyone who is not a Dark Elf.

Elven noble society is very competitive, with the fairest witch-queens of Darkside competing against one another at every opportunity. Lavish banquets of rare fungus and potent moss-wines are common, with everyone present attempting to score points off one another with acts of disdain, bitchiness and even violence. Despite their terribly regal bearing, all Dark Elves have a streak of pure evil running through their characters, which on occasion makes them very nasty.

TRADE AND SLAVERY

The merchants of Darkside have more power than their counterparts in surface towns, for the procurement of food, energy, slaves and precious metals requires careful planning and organization in the artificial environment of the underground city. While Dark Elves are feared by all races (for they will make a slave of just about anyone, if they can), they do trade with some Orc and Hill Troll tribes, giving silver and gems in exchange for human and Dwarf slaves, new giant insects and manufactured items. Dark Elf merchants meet with Orcs once every month or so, bringing their goods on the backs of tamed Giant Lizards and massive spiders to neutral caverns near the surface, where all exchanges are made.

Slaves are also very important to the running of the cities, for the Dark Elves are continually expanding their caverns and mining for more precious metals and gems. Slaves are usually taken in raids on the surface, though some are exchanged during trade with other evil races. Humans are most common, for they are the easiest to obtain, but Dwarfs are the most popular, because of their hardy nature (which can take all the regular beatings the Dark Elves inflict upon their captives) and because they know how to work rock and find the best seams of metal. Orcs, Trolls and Goblins are sometimes used for the most menial tasks, but they are weak, spiritless creatures, and the Dark Elves often kill them before their time out of frustration.

Elves are never kept as slaves. Those who do not die in the initial encounter (since Dark Elves inspire Wood Elves to amazing acts of suicidal fury) or who are not slaughtered immediately after, are commandeered by the sorcerers and witches for eventual sacrifice in one of their horrific rites, though most will be tortured interminably until this happens. Despite their mutilations and deprivations, Wood Elves have never been known to utter a single word to their Dark Elf captors, nor even to cry out in pain, and the Dark Elves have never learnt anything from their Elven captives.

RAIDING THE SURFACE WORLD

Slaves are exchanged for silver and gems with the Orcs and Hill Trolls, and captured in raids on the surface. Such raids are usually carried out by members of the Clan Camcarneyar, who creep about the darkened forests at night in raiding parties of not more than eight, hidden by black cloaks and clothing, and by protective magic which shields them even from the heightened senses of animals. They usually pick upon isolated farmsteads or small hamlets, where they know they will not be opposed by more than a dozen humans or Dwarfs, and always wait until the moon has set before attacking.

They first spread out around the target, and then cast a blanket of spells to stop them being detected by farm animals, who might wake the inhabitants. Flaming arrows on to the roof launch the attack, and are followed by a full-scale assault on all sides as the Dark Elves break in through windows and doors, dispose of any resistance with their long, jagged knives, and drag their captives off into the night. The raiders of the Clan Camcarneyar prowl the surface world most nights, ranging further and further afield in their search for victims.

SORCERER-KINGS AND WITCH-QUEENS – THE SHAËRN KERITHRION

The highest of all Dark Elves are the clan leaders, and the highest of all clan leaders are those of Clan Kerithrion, who govern the city as its royal family and reside in Aiù Lindàlé Kerithrion, the Palace of Kerithrion, at the heart of the dark city. The Clan Kerithrion is headed by a council of five, the Shaërn Kerithrion, who rule partly by common consent, and partly by playing the other members of the circle against one another.

King Eilden Kerithrion. He is the nominal leader of the Clan Kerithrion, and therefore king of Tìranduil Kelthas and ruler of the Dark Elf race. In truth, he is getting very old and weak, and retiring into a paranoid world where everyone around him is a threat to his rule. He trusts no one any more, least of all his sister Velicoma, and he leaves his chambers in Aiù Lindàlé Kerithrion only to attend the most important council meetings. He is an acolyte of the Demon Prince Myurr, whom he contacted by offering up his mother in living sacrifice several centuries previously. Myurr has told him that the throne of Kerithrion is threatened by the flaw of insanity, and Eilden is

224

now waiting for madness to show itself in one of the other four rulers – not realizing that it is he who is the flaw.

Princess Velicoma Endûl Kerithrion. Unlike her brother, whom she plans to kill any day now, Velicoma is in full command of her faculties, and has no illusions about any of the other four. She is the High Priestess of Darkside, and officiates at all important sacrifices. She too serves the Demon Prince Myurr, and it was she who first suggested that they exploit the paranoid side of King Eilden's character. Princess Velicoma is a ruthless, emotionless witch, and most Dark Elves feel afraid of her, without quite knowing why. She appears to be cold and icy, but very efficient and practical, and she deals harshly with foolishness. Around her there is an almost tangible aura of threat, due partly to confident arrogance and partly to pure evil. Should she ever come to power, everyone hopes they will not be the ones she makes examples out of.

Prince Astrëa and Princess Leya Garathrim. Astrëa and Leya are cousins of the king and his evil sister, and they act as a balancing force in the council. They are calm and intelligent, and have little time for Eilden's paranoia and Velicoma's schemings. They are worshippers of Ar Anwar Gerithan (Slangg), but somehow manage to offset his evil teachings with a careful concern for the proper workings of Dark Elf society. If Eilden and Velicoma get caught in a power-struggle against each other, they will be able to take control of Tìranduil Kelthas with the minimum of fuss, for Leya is the wife of Prince Taragûl Camcarneyar, head of the Clan Camcarneyar.

Prince Menel Ithilkir. The hothead of the Shaërn Kerithrion, Menel spends much of his time on surface raids with members of the Clan Camcarneyar and rarely has any time for the workings of Darkside politics. This is a great pity, for he is usually on the same side as the Garathrim, and could help them swing the power of the council towards a lighter, more workable base. As it is, he only attends council meetings when important military actions are being considered, or when an especially bloody sacrifice of a captured Wood Elf nobleman is due to be part of the entertainment. In truth, he is only a member of the Shaërn Kerithrion because he is head of the

Ithilkir branch of the clan, following the recent death of his much stronger mother at the hands of a nameless poisoner; this is widely suspected to be another of Velicoma's little plots, but was in fact the work of Astrëa and Leya.

The five members of the Shaërn Kerithrion live in separate parts of the palace, each protected by armed guards and strong magic 'just in case'. If they *were* ever to unite, the Dark Elves would finally be organized enough to look beyond surviving day to day. They would be able to make plans for a return to the surface world, to face the accursed Wood Elves in full battle at last, and to show them the true meaning of vengeance!

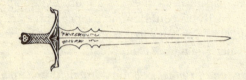

THE FACES OF EVIL AND CHAOS

There are many dangerous and Chaotic races on Titan, working for the complete overthrow of civilization with the supernatural help of awesome evil powers. But above all stands one race, as the most evil, most depraved, most decadent and most dangerous of all – mankind. For just as man has the capacity for great good, he also has it in him to do great evil, if he so desires.

In the years leading up to the cataclysmic War of the Wizards, the human race was split down the middle, with one side clearly opposed to the other, and with no room for neutral bystanders. Today, 280 years after the collapse, humanity is still struggling to reassert itself, but already there are men who have followed the path of Evil to its extremes. Indeed, there are far too many to detail here; all we can do is concentrate on those who are perhaps the most important, and shake our heads in despair for the many we have had to omit.

Razaak, the Undying One

One hundred years ago, Razaak was an apprentice to one of the Lawful wizards of that era. His master's name is surprisingly not recorded, but he could quite easily have been the Grand Wizard of Yore himself, Vermithrax Moonchaser. He was quite a promising pupil, as apprentices go, though like many he tried to run before he could walk. He was fascinated by what his master told him of the dark magic of shamans, Dark Elves and Demons. Peering through the ancient books in his master's study by the light of a flickering candle while the old man slept, Razaak quickly realized that he had the inner strength to become a powerful necromancer, who would one day be able to command everyone to obey him. Magic was too precious a tool to waste on doing good – he would use it to bring Allansia to its knees.

That very night, Razaak slipped back to his narrow bunk, packed all his worldly goods into a small sack, and left the way of Goodness for ever. He travelled to the remote wastes at the far side of the Flatlands, where he meditated and studied and practised the arcane arts in complete solitude for forty years, until he knew that his powers had become so great that he was a necromancer, capable of bringing the dead back to life to be his slaves! He felt confident, at last, that Allansia would soon be his.

Razaak sent messages to all the nobles of the land, demanding that they acknowledge him as their ultimate ruler. But they had never heard of him, and they ignored his threats as the work of just another lunatic sorcerer. Razaak's response came in the form of thousands of black insects, who brought plague and pestilence to all lands. He sent another message to all the rulers, this time with a deadline: they had until the next full moon to acknowledge his leadership, or things would get even worse. Many warriors were dispatched to slay Razaak, but all died in the attempt.

At last the warrior named simply Kull arrived. He owned a sword which he had found gripped in a skeletal hand projecting out of a mist-veiled lake, high up in the Moonstone Hills, which he was crossing on his raft. It was an enchanted blade, able to cut through the thickest plate-mail without its razor-sharp edge being dulled or notched. The sword had once belonged to Razaak himself, and was the one sword in all of Titan which could harm him! As part of his final pact with the demonic deities who accepted him into their ranks as a necromancer, Razaak had to discard all weapons save only for the sacrificial knives which he consecrated to Evil as part of his initiation. But there was no way of destroying his sword, so he threw it into the lake – from where it rose in the hands of the skeleton! An incredible twist of fate worthy of Logaan the Trickster himself brought the blade back to Razaak in the hands of the now invincible Kull.

But as the blade bit home, Razaak cast his curse upon the warrior. Kull's skin fell from his bones as dust around his feet, and he was transformed into a skeleton, who would wield the sword for ever! The mindless thing that was once Kull returned to the lake where he first found that blessed and accursed sword, and now sails back and forth, awaiting someone to take it from him and release him into death's sleep. Razaak's corpse was sealed in a stone sarcophagus, which was then placed in a deep fissure high in the hills, and the evil necromancer was forgotten. In recent months, however, reports have come through Trolltooth Pass of famine, pestilence and plague drifting across the Flatlands. The sky has become dark and menacing, the sun hidden behind a wall of grey. The source of the Evil has been pinpointed as a fissure in the mountains, blackened by fire and tainted with Chaos . . . could Razaak have been disturbed and returned to the Earthly Plane?

Malbordus, the Storm Child

Malbordus is a human sorcerer, a powerful servant of Evil and

Chaos whose time is only now beginning to dawn. His name means 'Child of Darkness' in Low Elvish, and it was given to him when he was nine by the Wood Elves of Darkwood Forest. To see the reasons for such a name, we must go all the way back to his birth.

Malbordus was born in a battered, ramshackle hut on the edge of Darkwood Forest in old Allansia, in the middle of the wildest winter for several hundred years. Who his mother was, no one knows, but it is thought she was just a simple peasant crofter. She certainly could not cope with another child, for the infant was abandoned in a snow-drift about half a league into the forest.

That night, black-cowled Dark Elves from Tìranduil Kelthas, the accursed city of Darkside hidden far beneath the surface of the world, were abroad in the forest, worshipping the full moon, Tiriel, with blood-sacrifices and bizarre rituals. One party, flitting quietly across the snow without leaving any trace, heard the child's cries. They found a pathetic, frozen bundle, a human child which screamed at the top of its voice. They took it to their ritual site, and offered him to the Silent Guardian in the sky for his blessing. He was a gift from the heavens, and was to be under Tiriel's protection for ever. After the ritual was done, the Dark Elves slipped away and returned underground to their city.

THE STORM CHILD

They named the child Aëren Tintathel, Storm Child, and reared him in their temple under the protection of the witch-queen Velicoma Kerithrion. As he grew, he was introduced by her to the ways of Myurr, the Demon Prince, and taught the ways of the Dark Elves as if he were one of them. His pale white face and his piercing blue eyes were very strange to the black-skinned Dark Elves. And the raw power of his human soul did not take long to assert itself.

By the time Aëren was seven years old, he was indistinguishable from young Dark Elf children in every way except physically; his skin, which seemed to get whiter as he grew older, marked him out as something special. But unlike the other children, he carried within him an intensity of purpose which was frightening to those to whom he chose to reveal it. He spoke, with deep feelings of hatred and anger, of the surface-dwellers who had left him to die in the snow all those years ago, and talked of a time when he would remind them of their so-called humanity. Such talk had never been heard in the mouth of such a small child before, and Princess Velicoma declared him to be a gift from the gods (though the gods she meant are very different to our own).

A year later, the child's intensity had developed a stage further, and began manifesting itself in spontaneous displays of wild magic. He could snap his fingers and cause plants to wither and die from sheer hatred. He would gaze deep into the eyes of a Giant Lizard ten times his size, or a wild Elven hound that he found in the street, and the dumb beast would vacantly follow him wherever he went until it died from starvation because the child had forgotten to command it to eat. Aëren was plainly destined to be a great wielder of the ancient magics.

THE FIRST TEST OF MAGIC

Elven magic is pure and graceful, full of the unstoppable power of nature itself. But Dark Elven magic is vile and degrading, a force of darkness which is so pure that it puts the cheap darkness of the night to shame. To be initiated into the very first stage of its arcane intricacies, a Dark Elf must prove himself or herself worthy by some test; a second test will then follow much later, and will herald the completion of his or her learning. Most Dark Elves take the initial test after half a century's study and worship, but the Storm Child was just turning nine years old when he was proposed for initiation. For the young Aëren, the test was one of his own devising. He would go back to the surface world, where he had not set foot since he was found in the snow on that terrible winter's night exactly nine years before, and start the first stage of his revenge.

And so, on a squally winter's evening, a small, black-robed shape skipped lightly from the hidden entrance of the caves which lead down into Tìranduil Kelthas, and disappeared into the shadows of the forest. He did not know where he was going, nor what he was going to do to prove his worthiness, but he knew that the nameless beings which he had felt watching over him for so long would protect him on this night.

Luck, if that is what it was, was with him that night, for he came, very soon, to an area of thick, tall trees, where the scent was strongest. His Dark Elven night-vision picked out the shape of tree-houses, far above the ground. The faint sound of laughter floated down to him on the wind, and he knew then that this was the place where his revenge began. Quite by chance the young child had stumbled into the middle of the Wood Elf town of Caëranos, completely bypassing the patrolling guards.

Summoning all the inner strength he could muster, Aëren began to think of fire. Small tongues of warmth, great towering flames, wood glowing with heat, the stench of burning flesh – Aëren thought it all. And the power began to form inside him; all the hate and anger and Evil in him flowed through his mind, where it was converted into thoughts of fire, fire, fire. The first tree caught, bursting aflame in a brilliant flash of light which blinded the small child. But he went on concentrating, letting the real fire feed the flames coursing through his mind. A second tree took, then a third and a fourth. And soon every tree, for as far as Aëren could see, was ablaze, and from the tops of trees, figures leapt to their deaths, their clothes alight with the flames of Aëren's Evil.

The entire tree-top town of Caëranos was alight now, with Wood Elves scurrying everywhere in vain attempts to organize the extinguishing of the fire. But it was already too late – too late for water and too late even for magic. As they ran round in

panic, several Elves knocked into the little human child who stood, wrapped in his cloak, staring up at the flames with wide eyes and a happy smile on his face. But they were too busy to take much notice of him then, for their lives were crashing down around their ears.

It was not until much, much later, when the Elves were counting the dead and asking how this could have happened, that the child was remembered. And they asked themselves who he was, this sweet-faced child who had appeared out of nowhere to watch their families and friends die. The Elves looked around for some clue, and they found a small black cloak lying in the ashes of the largest tree. It was made of a strange cloth, and it reeked of a musty smell, as if it had been buried in the earth for a long time, which made the Elves feel nauseous. The Elf who tried to pick it up let out a yelp, for it burned his hand with the intense cold of pure Evil. And then they knew that it was a Dark Elf cloak, and that the mysterious human child was in league with the Dark Elves of accursed Tìranduil Kelthas.

The story of the child who razed the Elf town spread quickly to all parts of the Elf nation, and he was given the name Malbordus, Child of Darkness, and his stature grew and grew in the telling. But far beneath the surface of Darkwood Forest, young Aëren, or Malbordus as even he would soon call himself, was settling down to study the rudiments of the first stage of Dark Elven magic. Since that solitary explosion of his powers, he has not set foot in the outside world again, and his name has been forgotten by all but a few.

But he must be approaching manhood soon, the time when he will have to take his second test of initiation, to allow him to finish his studies of the forbidden lore of Dark Elven magic. And this time he will not be satisfied with burning down a few trees. The next time Malbordus sets foot above ground, all Allansia will know of it.

Shareella, the Snow Witch

In the far frozen north of Allansia, the Icefinger Mountains loom over the ice-bound plains, their craggy peaks pointing accusingly at the sky. In the mountains live wild creatures such as Yeti and Toa-Suo, which prey on the smaller animals of their icy habitat. But in recent years the Icefinger Mountains have also been home to evil inhumans – Orcs, Goblins, Ogres and Trolls – who make sporadic raids on isolated hunting settlements in search of slaves. These foul beings serve the evil sorceress known as the Snow Witch.

This demonic harridan makes her home in an extensive network of carefully guarded caverns known as the Crystal Caves. These fabulous caves were cut from the ice of a glacier high up a mountainside many years ago by the same degenerate creatures which serve her still. What she is doing here, in this frozen land, is not fully understood, but rumours say that she is acclimatizing herself to the powers of ice magic, training herself until she is ready to unleash the cold and bring a new Ice Age to Titan, at which point she will take control.

Until fairly recently, no one knew where the Snow Witch had come from – one moment the mountains were quiet, the next she had arrived, with her army of Orcs and Goblins. But thanks to the indomitable spirit of Harlak Erlisson, an adventurer from Frostholm, we know much more about her, and can even begin to piece together the sorry life which led her to this point. Harlak spent nine months as a slave in her ice-bound caves, being forced to raid and kill human settlements by a magical collar which was welded around his neck, but which did not stop his mind observing and remembering everything he saw. The hardy warrior escaped after his collar was knocked off when he was caught in an avalanche, which killed the other members of his raiding party. He crossed the ice plains to Allansia and freedom, and then to us to report what he had seen and learnt.

The Snow Witch was once human. As a young woman in Zengis, where she was born and grew up, she was known as Shareella. In that far city, women have many important religious and social roles, while the men become soldiers or traders. It seems they believe that women are far more 'spiritual' creatures than the more physical men. However, to reconcile this fact, a sorceress had to wander the barren northern wilderness as a test of her survival skills and will-power. Young Shareella was trained as a sorceress, and for her test was sent to the fringes of the Icefinger Mountains in winter, where she would have to live – without the benefit of fire or shelter or any other comforts – for five weeks.

At first Shareella found the going very hard, for she was used to the warmer climate of more southerly Zengis. But by the end of the second week she was beginning to become acclimatized to the conditions, and started to explore her surroundings. Gradually she wandered higher and higher into the Icefingers, living off snow-deer she caught and killed with her bare hands, but cooked with magical fire. Four weeks into her test, Shareella was exploring, as usual, when she came to a secluded ravine-cum-valley which she had not seen before. She gazed down into it – and stopped in her tracks! At the far end of the depression was a gigantic statue of a Demon, apparently carved out of solid ice.

But when she approached it, and laid her palm on its surprisingly warm surface, a voice spoke in her head – the voice of the Ice Demon which rested inside the statue. It told her many things about Demons and their works, and about the 'perversions' of Goodness and the 'blasphemies' of Neutrality. And it showed her a vision of the world covered in ice, and her as its omnipotent ruler! Shareella was converted in an instant, and pledged her soul to do everything she could to attain that goal.

Under the tuition of the Ice Demon, she became a necromancer, able to raise up zombies or skeletons from the bodies of the dead to serve her. She was provided with hordes of Orcs and Goblins, who worship the Demon, to build her the Crystal Caverns, where she now resides, hidden within the mountainside by an illusory wall of ice. In their turn, the inhuman races brought her slaves, whom she keeps in order with special magical collars that deliver sharp jolts of pain any time she wishes. Shareella has become twisted by the powers given to her by the Demon, and now she is a Vampire, able to suck the souls from other people's bodies. But all the time she is studying the powers of the ice, and readying herself for the day when the glaciers will creak and then slowly set off to cover all of Titan.

The Demonic Three

Years ago, an aged sorcerer had three pupils, whom he taught in a secluded school of magic. Unlike the Grand Wizard of the Forest of Yore, however, he was a servant of Evil and Chaos, and his three pupils were being trained to be warlocks and necromancers. The coven of this evil wizard, whose given name was Volgera Darkstorm, was hidden among the grassy wastes of the Flatlands, near one of the many ancient circles of standing stones which litter the plains. There the four of them studied all the arcane arts, from sticking pins in voodoo dolls and simple spells for souring milk, to raising the dead and communing with Demons.

The three young apprentices were keen students, and they learnt their horrendous craft quickly, their capacity for evil surprising even the depraved old sorcerer who taught them. They would slip off in the evenings, long after their teacher had retired to his bed, and just for fun sneak up on the camps of horse-nomads under the cover of dark magic which would hide their smell from the sensitive horses. There, in the darkness, they would carefully set magical traps, which would later explode into flame, when from the safety of a clump of spiky bushes the three could watch the nomads desperately rush about, trying to beat out their flaming tents.

These three were named Balthus, Zagor and Zharradan, and their activities were soon to become known across much of Allansia. When they reached the age of seventeen, the trio decided they had had enough of learning, and enough of living out on the Flatlands. They killed their teacher by magic, left him lying in a pool of blood, and sneaked through Troll-tooth Pass and into old Allansia. There, in the shadows of Darkwood Forest, they said goodbye, wishing one another the luck of the Dark Lords in serving their aims in the years to come.

Balthus headed south, carefully avoiding the Forest of Yore. The sweet scent of Goodness hung over the forest, making the young sorcerer feel sick, but it was quickly past. He did not turn aside when he reached the foothills of the Craggen Heights, but continued trekking into them, walking until he could not progress any higher. There, on the bare mountainside, he slept, but early the next day he reached his goal – the citadel built by his grandfather and now inhabited by his father, both of whom were themselves practitioners of dark magic. Even as his father embraced him, welcoming him back, Balthus slipped a poisoned dagger between his ribs – and the Citadel of Chaos was his! He knew what he had to do. He would gather around him servants of Chaos, Orcs and Goblins – and he would make his own servants too, building them out of other creatures to give him the strongest armies in the land. He would show Zagor and Zharradan how evil he could be!

Zagor, meanwhile, headed north with Zharradan for a while,

skirting Darkwood Forest, before the other broke off and headed east into the Moonstone Hills. Zagor travelled for many days, until he came in sight of Firetop Mountain, a peak he had seen in his Demon-sent dreams many a time. Here, he knew, his destiny lay. At that time the legendary caverns underneath the mountain were occupied by Dwarfs, but that soon changed, as the evil Zagor marched in with a strong force of Orcs and foul undead creatures. Some of the Dwarfs fled into the endless maze-like passages and were never caught, but many were killed, providing yet more deathless troops for the necromancer.

Now, many years later, Zagor is lord and master over Firetop Mountain, where he rules over a motley collection of evil servants, guarding the fabulous treasures he stole from the Dwarfs all those years ago. At the other end of settled Allansia, the foul Balthus Dire rules over the Black Tower, a ghastly citadel which perches atop Craggen Rock like an angry finger pointing accusingly at the gods! Within its labyrinthine warrens, mutant creatures – spawned by Balthus in his own laboratories – train in the use of weapons and magic alongside Black Elves and many Orcs and Goblins. They are preparing for war, for their satanic leader plans to use them to invade the Vale of Willow and the ancient city of Salamonis, bringing Chaos and death to that pleasant land as a tribute to Dire's hell-spawned deities.

But what of Zharradan? Well, it is known that he headed east into the Moonstone Hills all those years ago. We can trace his path very well by the little clues he left behind him along the way – a burning Elven village here, a massacred Woodling settlement there and so on. When he came to the heart of the Moonstones, however, he seemed to disappear without leaving any trace. To say he is dangerous is an understatement – if he is alive. It is just conceivable that he has succumbed to the dangers of the world: let us hope so.

Sukumvit and Carnuss

They say there is no bond so strong in this world as brotherly love, but that clearly does not always apply. Once, many years ago, there were two young brothers, the sons of Baron Arkat Charavask, who at that time was ruler of the prosperous northern trading city of Fang. Fang was, and is, the capital of the small but rich province of Chiang Mai, which lies just north of old Allansia. The border with that land is the River Kok, a fast-flowing torrent which brings barges and merchant ships from as far away as the city of Zengis in Kaypong to the north, and from the Western Ocean and beyond the other way. Baron Arkat was exceedingly rich, and his two fine sons wanted for nothing.

But Carnuss was very jealous of his brother; he felt that Sukumvit was getting far too much of his father's attention. Sukumvit, as eldest son, could expect to inherit the rule of Chiang Mai on the death of Baron Charavask, so much of his time was spent in accompanying his father to learn the task of rulership: they were together on state visits, at the court hearing complaints from citizens, hawking or hunting, and on the training-fields where Sukumvit was learning the use of sword and lance.

While this was going on, Carnuss Charavask was being taught a great many very tedious things by the court sorcerer, Zaragan the Wrinkled, who was a very learned, but also very boring teacher. From the room at the top of the ramshackle tower where the wizard lived, Carnuss could see his brother jousting or hunting with the dogs – doing all the things that Carnuss longed to do. But no, he was not destined for such greatness. In his mind, even at that young age, he nurtured a hatred that would last for many decades.

When his elder son was twenty-one, Baron Arkat died, and Sukumvit was immediately proclaimed Baron of Fang. Carnuss, only a year younger, felt angry that his brother should acquire so much wealth and power just like that, and he plotted to get even. He began mixing with thieves and assassins in the seedy bars in the slum areas of Fang, getting in with a dangerous crowd. He would slump there, every evening, muttering how much he would like to kill his brother. Eventually a few of his 'friends' decided to take him up on the offer – but it would cost him 1,000 Gold Pieces, as the victim would be hard to get close to.

Carnuss, in his youthful stupidity, agreed – but the 'assassins' went straight to Sukumvit and told him of the plot, for they were members of the palace guard whom the Baron had hired to watch over his foolish brother. Carnuss's plottings were publicly exposed, and the young nobleman fled the city in disgrace. He travelled far and wide, but found that as soon as he mentioned his name people would laugh at him. Heading further and further south, he eventually went to live on Blood Island off the desert coast of southern Allansia, where he built a massive castle.

As the years in exile and isolation went by, Lord Carnuss's hatred for his brother festered, until it turned him quite insane. Sukumvit, meanwhile, was enjoying a long and peaceful reign over Fang, where he was quite well liked by his citizens,

despite a tendency towards violence. As a sadistic private hobby, he built Deathtrap Dungeon, a massive underground complex full of deadly creatures and fiendish traps. He offered a prize of 10,000 Gold Pieces to the warrior who could pass through it. When one finally did, Sukumvit's reputation suffered greatly, but he was undeterred, and immediately made plans for a few changes. When he had finally redesigned and rebuilt his 'Trial of Champions', as he called it, he sent messengers to every town and village for tens of leagues around, declaring that no one would *ever* pass through it alive!

Carnuss, brooding in his distant castle, suddenly saw a way of getting even with Sukumvit after all these years. He would find a champion, a warrior and adventurer tough enough to survive all that the Baron's feeble dungeon could throw at him. To this end, he set up the Arena of Death on Blood Island, which is still in use. He uses slaves obtained for him by the notorious pirate and mass murderer Captain 'Skully' Bartella; these slaves are often just normal people who have been 'persuaded' to join the good captain and his scurvy crew on a little sea-cruise. Once they are on the island, Carnuss subjects his trainees to mortal combat in the arena. He is trying to whittle them down to just a single warrior, who will represent him and win the Trial of Champions, but his tests are far too strenuous. When one does survive, however, he plans to send him or her north, to revenge himself on his sadistic brother.

The Archmage

There is far too much that we do not know about the Archmage of Mampang, far too much. We have no record of where he was born, of what nationality he is, nor of who his parents were – if he had any, that is. It is not known who trained him in the rudiments of dark magic, nor where he served his apprenticeship.

Whatever his origins, however, all know of him now, for he is lord and master of the foul citadel of Mampang, where he trains his evil armies of inhuman warriors, and from where he threatens to enslave all of Kakhabad under his rule. When he came to High Xamen, he was already in his late twenties, and the whole area was uninhabited. But he gathered around him all manner of Goblins, Orcs, Trolls and many other un-intelligent servants of Evil and Chaos, and began to build what was eventually going to be Mampang, the Citadel of the Archmage.

At first the makeshift camps of the builders were subject to attacks from the Bird Men of the area, the Schinn, who quite understandably did not want any foul sorcerer building his big black citadel in *their* lands. The Archmage made a pretence of wanting to meet and discuss the matter, but when the leaders of the Bird Men arrived to confer with the wizard, he had them killed. He then negotiated with other Bird Men, the traditional enemies of the protesting faction, offering to keep them supplied with gold and jewels in exchange for their help in keeping the Schinn away.

Eventually, after many years of construction, the fortress of Mampang was finished, and the Archmage and his evil

servants took up residence. For perhaps thirty or forty years the Archmage continued to study the arcane arts, summoning Demons and making pacts with them in return for greater and greater power, growing ever more proficient in the practice of dark magic.

THE SEVEN SERPENTS

At about this time, ten or fifteen years ago, legend says that the Archmage fought a notable battle. All the while the sorcerer was studying his black sorcery, his foul servants were raiding further and further afield, bringing terror to many isolated settlements in Baddu-Bak and along the banks of near-by Lake Ilklala. But it was while they were exploring caves overlooking Avanti Wood, on the far side of Xamen, that they found the Hydra.

The titanic battle lasted two full days, during which wild magic flashed around the mountain peaks and the Archmage received, apart from severe burns, a deep wound, whose scar apparently runs from his neck to his right knee. But the Hydra was finally dead.

So impressed was the Archmage by the strength and prowess of this formidable foe that he took its seven heads and cast powerful and intricate spells on them. Then, summoning all his necromantic skills, he resurrected them as seven winged serpents! As a cruel joke perhaps, or possibly because he still believed in them at that point, he assigned each snake to one of the gods of the Old World. Glantanka's power was given to the Sun Serpent; Lunara's to the Moon Serpent. Four more serpents were aligned respectively with earth, air, fire and water, and the last was given the power of Chronada, the obscure Kakhabadian god of time. The Seven Serpents serve him still, it is said, bringing information to him from all over the festering lands.

And now rumours say he has the wondrous Crown of Kings, stolen by Bird Men from the king of Analand! We can only shudder to think of the power he can now wield. He will not stop at Kakhabad, you can be sure of that, no matter how unruly it is – the whole of the Old World may not be safe from his plans of conquest, once he has tasted the rotten fruits of tyranny.

Lord Azzur, the Tyrant of Blacksand

Last, but definitely not least, we come full circle to where we started our journeying across Titan, in Port Blacksand, the heart of settled Allansia, the true 'land of adventure'. What a city! More evil even than Kharé, the Cityport of Traps from the wild lands of Kakhabad, it sits at the heart of Allansia like an open sore on a dying leper! Even those who dwell there call it 'the City of Thieves', for it attracts every pirate, brigand, assassin, thief and evil-doer for hundreds of leagues around. Danger lurks in every corner of every street, as the strong prey on the weak, and the weak prey on one another. Over Blacksand, however, rules the biggest thief of them all, the mysterious Lord Azzur.

Azzur has ruled over Port Blacksand for a least thirty years now. He came to power after he wrested control from its previous master, one Baron Valentis, in a subtle take-over of the city which involved poisoning the head of the militia, beheading Valentis's brother, blockading the harbour with pirate ships, and hanging the baron from the highest tower of his palace! As to who Azzur is, however, there are many theories – you will find several in every tavern of an evening – but few know the truth. Except for a few rare occasions, Azzur has kept himself out of view ever since he took over the city, and always works through the black-clad Azzur Guard.

The pirate connection worries many citizens, and some say Azzur is the brother of the famous brigand, Garius of Halak; others even say he *is* Garius of Halak! The fact that his crest shows a boat on a wave-topped sea flanked by the sun and moon, has added great weight to such theories. Extensive research by the great historian, scholar and traveller, Zelakar of Chalannabrad, however, has finally revealed Lord Azzur's true background.

AZZUR'S PAST LIFE

Lord Varek Azzur was born of noble parents in the city of Arion, far, far away from Port Blacksand in the north-eastern corner of Khul. Arion, like all cities, is inhabited by both the good and the bad, the Lawful and the Chaotic. To the young Azzur, the darker side of existence always held the most attraction. He was fascinated by the bizarrely clad worshippers of strange deities such as Kukulak, the Khulian god of storms, whose devotees always went about completely swathed in thick black-robes. When he reached the age of sixteen, he sneaked into Kukulak's temple during a mass, and learnt why his worshippers were always dressed so: as part of their initiation, burning brands were applied to their faces and bodies, causing great weals and scars. If the scars formed themselves into Kukulak's runes, the acolyte was accepted; if not, he was taken from the temple and disposed of. Azzur was caught that night, lurking in the shadows at the rear of the temple, after accidentally kicking over a large brass candle-stand. He was given a simple choice – either to take the test of the flame, or to die there and then.

The burns were made, and they formed themselves into Kukulak's runes before the disappointed eyes of the high priest. Azzur was suddenly an initiate of Kukulak, the god of storms! Fearing what his parents would say when they saw his face, Azzur fled Arion on board a merchant's ship bound for Corda. On the way, however, the ship was raided by pirates operating out of the Rockwall Islands, who enslaved the fitter members of the ship's company and threw the rest to the sharks. The pirate captain (his name and the name of his ship are not known) was intrigued by the black-wrapped boy with the scarred face, and he allowed him to become his cabin boy.

Here Azzur's trail went cold on Zelakar for some time, apart from a number of unconfirmed reports of a brave pirate warrior with a heavily scarred face who served with a captain operating out of the Arrowhead Islands. Nine years after he fled Arion, Varek Azzur turned up in Merluk, the small port on the extreme south-eastern tip of Allansia, in charge of a pirate galley called *The Face of Chaos*. He sailed into the harbour at Merluk flying the skull and crossbones, boarded three ships just making ready to set sail, and quite openly emptied their holds of several thousand Gold Pieces' worth of goods before sailing away again! Azzur had obviously learnt how to make an entrance in his years as a pirate!

Azzur spent the next six years raiding ships along the entire southern coastline, from the Strait of Knives to Kaynlesh-Ma, until he had acquired a fleet of galleys, several hundred fanatically loyal men, and enough money to buy most of the southlands! Instead, however, his attentions turned towards Port Blacksand, which at the time was a small, shabby principality run by the ageing Baron Valentis. Gathering together his forces, he quickly took control of the city, where he has ruled ever since.

PORT BLACKSAND UNDER AZZUR

Azzur's rule has been a harsh one. The city has become a haven for all kinds of evil-doers, and it is no longer safe for an ordinary man to walk the streets – not that most are actually able to, for Azzur has imposed a stringent system of passes. This is enforced by his black-clad town militia, which includes Trolls and Ogres among its number. The passes are expensive, and vary according to what a person wishes to do: one is needed to enter the city, another to leave again; one is required to drink in certain taverns, another to enter a temple, and yet another to trade. It gets quite impossible on the days when the militiamen are sticking to their master's rules and are checking everyone!

Of Lord Azzur the citizens have seen little, and only two people in Port Blacksand have ever seen his face. One is his personal holy man, who brings the wisdom of Kukulak to Azzur once a month; the other is an incredibly over-confident thief, who now rests in pieces in various parts of the city after creeping into Azzur's private chambers one night! Azzur drives everywhere in an ornate golden coach, his face hidden behind darkened windows. If he has to appear in public, which he does rarely, he always dresses in black robes which swathe him completely. The gates of his ugly, elaborate palace are never open to visitors.

The city is, as mentioned right at the start of this volume, built on the ruins of the dockland area of a much older city called Carsepolis. Some of the deeper cellars and sewers lead down into the ruins, which still lie beneath the city, and many tales are told of the strange beings which haunt them. Every so often people disappear from their beds in the night, leaving only a few scraps of clothing and a smell like a thousand rats. When people hear of another disappearance, they just make the appropriate signs to their gods and point to the ground beneath their feet with a gulp! Occasionally, young adventurers full of bravado (or ale) boast of making a special journey into the ancient ruins to search for treasure, but those who try it rarely return, and none who do speak of what they saw there.

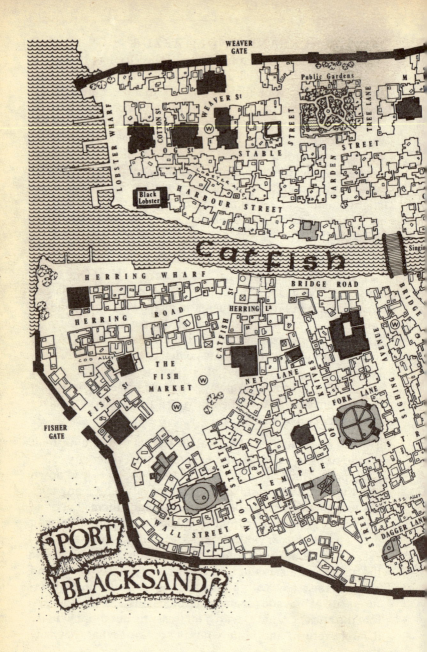

WEAVER GATE

Public Gardens

M

LOBSTER WHARF

COTTON St

CLOG St

WEAVER St

STABLE

STREET

GARDEN

STREET

TREE LANE

Black Lobster

LOBSTER ALL.

HARBOUR STREET

Catfish

Singin

HERRING WHARF

BRIDGE ROAD

BRIDGE

HERRING La

ROAD

CATFISH St

HERRING

COD ALLEY

THE FISH MARKET

NET LANE

KNIVES

AVENUE

SIGNING

FORK LANE

OF

FISH St

FISHER GATE

HOLMES St

TEMPLE

WOOL STREET

STREET

CUTLASS ALLEY

DAGGER LANE

WALL STREET

PORT BLACKSAND

STEVE LUXTON

250

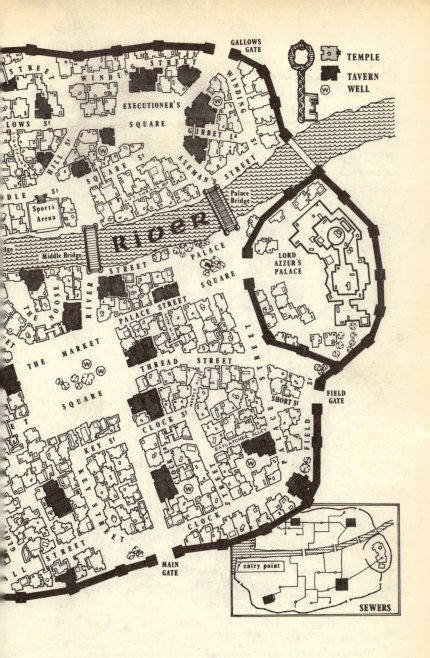

Since Port Blacksand is at the entrance to the Catfish River, right at the centre of settled Allansia, a lot of merchant traffic passes by it, generally in groups escorted by heavily armed galleys in case of piracy. Far fewer dock now than in the past, however, for they know that their wares will be stolen from their holds in the night, or their crews will be replaced by others who will mutiny and take their ships half-way through the voyage. Port Blacksand has an infamous reputation among honest seafarers the length and breadth of the coast, and even some pirates fear to enter it at certain times of the year.

It is a great place for hopeful adventurers, however, who seem to enjoy mixing with the rough and the violent. Many pass through in search of a boat and passage up or down the coast – or even out across the Western Ocean to distant Kakhabad or Analand. The taverns of Port Blacksand are always packed with warriors and would-be magicians, telling tales of their heroics or just sitting listening to those of other adventurers. But you need your wits about you if you are to survive even a single night in the City of Thieves. It is not a place for an inexperienced country boy with designs on being an adventurer. We say again – beware Blacksand!

THE UNDERWATER KINGDOMS

For hundreds, maybe thousands of years, tales have been told of the peoples who dwell 'under the sea'. The most persistent spreaders of such tales have been sailors, of course, who are renowned in all lands for being the biggest liars and exaggerators around! Put a salty old seaman in a run-down dockside tavern, stick a mug of rum in his tattooed hand to go with the dozens he has already quaffed, and he will give you a tale of such monumental catastrophe you will never contemplate going aboard a ship again! Such tales usually revolve around either gigantic sea-monsters which threaten to smash a galley into smithereens with one flick of a tail which has the dimensions of a city wall, or perilously beautiful Mermaids who perch seductively on stray rocks or the backs of passing dolphins and call love-struck look-outs to their doom.

Like most tales, those told of the underwater world are a mixture of half-truths and plain exaggeration. There *are* sea-monsters, and there *are* Mermaids, though they may not fit the descriptions you have heard. Moreover, they are far from being the only occupants of the world beneath the waves. Several races live in the oceans of Titan, though how they got there is anyone's guess. Some tell it like this . . .

The Children of Hydana

During the age of the earth before Time had been released by Death, and when the shape of the land was very different to what it is today, Hydana (the name the people of the Old World give the god of the waters) lived alone in a great palace at the bottom of the ocean. He was utterly captivated by the beauty of the sea and all the creatures which dwelt in it, and spent his time swimming in the depths observing all its wonders. But in time he became bored, for few of his brothers and sisters visited him (being too busy, for the most part, in fighting one another) and he wished for more sophisticated pleasures than merely playing with a few fish. Hydana had heard that his fellow gods had started to create their own beings, strange creatures which walked on two legs and had intelligence of sorts, and soon he saw some 'men', when they took their first tentative steps into the waters of their planet to swim and fish.

Hydana saw his chance. He captured a boat full of 'men' and 'women', and drew them beneath the waves to observe them; but he was dismayed to find that they wriggled a while, but then lay still, and would not move again, no matter how hard he shook them. He tried this several times, before it dawned

on him that the bubbles the things released when held underwater were what they breathed to keep alive on the land. Next time he captured a boat, therefore, he changed the lungs of his 'guests' into gills, so that they could join him in his wondrous world beneath the sea. At first, of course, the humans were terrified, but Hydana continued adding to their numbers, and in time they began to enjoy their new life under the waves with Hydana, and built their own towns and cities, and farmed seaweed and other crops. The god continued adding to his stock of 'little people', and soon had brought other beings such as Elves, Trolls and Giants to join the humans.

Hydana, however, was caught up in the First Battle against Death and his cohorts. During the battle he was so sorely injured that he retired to the deepest part of the oceans, from where he rarely emerges now, except at times of great disaster, or when called upon by his fellow gods for some special task – like the drowning of Atlantis, which we will come to in a moment.

The underwater races prospered in the oceans, and lived in small groups dotted around the ocean beds. They made their homes in caves at first, but soon began to build from stone,

learning the techniques by examining drowned villages near the coast which had been submerged by the sea's relentless advance. Their appearance gradually changed, and they turned into the Merfolk – green-skinned and scaly, with a fish-like tail instead of legs. They made friends with dolphins, seals and the other underwater mammals, and would often hunt and play with them; and each species protected the others from the attentions of sharks and sea-serpents. Life was peaceful under the waves, with few of the troubles which were coming to a head for their land-based relations.

THE DIVIDING OF THE RACES

But eventually, when the Forces of Evil began fighting for dominance of the land, their brothers under the waves were called upon to help. Although they had lived for many centuries in perfect peace and harmony with Mermen and Sea Elves, the Sea Trolls moved away and set up their own colonies, shunning the company of the beings which had once been their friends. Because the Mermen and Sea Elves dwelt in the warm, clear waters around the middle of Titan, the rebel races were forced to take the cold and silty northern waters. Petty disputes started over boundaries and who 'owned' particular stretches of the sea – something which had never happened in the underwater world before, though it would be familiar to any land-dweller. They led, inexorably, to war.

At the time of the first conflicts, the Merfolk were divided into four distinct groups, each based in and around a large underwater city in a different part of the ocean. They had no leaders as such, but were watched over by ruling councils of between three and twenty Mermen and Mermaids. And they were totally unprepared for war.

The first engagements came near the smallest of the four cities, called Buwalra in the strange tongue of the underwater people. A tribe of Sea Trolls which dwelt north of the city had gradually been encroaching on Merfolk lands, needlessly killing dolphins and setting sharks loose near by, and then destroying crops while the local inhabitants were distracted. Despite their peaceful nature, the Merfolk could take no more, and sent a delegation to the chief of the Sea Trolls, who was known as Krulliagh Stormtooth. The delegation went in peace, escorted by more dolphins and with Sea Elf observers. Before they could arrive at the craggy plateau-side where the Trolls had their settlement, they were ambushed by a combined force of Trolls, Giants and sharks, and as one they were slaughtered in a frenzy of blood-letting. Their bodies floated slowly back into Buwalra on the current, and messengers were sent to the other three cities, informing them that the citizens of Buwalra were about to declare war on Stormtooth's forces, and asking for aid in their fight.

A strong force of warriors was dispatched and swam with all speed for the city, but several leagues outside Buwalra they met the first Merfolk bodies drifting in the water. By the time they reached the centre of the city, they realized that a terrible massacre had taken place. The central square itself was a mass of writhing sharks, frenziedly chewing away at a large pile of bleeding bodies; the entire population of the city had been slaughtered – apparently without putting up any resistance, for there were few Troll corpses around.

The Massacre of Buwalra, as it has been called to this day, was only the first engagement in the unceasing conflict between Merfolk and Sea Trolls. The Merfolk have become very bitter and battle-hardened, for they are always on the alert for the bulky silhouettes drifting over their reefs, which indicate the presence of another Troll raiding party. The conflict is intense in some parts of the ocean, while an uneasy peace exists in others, but all Merfolk are always on their guard against the Trolls, whom they now call the Sharadrin, or 'Deep Ones'. Buwalra itself has been left empty, as a shrine to those who were so cruelly slaughtered there all those centuries ago. Silt and debris is cleared from its streets and buildings every so often, but the only creatures who live there now are fish.

Merfolk have little to do with land-dwellers, for there are weightier matters which concern them more. Tales are some- times told of sailors who have been saved from shipwrecks by dolphin-riding 'fish-men', but such occurrences are very rare. Mermaids still lure men into the water, to take them as lovers for a short while, but no one can ever be sure how many men have been lost in this way. Adventurers and curious sages who have perfected magical gills or spells for breathing underwater are greeted cordially, but with some reserve, and their stays have been short.

MERFOLK RAIDING PARTY

This is a typical Merman war-band in the formation they take while out patrolling for sharks or raiding Sea Trolls. At the front, scouts swim with the fastest dolphins and seals, looking out for likely threats. Behind them come the forward guards, riding dolphins or sea-horses, followed by the main band of warriors again riding sea-horses or swimming. The rear is taken up by several more dolphins and seals. All the Mermen are armed with spears and nets.

= MERMAN   = DOLPHIN

= MOUNTED MERMAN   = SEA-HORSE

THE OTHER RACES

Sea Elves are much fewer in number than Merfolk or Deep Ones, and they keep themselves very much to themselves as far as they can. Like their land-bound cousins they can live for many, many centuries, and also like them they have taken on the role of gardeners. They have had few troubles with Sea Trolls, for the latter have learnt to leave them well alone, after a few disastrous attempts at attacking Elven settlements at the start of the conflict.

The Elves have adapted so well to their underwater environment that they are more like fish than humanoids, and are able to swim at great speeds and with great dexterity. It is even thought that they have become colour-changers like chameleons and can blend in with whatever surface they are passing over (sand, say, or rocks), which allows them to sneak up on prey without being seen. Mermen only use spears, knives and nets, but Sea Elves have perfected the use of small crossbows, which fire sleek darts carved from bone at quite a speed through the water. They have also learnt how to use paralysing poisons taken from scorpion fish, which they smear on their darts and spear-tips.

Sea Elves make their homes in small, well-hidden settlements, camouflaged by forests of kelp and weed and protected by giant spider-crabs and octopi which are enough to warn off most creatures. They are governed by their priests, rather than by chieftains or kings, and their magic is powerful and totally connected with the lore of the sea. Unlike Merfolk, they keep in close contact with their land-based relations, and attend the Elven Councils once a century, residing in large tanks in the council chamber for the duration of the council!

Sea Giants are much like other giants, being massive, slow-moving and solitary beings. They tend to dwell in large caves or crude stone buildings, living alone or, sometimes, with a few pet fish or some other sea creatures such as squid and octopi. They are slow-witted, gentle creatures, who rarely realize how much damage they can do. They are friendly towards Sea Elves, but enjoy the company of Mermen more, for they despise Sea Trolls for the damage they cause, and occasionally help in raids against them. Mermen get very annoyed with Sea Giants, for they tend to go stomping over their prize crops by mistake, but they are always grateful for their help during their constant skirmishes with the scaly green Trolls.

Atlantis, the Sunken City

Such is the general situation beneath the waters of this world's oceans, but what of Atlantis, that infamous city of legend? Ever since people have been telling tales, there have been legends about the city which was deliberately drowned by the gods, and the stories are not restricted to coastal regions – even the primitive peoples of the Scythera Desert and the Desert of Skulls have tales of 'a city over running land [water] buried by the gods'. The story of Atlantis and its cataclysmic destruction has passed around the whole world.

Once there was a large island in the centre of what is now called the Western Ocean. In those days, this stretch of water was much larger, for the three main landmasses we know today were joined where the Ocean of Serpents and the Ocean of Tempests now flow. The gods had departed from the Earthly Plane by this time, but the races of man had started their rise towards civilization. The island was known as Atlantis, after Atlan, the messenger of the gods, and it was the greatest centre for wisdom on the whole of Titan. In its capital, Atlantis City, the wisest scholars of the day would gather to discuss deep philosophical questions about the nature of life.

Atlantis was very rich, for in the mountains which made up perhaps half its area the Atlanteans had found gold in abundant and seemingly inexhaustible supply. With this gold, the people of Atlantis bought the finest goods the world could offer and lived in extreme luxury in Atlantis City, which was without doubt the most beautiful metropolis ever to have graced the surface of Titan. The wealth of the Atlanteans attracted the attentions of many poorer nations, and invasions were attempted at a rate of perhaps two or three a decade. But with their riches the Atlanteans could easily afford the best mercenaries, and the invading nations were quickly repulsed, their forces sent fleeing and broken back to their home ports.

So Atlantis thrived, growing ever richer and ever stronger. It quickly became the centre for trade and learning for all the western lands. But all good things come to an end sooner or later – and Atlantis's doom was set when its greatest king, Faramos XXII, died after reigning for eighty-one years without leaving a son. A search was started, a search which lasted for four years, until the 16-year-old son of a second cousin from the small kingdom of Kelios (now part of the Isles of the Dawn) was found, and declared king of Atlantis, taking the name Faramos XXIII in memory of his noble predecessor.

The new king was very young and inexperienced, but according to Atlantean law he was granted absolute power over the entire land – the richest and most powerful land on Titan! The power went to Faramos's head surprisingly quickly, and within four months he had launched an invasion against the last nation to threaten Atlantis, a large merchant-governed democracy called Taralak. This soon fell, and the victorious mercenary armies swept on into the lands beyond, which fell almost as rapidly. Within four months the armies of Faramos had carved a massive swath across the whole of the centre of the continent, and were busy putting most of the northlands to the torch! Deeply impressed by this new method of proving Atlantean superiority, the whole country united behind Faramos, and Atlantis geared up for the eventual take-over of the whole world!

The gods could not stand back and watch any longer, especially as it was (rightly) suspected by this time that the boy Faramos was in fact the infernal Demon Prince Myurr in

disguise. During the most spectacular thunderstorm this world has ever seen, Hydana the god of the waters rose from his secret domain at the bottom of the ocean, and blasted Atlantis with a monumental tidal wave. At the same time, Throff, goddess of the earth, caused Atlan's Beacon to erupt, and the nation was destroyed amid raging torrents of lava and water, before sinking to the bottom of the ocean (though not before Myurr had made his escape back to the Demonic Planes, unfortunately). The angry sea carried the wrath of the gods to the mainland as well; the land was swamped, and great channels were gouged, which turned it into three separate islands. These gradually drifted apart, creating the three continents which we know today.

As for Atlantis, it rests there still, at the bottom of the Western Ocean, home to Merfolk and Sea Trolls who war continuously for the prestige of dwelling there. Its treasures have never been recovered, but every so often a few strange Gold Pieces get hauled up in fishermen's nets, reminding us all of the city which sank beneath the sea, and of the power of our gods!

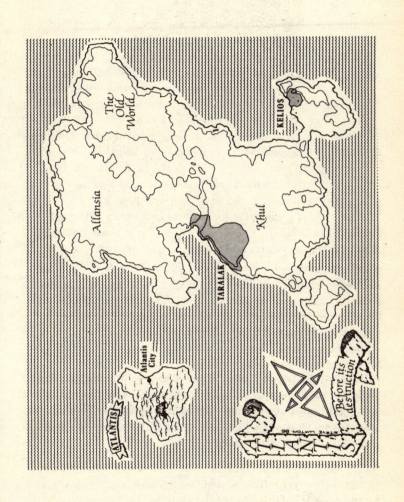

The Old World

Allansia

Khul

KELIOS

TARALAK

Atlantis City

ATLANTIS

ATLANTIS

Before its destruction

STEVE LUXTON 86

THE TITAN CALENDAR

In the so-called civilized countries, which are stretched out along the narrow coastal strips as if trapped between the impassable ocean and the hostile interior, most people make a living from the land. Their entire lives revolve around the seasons of the year, for thus the farmers know when to plant their crops to reap the most fruit. In the small towns too, the citizens live strictly by the calendar, whether they are waiting for the regular visits of the travelling merchants, trying to remember when each type of fish can be found off the coast, or observing the feast-days of their gods. In any land visited by the caravans of the merchants, you will find that they reckon the passing of time in much the same way as anywhere else, but in wilder lands you may discover entirely different systems. Wherever you travel, however, you must respect the culture of the people, and try not to give offence – or you will soon find that their smiling hospitality hides glinting daggers grasped tightly behind their backs!

Reckoning the Years

During the Time of Naming, when everything was given the title it would carry until the end of time, the years were allotted names in honour of the greatest of the beasts that walked the surface of Titan. The years still pass in twenty-year cycles in honour of the creatures whose names they bear. The cycle is as follows:

1. The Year of the Dragon

2. The Year of the Lion

3. The Year of the Snake

4.	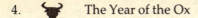	The Year of the Ox
5.		The Year of the Tiger
6.		The Year of the Goat
7.		The Year of the Mouse
8.		The Year of the Deer
9.		The Year of the Bat
10.		The Year of the Wolf
11.		The Year of the Eagle
12.		The Year of the Dog
13.		The Year of the Spider
14.		The Year of the Rabbit
15.		The Year of the Fox
16.		The Year of the Crocodile
17.		The Year of the Owl
18.		The Year of the Cat
19.		The Year of the Shark
20.		The Year of the Horse

Some astrologers in Allansia and elsewhere believe that people born in a particular animal's year take on the characteristics of that animal. People born under the sign of the Owl, for example, are said to be wise and noble, but with a hidden savagery; those born in the Year of the Deer are said to grow up shy and nervous, always fleeing from the least danger. Whether or not it is true, many people give great honour to the animal of their birth-year on their twentieth birthdays, when they come of age and become recognized adults.

Each passing of the twenty-year cycle is called a 'Turn', so an old man may talk of being born in the Year of the Spider, three Turns ago. Of course, as you already know, the more civilized cultures also talk in terms of real dates, according to the system standardized by the scholars of the various seats of learning of the known world after the War of the Wizards, and instituted the After Chaos reckoning, of which we are now in the 284th year, the Year of the Fox. Thus, if he were a little more educated, and were proficient enough at the generally unknown discipline of mathematics, our elderly gentleman may tell us that he was born in 222 AC, and that he is a venerable sixty-two years old.

In other lands, they use very different systems for reckoning the years (though in some lands, such as Frostholm in the frozen north-east of Allansia, the people have no calendar at all, for they neither know nor care about their birth-dates or the time of the year!). Many people simply date their lives after noteworthy events, such as 'four years after the Battle for Vymorna Pass' or 'seventeen years after Hurlinn beheaded King Shakash of Kaynlesh-Ma'. The calendar of the semi-human nomads of the Baddu-Bak Plains in Kakhabad is based on years being a certain number 'Away' from the present; in other words, last year is One Away, and our old man was born in Sixty-two Away. The people of Hachiman in remote Khul reckon years by a cycle of eight named years (the Tree, the Fish, the Stone, the Sun, the First Moon, the Second Moon, the Sword and the Arrow) and also by the year of the reign of their ruler. Thus our old man might tell us that he was born in the Year of the Fish in the fourth year of Shogun Aykira (the grandfather, incidentally, of the current Shogun, Kihei Hasekawa).

Measuring the Months

Again, in different parts of the world there are differing names and reckonings for the months of any given year, but in most civilized regions each year is divided into twelve months. Within each month, the days are counted out, so that in Allansia, for example, a day might be Seaday, 8th day of Dark. However, there are two separate reckonings for the days within such months.

The Allansian Reckoning. This sytem makes the months all different lengths, called by the following names:

1. Freeze (31 days)
2. Dark (28 days)
3. Unlocking (31 days)
4. Sowing (30 days)
5. Winds (31 days)
6. Warming (30 days)
7. Fire (31 days)
8. Watching (31 days)
9. Reaping (30 days)
10. Hiding (31 days)
11. Close (30 days)
12. Locking (28 days)

The days are grouped into weeks, each consisting of seven days. Careful study, however, will show that this adds up to three days less than a normal 365-day year. After Locking, the Allansian calendar adds three uncounted days for the celebration of New Year. Children born during this celebration time are considered very well blessed, and great things are expected of them. During this time, the cold stillness of the winter is broken by 72 hours of riotous celebration (see below for more on New Year and other special days).

The Khulian Reckoning. For as long as people have reckoned days and months, the countries of the mysterious continent have had twelve months, each exactly 30 days in length, and each made up of five weeks of six days apiece. The months are named as follows:

1. Snow's Cloak
2. Skies in Darkness
3. Land's Awakening
4. Heaven's Weeping
5. Birds Chatter
6. Days Lengthen
7. Corn Ripening
8. Man's Harvesting
9. Forests Golden
10. Nature's Curling
11. Sun's Hiding
12. Land's Sleeping

At the end of the year, after a month of Land's Sleeping, the peoples of all the countries of civilized Khul mark New Year with not three but *five* days of merry-making, though it must be said that in many parts of the continent the celebrations are more sombre, as the people give thanks to their various gods and pray for a prosperous year to come.

Pacing Out the Days

In Allansia (and in the Old World) each week has seven days, while in the distant continent of Khul the people measure a week in six days. The days each have these names:

Day of the week	Allansian	Khulian
First	Stormsday	Rageday
Second	Moonsday	Freezeday
Third	Fireday	Fearday
Fourth	Earthday	Lifeday
Fifth	Windsday	Wildday
Sixth	Seaday	Spiritday
Seventh	Highday	—

On Highday in many civilized parts of Allansia and in some of the principalities in the western continent, and on Spiritday in Khul, most work stops and those of religious persuasion attend the temples and chapels to worship their various gods for much of the day, spending the rest relaxing in comfort. As with the various years, astrologers insist that the day of week determines the character of a child from its birth. A baby born on Earthday, they say, will be good with his or her hands, and destined to be a craftsman, or a farmer, but one born on Moonsday will be a scholar or priest, and will follow the path of learning and enlightenment. (Incidentally, it is also believed that most twins are born on Moonsday, and surprisingly this appears to be true, at least in Allansia.) It is very definitely true that different types of magic work better on the days associated with them than on the days of their opposing elements, to such an extent that some specialized sorcerers dare not leave their towers on certain days; such is the power of the elements and magic on Titan!

In some distant lands, primitive tribes still believe that the world is flat, and that the sun (or in many places, the sun goddess) crosses the sky on a gleaming golden chariot once a day. During the night she fights her way through the under-world, facing terrible dangers in her struggle to balance Good and Evil and keep the world alive. She returns again at dawn the next day, starting the whole cycle over again. Of course, no *civilized* people would ever believe in such things!

FEAST-DAYS AND FESTIVALS
The list which follows gives details of just a few of the many rituals and celebrations to be found across the world; we are sure you will encounter more on your travels.

Night of the Ancestors (first day of Hiding): In the land of Kaypong, in the city-states around the Glimmering Sea, and in many other more isolated areas, the people celebrate the Night of the Ancestors, where they welcome into their homes all the ghosts of ancestors gone by. Most years, this consists simply of an awful lot of singing and dancing, with everyone dressed in ghoulish masks and costumes decorated to look like skulls and skeletons. As dawn breaks they run yelping through every

building and out through the gates of the settlement, symbolizing the departure of the ancestors' spirits for another year. However, perhaps every ten years or so, the ghosts of their ancestors take it upon themselves to appear in person, whereupon the night passes in a seriously happy ritual dance of celebration, with each reveller entwined in the arms of ghostly forms which keep them dancing all night, before the spirits themselves flee with the dawn. The Night of the Ancestors helps the people rationalize the deaths of their loved ones, and demonstrates most forcefully that life and death are inseparable on Titan.

Children's Festival (first Highday of Warming): In many small villages across Kakhabad and Ruddlestone, the citizens celebrate the joys of childhood, by allowing the children to exchange roles with all the adults for a day, and to have the freedom of the village. Everyone over sixteen years of age must serve the children all day, often putting up with beatings or

thoroughly ludicrous requests according to the whims of the impish children! The children do exactly as they want for one day, secure in the knowledge that the adults are not permitted to get their own back the day after. It helps the adults see what it is like to be a child for a day, and is, of course, incredibly good fun for the younger participants!

Feast of the Waters (various days in Unlocking): Along the banks of rivers like the Eltus in Arantis and the Tak in southern Khul, life depends upon the regular flooding of the farmland, when the river brings a wash of fertile soil in which crops can flourish. Therefore, at the first sign of 'Nature's Unlocking' (after which the month is named), the riverside-dwellers bring out carved boats and symbolic wheat and rice stalks, and offer prayers to their river gods for a heavy and fruitful flood, so that they may eat over the lean winter months to come. In some lands it is said that animals and sometimes children are sacrificed when the water is not forthcoming, though the truth of this barbaric practice has never been properly determined.

New Year (last three or five days of year): Year's End is the greatest of all festivals, and is celebrated almost universally among the human races. It is not known whether Elves celebrate the passing of another year; Dwarfs certainly do, typically in one vast fit of drunkenness! Orcs and other non-humans occasionally celebrate the New Year, usually by sacrificing and eating a lot of other non-humans in a debauched feast of monumental proportions!

Humans celebrate the New Year in many ways. In Khul, the highly religious citizens of Ximoran and Buruna spend five days in solid prayer in their temples, stopping only on the evening of the fifth day for feasting and celebration, activities which seem all the more jubilant because of the sombre prayers beforehand. In Analand and Lendleland, the people celebrate with hunting and fairs, with travelling traders setting up in village markets to sell all kinds of exotic wares. In Port Blacksand in Allansia, however, Lord Azzur usually celebrates by executing several prominent citizens (and then kindly donating their riches to the city's poor – what a benevolent ruler!).

THE ADVENTURING LIFE

So now you know where to go, whom to make friends with, and whom to avoid on your travels. But how do you get to where you want to go, and what hazards will you face as you journey around this wide world of ours? Read on and we will tell you.

Travelling from A(llansia) to B(addu-Bak)

In the first place, you must remember that there are few fast methods of travel on Titan. While some wizards have perfected crude 'Teleportation' spells which can take them anywhere they want to go in the blink of an eye (or more usually take them anywhere *but* where they wanted to go!), and some races, such as the Mountain Elves, have access to fast flying beasts such as Giant Eagles, most people simply journey by foot, and as a result rarely undertake long journeys. Apart from the desert nomads, most common people never stray more than a day's walk from their birth-place!

Those people who do move about, especially in the wilder areas of Titan, are therefore quite unusual. These exceptions to the rule can include noblemen and those in their service, who often travel beyond their own borders to consult or attack other leaders; merchants, who carry goods from where they are made to where they are sold; pilgrims and scholars; soldiers and errant mercenaries; a few specialists, such as wandering minstrels, circuses and the like; and wandering adventurers, thieves and outlaws. In a thickly settled part of the world, the roads will be quite crowded with this sort of traffic, as people move from one town to the next. In outlying areas, you are far more likely to travel for days without meeting anyone.

WALKING

While the use of 'Longshank's pony' is all right for short journeys of no more than a week, no one in their right mind would want to walk for greater distances. While it may be the source of some esteem to become the first adventurer to walk across the Flatlands, for example, it will take you four months, and you could do the journey in half the time on the back of a horse.

However, horses are expensive, and walking does give you a chance really to get back to nature. As you stroll along, you can take in everything around you and enjoy the feeling of being out in the wild. For walking any great distance you will need a good pair of stout leather boots, and a staff made from the smoothed branch of a hardwood tree. The boots will last you for a long time, as long as you remember to take them off when fording rivers, and the staff will help you stand up when you are tired and will come in useful to push your way through scrubland.

MOUNTED TRAVEL

Horses are the most common mount, and you can buy an average-quality horse in most villages and towns. The best horses in all Titan, however, come from the plains of Lendleland, where gorgeous black and white horses run wild on the grassy expanses. A Lendleland horse could cost as much as 1,000 Gold Pieces, unless you capture and tame it yourself, but it will serve you faithfully until it dies.

Most races use horses and ponies, even Orcs, who use them for pulling ore-wagons in their mines. Most people learn to ride a horse when they are very young, even if it is just the farm's cart-horse, and once learnt it is not something one ever forgets. The nomads who roam the Flatlands on their shaggy ponies are experts at performing all kinds of tasks while on the move, from firing a bow to sewing up holes in their tents – all without their hands on the reins! You will not need to be quite that proficient, but if you can swing a sword in one hand and hold on with the other, you will do better than many would-be highwaymen and bandits!

Another advantage of using a horse is that you can hitch it to a cart or a travois (two long poles with a sheet of cloth slung between), on which you can carry your belongings or a wounded comrade. In some lands, nomads actually pull complete houses on wheels behind them, moving their village wherever they wish!

Mules and donkeys are slower than horses, and can be quite uncomfortable to ride, but they can cross terrain which a horse would refuse to attempt. They are more useful as pack animals, however, for carrying treasure or goods across long distances. In northern lands, most merchants use long trains of mules to carry their wares to their distant markets; when they get there, they may even sell the mules too, and return on horseback in comfort.

In the hotter regions, camels take over from horses as the commonest mounts. They are temperamental beasts and can be quite frustrating, until you discover the right commands to make them lower their bodies for you, or rise up and start walking again. After some extensive (and infuriating) research, we can reveal that all camels will drop to their knees for you to mount if you simply say '*Hcchhtt!*' in your throat, and will rise and start walking on '*Hutt! Hutt!*' – simple when you know how, but dreadfully irritating if you do not. The big advantage of camels, as you may know, is that they can go for several days without needing food and water, which can come in handy when you are lost in the middle of the baking expanses of the Scythera Desert!

Giant Lizards may strike you as being very impressive to ride about the world on, but they are surly beasts, and you need a hide like a Lizard Man's to save you from getting sore! They do not like cold climates, have to be fed on a lot of fresh meat every day, and most villagers will lock their gates if you try to bring such a beast near them, so they cannot really be recommended as mounts.

Similarly, you should not think of trying to ride a wolf. It is true that Orcs and Goblins do, and that it can look very heroic and impressive, but where would you get a tame wolf from anyway? You cannot just go up to the first one you meet in the wilderness and jump on its back, yelling, 'Hiyo, wolfie!' Orcs have reared wolves for centuries, and even now the mounts turn on their riders when there is no better food around.

The fastest way of travelling (short of teleportation) is to fly on the back of a Giant Eagle. As with other wild creatures, you have to persuade the Eagle to take you in the first place. Giant Eagles usually allow only very gentle creatures, such as Elves, on their backs, and then only under protest. They are noble creatures, and may feel it is beneath them to carry a lesser being! If you ever do manage to fly on the back of a Giant Eagle, however, you will never forget the experience, for they can fly faster than the wind!

CROSSING THE WATERS

To see all of Titan, however, you will need to sail the wild oceans in the company of pirates or merchants. Because of the large distances between the continents, you may find you have to resort to island-hopping to reach your goal, but with patience and in time you will find that you can sail all the way round the world, if you so desire! The easiest way to cross the seas is to pay for a passage in a merchant's ship or a warship. Many captains, however, will want you to work your passage. This is an ideal opportunity to learn about shipboard life at first hand, but it can be very hard work, sixteen hours a day even in the baking sun or a raging gale. If you are not used to the rocking motion of a small boat on the sea, you may also learn a lot about sickness!

Barges. Long, flat barges operate only on rivers and along the calmer coast-lines, for they are easily swamped by large waves. The water-borne trade between Port Blacksand and Zengis, for example, uses trains of barges which are sailed up and down the wide River Kok. You can usually buy passage on a barge to most riverside destinations in settled lands.

Galleys. These are long, oar-driven ships (though they carry a few small sails for when the crew needs to be rested), usually manned by slaves. They are often used by coastal pirates, as they can be very manoeuvrable in combat: skilful rowing can make them go backwards, for instance, or turn quickly. They may be armed with a ram, or a catapult to fire blazing bales at other ships. The northmen of Frostholm in Allansia use long, square-sailed galleys decorated with Dragons, which they sail far from home to raid isolated coastal farmsteads and villages.

Merchant Ships. These are typically the same size as galleys, but wider, with a single mast and a triangular 'lateen' sail. Some also have ports for oars, which can be used to move the ship around a dock, or when becalmed. Pirates, however, often use similar ships for making raids on merchant ships. In this way, they can get very close to their quarry before ramming them and swinging men across on ropes to kill and plunder.

Warships. These are few and far between, for there are few nations rich enough to support a proper navy. They are fast and manoeuvrable, and can usually outrun a pirate ship. They are not very seaworthy, however, and are prone to sink in very rough seas. Larger than merchant ships, they usually have two or three masts, a battering-ram just below the waterline at the front, and strange castle-like constructions at the prow, from which warriors can leap on to an enemy ship as soon as it has been rammed. They may also have large catapults or ballistas.

Roughing It!

When you are wandering through wilder parts of the world, you will initially have difficulty eating, drinking and camping, and you may be prey to any number of dangers. There are many hazards to catch the unwary or inexperienced traveller, and you will quickly learn from your mistakes – if you are not eaten, poisoned or whatever first!

Food in the wilderness can be quite a problem, especially if you are in unfamiliar lands. Many travellers carry plentiful supplies of provisions with them when they set off on a journey. In Analand they prepare something called vittles, which are small pastry balls filled with dried meat. They can last for days, and although you may get bored of eating the same thing, you can at least be sure you are eating something which will not poison you.

The same, alas, cannot be said for many fruits and berries. When you are a long way from the last outpost, and your food is running low, all bright red berries look very appetizing, but you should perhaps remember that they may be bright red to warn creatures not to eat them! While succulent delights like the bomba-fruit (a red, apple-like fruit found in many warm lands) will refresh you, there are things like the bitter-sweet, which looks like a bomba-fruit but causes terrible stomach pains in humans, to catch you out. You are much safer snaring a few rabbits or a hill-fox – at least you will know what the food tastes like, even if you have to go through the stomach-turning ritual of skinning and cooking it!

Some experts believe that when camping for the night you should light a fire, and keep it burning all through the night, to keep wild beasts away. Unfortunately, we have found that a fire may also serve to *attract* all the wild beasts in the area, who would otherwise have ignored you! If you have already attracted the attentions of something dangerous like a pack of wolves, however, a fire will keep them off for a while, though the hungrier they get, the braver they will get too. If you find

yourself stuck in the open surrounded by a pack of wolves, it is likely that you will not be doing much sleeping that night! If you are really worried about wild animals in the night, sleep with your back to a large tree, or, better still, sleep *up* the tree.

There are other dangers in the wild too, but these we must skip over here: we would not want to discourage you from venturing out into the world with tales of wolves and bandits and violent death, now would we? There is one thing you should know about, however. In recent years, the yellow plague has re-established itself in a number of outlying villages in the wilder parts of Allansia and Kakhabad. While it can be cured by drinking the juice of the blimberry if spotted in time, it is often far too late by the time the victim learns he has the disease. If you enter a country village and you do not hear the chirping of birds, and dogs do not run to greet you, and children are not playing in the streets, then you should be on your guard!

As you travel around the wide world of Titan, you should be careful, but not over-cautious. It can be a wild, dangerous place at times, but danger is surely what heroic adventurers like yourself thrive upon!

Money

Everyone needs money, in one form or another, if they are going to make their way in the world. However, in different lands what is regarded as money can take many different forms.

GOLD PIECES AND OTHER COINAGE

As you may already have gathered, the standard unit of currency in most civilized human areas is the Gold Piece. Due to the efforts of traders and merchants, their size and weight has been made much the same across the world. They are circular coins (though in some lands they may be square or octagonal, or have a hole through the centre), typically between four and six centimetres across, and weighing eighty or ninety grams. Depending on the part of the world they are found in, Gold Pieces may be decorated with embossed pictures of local kings or gods or even popular heroes, though most are rubbed almost smooth after having passed through the hands of so many people. Some conniving metal-smelters cast their own gold coins, mixing lead or brass with the more precious gold to make the latter stretch further. The penalty for such counterfeiting is typically execution (usually by a particularly unpleasant method, such as pouring hot lead into the ears). In some lands Gold Pieces are given nicknames, such as Kings, Regals, Sovereigns or Suns, or after a popular version of the name of the local ruler (coins in Kaypong, for example, are known as 'Coggies', after the city's ruler, Baron Kognoy).

A single Gold Piece would typically buy you one night's stay in an average-quality inn, or a new dagger, in a busy city, though quite considerably less in an isolated area which is served only by the infrequent caravans of swindling merchants (see later for more details of typical prices). But what happens if you want to buy just an apple or a loaf of bread, or any other small item which obviously costs less than a Gold Piece? In a few countries, smaller Gold Pieces, perhaps half or quarter the size of a standard piece, have been minted; these are sometimes known as Princes or Half-Regals. In other lands, they use Silver Pieces of much the same size as a Gold Piece. These are typically exchanged at a rate of ten Silver Pieces to one Gold Piece (though some Orc tribes use much larger Silver Pieces equal to a single Gold Piece, along with their more usual crude lead and bronze coins). Silver Pieces are typically nicknamed Silvers, Moons, Stars or Queens. In some lands, they even cut their coins into halves, quarters or eighths to give change. This tends to happen only in lands where gold is in plentiful supply, however, as all those little slivers of gold soon get lost!

In some lands, coins have not yet taken over from more traditional forms of money. Among the primitive tribes of the eastern Flatlands in central Allansia, rods of copper and bronze are used as money, exchanged in just the same way as Gold or Silver Pieces. To the subhuman Troglodytes which live beneath the Icefinger Mountains, the number of human or Dwarf bones a person possesses shows how wealthy they are; each small finger-bone may be worth a Gold Piece to them. A complete set of ribs or a skull would be a great – if rather morbid – fortune!

BARTERING
In every settled land, from barren regions wandered by desert nomads to the teeming vermin pits of cities, people swap things instead of using money. Indeed, in many isolated lands, money and coins are completely unknown, and people trade only by exchanging things they do not need for items they do. This 'barter' system works at all levels, depending on the quality of the goods involved and the status of the trading parties: a top-class armourer would not accept two dozen

chickens in exchange for a decorated breastplate, for example, though a fine jewel-encrusted sword would be gratefully accepted; similarly, one would not try to buy some cheese with a bag of gems or a golden holy symbol! Bear this in mind and keep a sense of proportion, and you will not get into any difficulties, no matter what you want to trade, or where you are.

TAXES

Taxation is the heaviest burden on anyone wishing to live in a civilized area under the protection of a king or nobleman, because armies and fortifications need to be paid for – as do the luxurious trappings of a king's lifestyle! Some lands, such as the kingdoms of Arion or Analand, take only minimal taxes from their citizens, because the money gained from taxation is used sparingly and with careful thought, to maintain the upkeep of the armies and little more; in Analand, most of the king's income comes from his own trading and farming concerns, and he asks for next to no money from his devoted subjects. Many lands, however, have rulers who rely on the money gained by taxing their citizens to keep them in the style to which a ruler rapidly becomes accustomed!

In most cities, the ruling family is allowed to take as much money as they like in taxes. However, every king knows that taking too much from the citizens leads to riots and maybe even the overthrowing of the monarch, so most play it safe and rely on a few common taxes at regular times of the year. In a large city, such as Salamonis in Allansia or Ximoran in Khul, taxes are typically imposed in two ways. There is usually a standard tax on anyone passing through a city gate to trade, and on anyone bringing large amounts of money into the city – adventurers take note! Similarly, ships bringing cargo into a port may have a small tax imposed on the goods they carry, depending perhaps on their worth to the citizens of the city. City gates occasionally also carry a small tax for being opened after sundown for someone to enter or leave the city.

When harvest-time comes around in the middle of autumn, the second tax is usually imposed, this time covering all lands surrounding the city as well as its residents. On all farmers and landowners, a tax of between 10 and 15 per cent of the value of all crops and animals is imposed; in the city, the rate may be anything from 2 to 25 per cent of a man's wealth in real money (but where money is in short supply many collectors will take property just as happily!). The 'Summer's End Tax', as it is known in some lands, is resented by just about everyone, because no one likes losing any more money than they have to, obviously. It often results in a frantic dash to hide money and property from the prying eyes of the hated tax-men, or, more ludicrously, in farmers putting woolly jackets on their cattle and calling them 'sheep', because sheep are worth less than cows, and to citizens moving furniture into their neighbours' residences while they are being assessed, and then back again before the tax-collectors move next door!

For their own part, the tax-collectors use very devious means to catch the citizens out. They keep the dates of the collection secret as best they can; they set up checkpoints at all city gates to stop wealthy citizens smuggling their fortunes out of the city for the duration; they even dress in disguise and snoop around beforehand, preparing a list of everything usually present on a farm before they arrive to count it officially the week after. It can be very dangerous being a tax-collector, and many have taken to travelling under a heavily armed escort! For all these reasons, when taxation time comes around, whole countries slow down almost to a standstill, and everyone takes part in the generally good-humoured game of tax-collecting!

PRICES ACROSS TITAN

From a very early age, everyone on Titan learns the value of money. Despite the miserable citizens of Brice insisting 'Gold and all its power are the root of all that's sour!', money has a very special meaning to most people. To the rich it means another galley, another slave-girl, another fur from Vynheim or another pet Black Lion from the Plain of Bronze. But to the poor it can mean the difference between eating today or tomorrow, between sleeping in the street or in the warm, between life or death itself.

TYPICAL COINS

On the left is a typical Gold Piece. This one is from Port Blacksand, bearing the arms of the city's evil ruler, Lord Azzur, on the front and a picture of a Dragon on the reverse.

To the right is a slightly smaller Gold Piece minted in the Dwarf citadel of Fangthane, at the far eastern side of Allansia. It bears the crossed axes of Fangthane's ruler, King Namûrkill, and the Dwarf Rune on the reverse. The runic inscription reads 'Cast in sacred Fangthane – may it never fall!'

On the left is a small lead coin used by Orcs and Goblins, which appears to have been stamped out of a sheet of metal, as the two sides are not properly aligned. They both show the head of some Orc chieftain, whose name seems to have been 'Scurfric'.

The final coin, on the right, is a Silver Piece from Tak in southern Khul. It is pierced in the centre for hanging on a cord around the owner's neck – a protection against that city's zealous thieves! It shows a trading galley on one side, and some stylized silver ingots on the reverse side. Twelve of these coins are worth 1 Gold Piece.

From the time he or she can talk, most children of poor or averagely moneyed families are taught to haggle. Haggling is a sophisticated form of arguing between a trader and a buyer, where they try to establish a price both of them are willing to accept. Sometimes it seems as though the rich disdain to haggle for common goods, but in fact they usually employ someone to haggle for them – and even the rich openly haggle for jewels, furs or slaves. In some lands it is a mark of great wealth and prosperity not simply to accept and pay the price a merchant first asks for his wares; in other lands it is a great insult, as merchants tend to get left feeling they should have asked for more in the first place! As you travel about the world, you will very quickly learn where to haggle and where not to haggle, where to refuse to pay what's asked and where to give in and not buy somewhere else.

Across Titan, depending upon their availability, things cost different prices. In the centre of a busy trading city such as Port Blacksand, Royal Lendle or Ximoran, even quite rare items are likely to be fairly cheap compared to the price you would have to pay if you relied on the efforts of a single merchant to get them to your isolated part of Kaypong or Arantis. The following list details some of the things you may need as you travel around Titan; it should help you haggle down to the right sort of prices in different parts of the world. Column A is for a large city where goods are plentiful and merchants make regular visits. Column B is for towns and villages where there is some local produce, and regular visits from a few merchants. Column C shows prices for isolated regions where there is little exotic food and only intermittent visits from a single, extremely greedy merchant! Remember that 10 Silver Pieces (sp) = 1 Gold Piece (gp).

Description of Item	A	B	C
Ale, flagon	4sp	3sp	3sp
Arrowheads, dozen	2gp	2gp	4gp
Arrows, dozen	3gp	3gp	5gp
Battle-axe	35gp	50gp	75gp
Blanket, large	2gp	2gp	4gp
Boots, strong leather	6gp	5gp	10gp
Bow, long	15gp	12gp	25gp
Bow, short	12gp	10gp	22gp
Breastplate	65gp	70gp	150gp
Candles, dozen	1sp	1sp	4sp
Cloak, wool	3gp	2gp	5gp
Cloak, silk	10gp	18gp	25gp
Crossbow	90gp	120gp	150gp
Crossbow bolts, dozen	6gp	9gp	15gp
Cuirass, chainmail	40gp	60gp	130gp
Cuirass, leather	20gp	25gp	55gp
Dagger	1gp	1gp	2gp
Dagger, throwing	3gp	5gp	10gp
Gloves, leather	3gp	4gp	7gp
Grappling-iron	12gp	15gp	30gp
Grindstone	8sp	8sp	12sp
Harness, horse	4gp	4gp	9gp
Hauberk, chainmail	55gp	80gp	175gp
Hauberk, leather	25gp	30gp	65gp
Herbs, common, per bunch	1sp	1sp	2sp
Herbs, rare	3gp	6gp	8gp
Horse, common type	40gp	40gp	50gp
Horseshoe	3sp	2sp	3sp
Lantern	2gp	3gp	6gp
Meal, hot, in tavern	2gp	2gp	2gp
Meal, cold, in tavern	8sp	5sp	5sp
Quill, ink and paper	1gp	2gp	4gp
Quiver	1gp	12sp	2gp
Robe, linen	2gp	3gp	7gp
Robe, silk	10gp	16gp	24gp
Rope, per metre	6sp	7sp	15sp
Room, shared, per night	1gp	15sp	2gp

Room, single, per night	2gp	4gp	5gp
Sack	2sp	3sp	5sp
Saddle	6gp	7gp	10gp
Shield, small	5gp	6gp	10gp
Shield, large	12gp	15gp	25gp
Spear	6gp	8gp	12gp
Stable, per 24 hours	1gp	8sp	2gp
Sword, long	30gp	40gp	65gp
Sword, short	20gp	25gp	50gp
Tent	3gp	4gp	6gp
Tunic, leather	5gp	6gp	12gp
Tunic, wool	2gp	3gp	5gp
War-hammer	35gp	40gp	75gp
Wine, flagon	4sp	6sp	7sp

MERCHANTS AND CARAVANS

'Never trust a merchant with gold in his ears' is a very peculiar saying from Arantis in southern Allansia, but it reflects the natural distrust common people have of all merchants and traders. They seem certain that if someone is selling something – and even worse, has actually *travelled* to you to sell something – then he must be out to trick or cheat you in some way. Of course, this is not completely true, but it does have a basis in truth, and there are real-life examples of the classic 'cheating merchant' everywhere you look. Despite their rather shady reputations, however, merchants are a vital part of the commercial system in all settled lands.

In cities and larger towns, there are always many specialist craftsmen, such as jewellers, dyers, herbalists and perfumers, who sometimes need very exotic ingredients. However, it is an interesting fact that cities are always situated extremely far away from the places where the exotic items come from, so merchants and traders are needed to bring the goods from the outlying lands to the cities. In the outlands, there are few craftsmen good enough to produce fine swords, armour or clothing: the lack of customers makes them stay away. But there are always people who *do* want to buy a few choice items, from local nobility to peasants with their sights set on higher things, and such people can provide a good market for a crafty trader. So trade can work in both directions – providing, of course, the merchant is willing to travel the long distances needed to get from the cities to the outlying lands, and then back again.

If the journey is long, most traders travel as part of a caravan, accompanied by other merchants, a few porters and servants perhaps, and a hired escort of mercenary guards. Bandits are a fairly frequent hazard to caravans, especially on the prosperous routes, but the presence of a dozen or so heavily armed professional soldiers should be enough to scare away all but the strongest threats. Hiring yourself out as a guard for a merchant is often a good way of travelling for long distances –

it beats walking, certainly, and has the added advantages of company, security and payment at the end of it! There are certainly far worse ways to travel.

The most popular pack animals are mules, though they are often replaced by camels in hotter, desert regions because the latter survive better without water. One famous merchant, Tadeus Lecarte, was escorted by two Sabre-toothed Tigers wherever he went! He had bred the pair, named Fangy and Carny, since he had found them as cubs on the Plain of Bones, after they were abandoned by their mother. By the time they reached adulthood they had become domesticated enough to be safe even around humans they did not know – but it would take only a single word from Lecarte and they would come running to his aid. Unfortunately, Lecarte died eight years ago, after attempting another crossing of the Plain of Bones – mauled, ironically, by a Sabre-toothed Tiger he tried to pat, mistaking it in the dark for his own Carny. It is not known what happened to his two pets.

MAIN TRADE-ROUTES

Although many traders prefer striking out on their own, increasing numbers of bandits, roving Orc bands and other threats have meant that more popular trade-routes have arisen, where one can be sure of meeting with a fellow traveller at least once a day, and where one knows that there are always regular armed patrols. There are many trade-routes on all three continents, but the main ones, and the special goods they carry are as follows:

Zengis to Salamonis, via Fang, Anvil, Stonebridge and Chalice: spices, furs, silver, gold, Dwarf goods, northman goods from Vynheim. The route from Zengis to Fang is open from Sowing to Hiding only.

Pollua to Royal Lendle, via Chalannabrad and Crystal City: glowstones, minerals, spices, cloth, leather goods.

Kalagar to Ximoran, via Ashkyos and Djiretta: gold, copper, ivory, furs, metal ware.

Inns and Taverns

So now you know about money; perhaps you would like somewhere to spend it? Well, where else but an inn or a tavern, where you can boast about your heroic adventures, meet up with other brave adventurers, and relax with a flagon or six of ale? You will also need inns, since safe places to stay in the open are rare; most sensible adventurers time their day's journey, wherever possible, to arrive in a village with an inn just as the sun sets. And while you are resting between adventures, you will certainly have need of an inn, for an active, danger-seeking hero like yourself would never settle down in one place long enough to buy a regular home – well, not for a few years anyway!

'Inn' and 'tavern' are, in fact, the names of two quite different types of drinking establishments. In a tavern, you can always get a drink, and occasionally some food and entertainment too; in an inn, you can stay the night, and maybe even stable your horse, as well as drink and eat. While you are on the road you will definitely need the services of an inn; at other times a tavern will suffice.

Both types of establishment serve many functions for the people who use them. The local alehouse is always the heart of any village, and it is here that all the men meet of an evening. Gossip and local news are exchanged, stories are told, legends are retold, and usually all in an atmosphere of great conviviality. If you find yourself in a country inn or tavern for the evening, you will more than likely find yourself asked about events in other parts of the world; for many country people, travellers such as yourself will be the only carriers of news they ever see. Gossip can be great fun to listen to, though it can sometimes turn out dangerous. In a tavern frequented by the local thieves, the last thing you want to do is get caught eavesdropping on someone planning their next 'big job'!

In any good inn there will be plenty of travellers staying the night rather than spending a risky night out in the open:

highwaymen, wolves, bandits and worse are enough to persuade most people to stay indoors until sunrise! There may be adventurers like yourself, rich merchants and their entourage of bodyguards and maybe a few slaves, or pilgrims on their way to worship at some nearby holy shrine. All have their stories to tell, and any one of them can prove most entertaining. In city taverns, the clientele enjoying their drinks might range from professional people, such as scribes or slavers, militiamen or assassins, to local citizens, ruffians or even beggars. You will quickly learn that every inn or tavern has its own peculiarities, which may turn out to be entertaining or perilous. Every inn and tavern looks different too, but for simplicity's sake we have divided them up into a few types.

City Taverns. These are likely to be small and cramped, and often very hot and crowded by the evening. Consisting of only one, or perhaps two rooms, they may nevertheless be divided into small booths for the privacy of their customers. While personal service is not out of the question, many use the new-fangled method of buying one's own drinks at the bar rather than calling someone over to your table. The atmosphere may be rowdy and sweaty, or tense and conspiratorial, depending upon who uses the establishment, but a stranger will rarely attract much attention.

Some cities impose rather annoying opening and closing times on their taverns, in the hope that some of their citizens will do some work in the afternoons instead of sitting drinking; unfortunately, to get around the closing times many revellers drink more than they should before the tavern shuts, and spend their afternoons at their work in a very unproductive drunken state anyway! Typical city taverns include 'The Hog and Frog' in Port Blacksand, 'The Battle of Skynn' in Royal Lendle or 'The Man Upside Down' in Ximoran.

Country Taverns. Unlike their city-based counterparts, these may be massive alehouses, built out of stone and large beams of timber, and made up of a dozen or so small chambers gathered around a central taproom, where barrels line the walls and serving-wenches fill flagons of ale to bring to your table. There is likely, especially in winter, to be a great fire in the centre of the room, and cartwheels of candles hanging from the ceiling to give plenty of light (these are also useful for swinging across the room during a punch-up!). The atmosphere is likely to be dense with smoke and the smell of soil, and the straw floor may be thick with mud by the end of the evening. In a country tavern, the arrival of a stranger may result in a sudden, highly embarrassing silence, especially if the tavern is an isolated one. We do not have any advice on how to cope with moments like this – one usually just tries to ignore it and order a drink. You should let the other drinkers see that you are just a normal human being like the rest of them . . . unless, of course, you are an Orc or a Werewolf or something! Examples of typical country taverns include

'Hullgrim's Alehouse' in Anvil, 'The Bristling Bristle-Beast' in Florrin or 'The Bent Spear' in Fenmarge.

City Inns. There are two distinct types of city inn. The first type caters for any local adventurers, professional people and others who prefer to stay in an inn rather than purchase or rent accommodation. Such inns may also be found alongside docks in harbour areas, providing temporary accommodation for ships' crews – and maybe even stringing up hammocks instead of beds and serving traditional seafarer's grog in preference to ale! These inns are typically quite small, with a single bar-room for customers and guests alike. 'The Black Lobster' in Port Blacksand is such an inn.

The second type is often found on the edge of a city, near a main gate, for it caters almost exclusively for travellers entering or leaving the city. Indeed some, such as 'The Way Inn' in Chalannabrad, are actually built into arches over one of the main thoroughfares. They usually revolve around a central courtyard, which the guest-rooms overlook. There will also be stables, and probably the services of an ostler, blacksmith or wheelwright, either on the premises or at least close by. The bar-room may be quite small, or divided into a number of small rooms, where individual parties of travellers can relax together away from other guests. Inns of this sort include 'The Wayfarer's Rest' in Kharé and 'The King's Highway' in Djiretta.

Country Inns. Out in the countryside inns are more like taverns, unless they are on very busy roads, in which case they will be much like a city inn. They will again be based around a courtyard, and have stables for travellers' horses or carriages. They may have a number of small guest-rooms, as does a city inn, but will usually also have a main drinking-room for the more local clientele. Such inns are the usual haunts of highwaymen or smugglers, and may prove to be quite perilous places if you are not careful. The best advice we can give is to go to bed as usual and not investigate any strange noises you hear in the night (unless there is someone rifling your pockets, of course!) – and always keep your sword handy, just in case. Very strange things go on in some country inns; though it must be said that there are just as many where nothing out of the ordinary ever happens. Typical country inns include 'The Hanging Party' near Silverton, 'The Great Wall' in Cantopani and 'King Gregor's Fingers' on the road south of Ximoran.

ALE AND OTHER DRINKS

One of the most important activities which people visit taverns for is, of course, drinking. In some areas there is no choice: you drink the local ale or you do not drink at all! But in towns and larger villages things can be a little more civilized, with ales, wines and spirits from all over Titan. Some beverages are very famous across whole continents for their potency or peculiar flavours; on your travels you will find it worthwhile to sample many different types, but be warned – some drinks are a little stronger than others!

FAMOUS ALES AND SPIRITS

Holdgut's Special Blue: A weird, blue-tinted ale found in western Allansia. Two flagons are enough to stun a large Hill Giant with a cold! It costs 4gp a flagon.

Quillian Water: Found only in Quill, in Brice. It looks like water, tastes like water, and three small measures will kill a man. It is usually served in tiny thimbles, around 10gp a shot!

Buruna Catsblood: A very light sweet ale from Khul. Thought by most to be brewed from the water of the Catsblood River, and dyed red for effect. It is actually made by taking two dozen cats, and slowly . . . It costs 5gp a half-flagon.

Skullbuster: A Dwarf speciality, a deep brown spirit made from distilling wheat through cracks in granite boulders. You have to be a Dwarf to enjoy the very gritty taste, but it will put any non-Dwarf under the table in three minutes flat. It costs 2gp a shot, and is found only in north-west Allansia.

Guursh: Orc ale. Do *not* drink it, if you value the lining of your stomach!

OTHER AMENITIES

Tavern food is usually not as bad as many make out (though sometimes, of course, it is far, far worse!). It is just that, in some parts of the world, the names of some foods sound a little strange. Our stomachs, too, would initially turn over at the thought of something like 'devilled Bristle-Beast kidneys', but in fact this is a very tasty, filling dish found in southern Kakhabad and northern Analand. If you keep an open mind, and are courteous when you casually ask what a particular dish contains (and even more courteous if the description which follows makes you want to spit it out immediately!), you will have few problems with food when you travel the world.

Many taverns have their own special brands of smoking-weed, which they sell to anyone who wishes to have a relaxing smoke after their meal or with a drink. If you bring a foreign type of tobacco into a tavern with you, do not forget that you may be expected to offer a sample to anyone who inquires after it. Whatever you do, beware any smoking-weed offered you in very hot places, such as any of the cities around the Inland Sea in Khul. If you have never tried it before, you can guarantee that the stuff will send you to sleep or make your mind go fuzzy, and you will be robbed of all your belongings in an instant. In some parts of the world, smoking *can* damage your health!

ENTERTAINMENT!

One of the highlights of visiting any inn or tavern is the entertainment which may be found there. Regular appearances by minstrels, exotic dancers or performing animals are guaranteed to bring crowds of customers flocking to a particular hostelry for an evening, thus bringing extra profits for the innkeeper! In small village taverns the only entertainment might be one of the locals with his finger stuck in his ear yelling a few popular songs at the top of his voice, but there are sometimes visits from wandering minstrels, players or circus acts. In the larger towns or cities, and especially sea-ports, there may be entertainers from all corners of the globe. Just about any act you can imagine, and a great many you cannot, can usually be found in a vermin pit like Port Blacksand or the City of Mazes.

Also very popular in taverns and alehouses across the settled world are gambling games. There are a great many different games – every little corner of Titan seems to have its own favourite, and even when particular areas have a game in common, the rules are often different. Here are three of our favourites; we know you will find your own, whether it be in the infamous Gambling Halls of Vlada in Kharé, or in some windswept little tavern hidden in the wastes of the Pagan Plains.

Mumblypeg. Also known as Pinfinger in some places, this is a very simple game, but requires good dexterity to be played well. All you do is take a dagger, and stab the point between the fingers of your hand as it rests on the table-top. As the stakes get higher and higher, the stabs get quicker and harder. Flowing blood indicates that the game is over!

Knifey-Knifey. Also known as Kharéan Roulette, this game is outlawed in most countries, for it invariably ends in death. Six identical daggers lie on a table; one is real while the other five have retractable blades which will do no harm. In turn, each player selects a dagger and quickly stabs himself in the chest with it. If it is a fake, it is returned to the table, shuffled together with the others, and the game continues; if it is real, death for the unfortunate player is certain. The game continues until only one player survives. This is a very exciting game to watch, but not to play (Knifey-Knifey experts are few and far between, but usually very, very rich).

Ten-Ten. This is probably our favourite game (you will often find us playing it in our local tavern, 'The Sage and Scholar', of a lunchtime). It uses a board, covered with 64 squares, in each of which there is a number from 1 to 9. Half the squares are black, while the other half are white. Each player simply throws a dart at the board in turn. Black numbers count *towards* the total, but white ones are *subtracted* from the total. The game continues until a player hits a number which takes the score to exactly ten or minus ten, whereupon he takes the contents of the pot. This game is especially popular in Analand and Ruddlestone on the western continent, but is played in most civilized cities across Titan.

DANGEROUS DRINKING
Occasionally, without warning, you may suddenly find yourself in the middle of a bar full of burly warriors, all intent on bashing lumps out of one another! Bar-room brawls are especially common in rough taverns in dockland areas of evil cities such as Blacksand or the City of Mazes, and once someone wants to start one, there is precious little you can do except grit your teeth and lay into whoever comes close, and remember to get out before the Watch arrives! But brawls are sometimes the least of your worries, for there are much more sinister things going on in some inns and taverns.

Smugglers are very common in some coastal areas, especially near ports which charge extortionately high trading-taxes. Taverns offer an ideal base, for most have deep cellars in which great amounts of contraband can be stored. Theirs is a very dangerous game, and they can be very ruthless people. So are highwaymen and bandits, who operate in country areas away from large towns but close to the major trade-routes. The most famous highwayman of all, Grinning Lord Dorian, worked along the roads between Port Blacksand and the interior of settled Allansia, robbing merchants, carriages, messengers and lone travellers, and operating out of 'The Orc's Torso' on the road to Stonebridge. He was a master swordsman and a superb shot with a crossbow, but ironically he was killed when his horse, Blue Boris, ran into a tree after an unsuccessful attempt to rob the wizard Nicodemus (who was travelling in disguise).

Most dangerous of all are crooked landlords who throw in their lot with thieves and prey on their own guests. The near-legendary Erlik Vinner of Rorotuna constructed an entire death-trap within his inn. Guests would lie in their beds, and suddenly be flipped backwards, down a chute and into a steaming vat of boiling water. Vinner would steal their belongings, and then claim next morning that the guest had fled without paying his or her bill! Vinner's inn, 'The Happy Landlord', was also famous for its peculiar but tasty stews . . .

A TYPICAL INN: 'THE BLACK LOBSTER' IN PORT BLACKSAND

'The Black Lobster' is a renowned dockland inn, much frequented by pirate crews and their captains. It is owned by 'Laughing' Guidon Allierté, who also owns two taverns in Rimon, and three in Halak, further down the coast. As a result, 'The Black Lobster' is left to itself most of the time, run by a succession of barmen under the watchful eye of Allierté's nephew, Halron, who is more concerned with drinking the profits than making them! The Allierté family have owned taverns in Allansia for many years, and they have built up strong ties with several pirate captains, who always bring their custom to Allierté's joints when in port. It is thought that Garius of Halak is one of these, though he has never been caught there by the militiamen who raid the place infrequently.

'The Black Lobster' is a typical city tavern, with a single, average-sized bar and a number of small booths. Its rooms are filthy and bug-ridden, but at least they are not shared with other guests, and they are not overpriced at 1gp a night. The

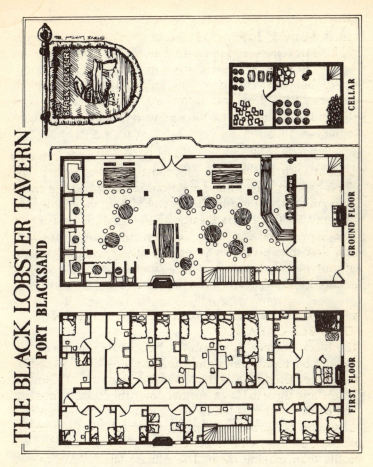

THE BLACK LOBSTER TAVERN
PORT BLACKSAND

CELLAR

GROUND FLOOR

FIRST FLOOR

bar serves a number of local ales and spirits, as well as seamen's grog made from cane sugar all the way from Arantis. Its clientele is invariably half pirate and half adventurer (often looking for passage on a pirate ship).

FAREWELL, BRAVE ADVENTURER!

So now you have reached the end of our book, and where better to end than in a tavern, relaxing with a flagon of ale while you slowly take in all that you have seen and heard on our massive trip around the world of Titan? We are sure you will agree with us when we say that it is a very strange and perilous place, but it is true that it can be a very rewarding one too, if you keep your wits about you.

All that remains now, of course, is for you to go and put all this information into practice! If you were not an adventurer before you read this book, we hope we have woken your mind to such a possibility. There are fortunes to be made out there in the big, wide world, wrongs to be righted, evil to be fought, heroes to be made. Perhaps you will be one of the heroes of the future.

And if you are already an adventurer, we sincerely hope that you have learnt something from our humble work. To you, sir or madam, we tip our conical hats and pray forgiveness if we have made any errors in this book, or under-emphasized some dangers, or let some evil beings off a little lightly compared with your condemnation of their wickedness. We are only human, and we have not benefited from the first-hand experience which is the sole province of adventurers such as your very good selves.

To all our readers, we wish a long and happy life, though we hope it is an exciting one too. If you should ever pass through Salamonis, we would be delighted to receive you in our humble chambers in the Palace of Learning, and to hear something of your marvellous adventures.

May the gods protect you always!